The

Book

Fate of the Devil

Kennedy Cormack

Published in 2019
by Kennedy Cormack

Interior layout and design
by Kennedy Cormack

Book cover design
by Kennedy Cormack

Facebook: Kennedy Cormack Author
Twitter: KCormack_Author
Instagram: Kennedy_Cormack_Author

Also by Kennedy Cormack

The Chosen Series

Prey for The Devil

Race with The Devil

The Devil's Deceivers Series

Mathim

Sallas

A sad note

This book was written before the fire at Notre Dame. Any similarities contained in its pages is entirely coincidental.

My heart goes out to the people of France and all around the world at the damage caused to this most beautiful of historic landmarks.

As always, this book is dedicated to my mum and dad but also to a guy I don't know. I don't know his name or his story, but he touched my heart in a way he'll never know.

Before I sat down to start this tonight, I went out with friends for lunch. As we were walking back to our cars, we stopped at the most beautiful church as one of us wanted to go inside. As we walked in, I noticed a man lighting a candle, pacing up and down, and praying. He was obviously really struggling with something, so I moved away, respecting his privacy. After a while we began to walk to the exit, and I saw he'd moved to a pew at the very back. Then I noticed the bottle of wine at his feet. He looked at me and said "Never rush, flower. Demons are always in a hurry; good people take their time." In amongst the battle with whatever demons he was fighting, he took the time to share words he thought would help me.

So, to the man who will probably never read these words, thank you. And to anyone struggling with their own demons, keep fighting.

As I bring Jax's story to an end, it strikes me just how many people I have to thank for all the help, support and love they've all given both me and my bookbabies. So, here goes. If you're reading this and think you should be in here, then trust me, you are.

To Becky and Rocky, the two ladies who convinced me to just try. Either with words or by example, you both showed me the way.

To Yogi, Bags and Beth, thank you for being the best beta readers on the planet.

To Glenys for all your advice on locations, but also for loving my bookbabies as much as you do.

To my Haven gang, especially my voice buddies. Thank you for making me laugh, keeping me sane, and offering help and inspiration through everything. You guys know how much I love you all, but it doesn't hurt to remind you.

And to everyone who read Jax's story, she wouldn't have got this far without you all cheering her on.

"It is said that the fallen son will seek revenge upon his father, wreaking havoc upon his favourite creations. Three children, borne of the son, will come into their own, and will be the deciding factor in the final outcome. No angel or demon may approach them, their decisions must be made of their own accord. Only one may have any sway, one from their own kind; the Chosen One."

(The Lucifer Prophecies, date and author unknown.)

A Satisfying Sight

I push the humans out of my way as we arrive in the more crowded streets. To transport Jay straight to our destination may have been too much for him the first time he travelled in such a way and so we find ourselves hurrying through the busy throng to reach it. Checking over my shoulder, I see that he is close behind me, but no other is in pursuit.

"Stay close, Jay. We will be there soon," I order.

He does not question me; he simply nods in answer. Good. He will need to take instruction as easily as this when my Master meets him. I continue to brush past those around me until the numbers lessen as we near our temporary home. The dark building looms over the street, blocking the sun and creating long shadows that stretch across the ground at its front.

Only when we are safely inside do I allow myself to take a moment's pause to catch my breath. I hear Jay panting beside me and turn to look at him. Bent forward, his hands on his knees as he rests against the closed door, he stares at the blood on his hand as though mesmerized by the sight of it.

"Your first?" I ask.

"First what?" he replies, turning his head to look at me in confusion.

"Was that the first life you have taken?"

It is no small thing to end someone's existence. For us demons, it is a thing to be celebrated. But for most humans, this is often not the case. Curious about his feelings on it, I watch him carefully for a reaction.

"Oh, right. Yes. It was." He pauses for a moment, allowing himself time to think. "I thought it would feel different. I thought I would feel … more."

I force myself to keep my passive expression. Guilt, excitement, either of these would be an expected reaction, depending on the type of human who had committed the act, but to feel nothing? That is very different to the norm of this race.

"You had considered what it would feel like to kill someone?" I ask.

"Yes, often. I put it down to morbid curiosity, nothing to worry about. Now I wonder if I have always known it was in my future."

"Perhaps. From what I saw of your sister, it would not surprise me if you had a heightened intuition. And the act itself could not have been timed better."

I speak no lie here. To see the utter desolation upon Jaqueline's face as her most beloved friend fell to the ground before her, his life oozing out of him from the wound left by Jay's blade, was a sight I will never forget. Although, if not for Jay's being a child of Lucifer, I may have ended him for taking the opportunity away from me. Years of torture and suffering I placed upon Jax, but to no avail, and ending up fooled by angels and traitors alike, my blood still boils when I think how I was deceived. I would have liked to inflict this pain upon her myself. Bathin too. I cannot wait for the day I drag him back to the Master he turned his back on, I will watch as Hell's own torturer tears him piece by piece.

"Tell me, Astaroth. Tell me everything."

There is no demand in his tone, just a desire to know the truth of his situation. I nod towards the seat near him and take my place in one behind me, settling to tell him what he requests.

"Very well, Jay. It is important that you are prepared for the journey you have ahead of you. You are one of three children of my Master. Well, that is to say, one of the three told of in the prophecy. He has offspring all around the world, but they are not the important ones.

"You will be responsible for his ultimate victory. The prophecy, however, also tells of the Chosen One. The one human who can bring about the success or demise of Lucifer. She chose to side with the angels and attempt to thwart his plans, rather than aid him in them. For that she will not go unpunished. Eventually. She works to persuade you all to join her. So far, we are even. They have your foolish sister, and we have you. You made the better choice, Jay. Your loyalty to your Father will be greatly rewarded."

"And what are his plans?" he asks.

"I cannot claim to know all of the details. I only know that I will be by his side in all he aims to do. And so will you, now."

He sits back in his chair to take all of this in. After a few quiet moments, his eyes meet mine.

"I am ready, Astaroth. What do I need to do?"

I smile at his eagerness. He will do well, this son of Lucifer.

"All in good time. For now, I make sure that any questions you have are answered before we speak to my Master. And then, we do as he decides."

I wait for a moment, watching him as he ponders.

"What would you ask of me, Jay?" I prompt.

"Those people that came to her rescue. Who were they?" he asks.

"Eremiel, the angel. Xander, her human friend that met with such an unexpected end. And Bathin. His story is more complicated. He was once one of Lucifer's most favoured demons, raised high in his ranks and Captain of one of the most formidable armies Hell has ever seen. I never trusted him, and, in the end, I was proven correct in my suspicions. He betrayed my Master, helping Jacqueline escape from Hell, and siding with the angels in their quest."

"But why would he turn on my Father? I mean, if he was so well-respected, what would make him throw all of that away?" A frown wrinkles his brow as he looks to me for an answer.

"Bathin worked to raise himself high in the eyes of Lucifer, but he and his friends always remained close. When two of them were killed for betrayal, he refused to believe it of them, despite all the proof laid out before him," I explain, the memories almost bringing a smile to my face before I can stop it. The demise of Bathin's closest comrades is one of the things I am most proud of, although I cannot say this aloud. To see the pain that it caused him to lose them satisfied me in a way no amount of bloodshed ever could.

"Do you think he's really dead?" he asks quietly, looking back at his hands.

"You begin to regret your actions?" I am surprised at his question. He seemed so accepting only a few moments ago.

"No. Not at all. I was just wondering. I mean, it can't have been a deep wound. If it wasn't in the right place, it might not have been enough. If it's something that would please my Father, I don't want it to have failed." He regards me closely, waiting for my answer.

"Ah, I see. You wish to make sure you completed the task. Commendable, Jay. Come, let us make sure."

I stand up and motion for him to follow me through the door at the other side of the room and through the hall until we come to face the large mirror. I arc my arm over it and bring the cathedral into view. I refocus its gaze to the small group huddled around a still shape on the ground.

"It does not look like you were unsuccessful," I say, distractedly. My eyes are trained upon Jax. Tears stain her face and for the first time, I see hopelessness in her eyes. She looks to Bathin and Eremiel in turn, but getting no help from them, she goes back to stroking the hair of her dead friend.

"They cannot help him?" he asks.

"They cannot. Angels and demons alike can only heal, not resurrect. Well, that is not entirely true. I have heard lore of resurrection but not for the likes of Xander. It must be one who truly deserves to be saved. And even then, it has never been heard of within my lifetime. It takes great one of great power to do such a thing."

"I have another question. My last one in fact." He turns to face me, spine straight and taking a deep breath. "When do we go home?"

"Soon, Jay. Soon. First though, I think there is someone you should meet."

I clear the image from the glass and leave it showing only our reflections as I begin to speak, signalling Jay to step to one side.

"My Lord, it is done."

The mirror blurs for a second before clearing to show my Master.

"You have him?" he asks.

"I do, Sire. He came most willingly and already shows himself to be very useful. He waits to be introduced."

I beckon Jay back in front of the glass, and he steps quickly to my side. This boy impresses me once more with his eagerness to meet his Father.

"Well met, my son," greets Lucifer. "I watched your altercation with the angels, and I have to say I was not disappointed."

"Thank you, Father. I hope I will never be a disappointment to you."

"And I. Very well, Astaroth. You may bring him home," he says, and I see Jay quickly force a grin from his face. "Bring him to me and then we will discuss your next move. You have done well, my Grand Duke,

as always, I would not lose momentum by delaying you."

"Indeed, Sire. It will be done."

He nods and looks away briefly.

"Scirlin, create the doorway," he orders.

The mirror flashes and blurs once more, snapping back into focus when the connection is forged.

"Well, Jay, are you ready?"

He steps towards me in answer and I turn back to the glass. Stepping through the surface, I feel the change in the air and the heat surround me, Jay only a second behind. We are home.

2

A Loss

"This will do, Xan," I say, before realising he is not as close behind me as I thought. "Xan?"

I watch in awe as Mathim parries another attack from Astaroth, Eremiel recovering from something I haven't seen before leaping back into the fray. I scan the scene for Xander and breathe a sigh of relief when I see him jogging towards me.

"Where did you go?" I ask. "Xan, look out!"

My cry of warning comes too late, as Jay slams a fist into his side. It's only when the sunlight catches the blade that I see it and realise it wasn't a punch that created the look of shock on the face of my friend. He falls to the ground and I scream and begin to run towards him; the noise distracting both angel and demon from their battle with Astaroth.

"To me, Jay," he barks, and Jay does as he's told and runs towards him. Astaroth places a hand on his shoulder and they both vanish from sight.

But the only thing I see is Xander, by now lying prone on the floor, the red pool beneath him spreading with every second that passes.

"No," I cry, "please, no."

His hand searches for mine while he struggles to breathe.

"I'm sorry, Jax," he says with his last breath, as the last flicker of life fades from his eyes.

"No, Xan. No." I shake his shoulders, wanting even the smallest sign that I haven't just lost him.

"Please," I beg, looking at the angel and demon before me in turn. "You have to do something. Anything."

Eremiel remains silent and I see the pain on Mathim's face as he moves to his knees beside me, taking my hand.

"There is nothing we can do, Jax. I am so very sorry."

"No, that's not right," I argue, pointing a finger at Eremiel. "He's an angel, he should be able to fix this. Please, it's Xander. He doesn't deserve this. He wouldn't have ever been drawn into all of this if it wasn't for all of you. I can't lose him, I can't—" My words run out when I see a tear roll down Mathim's cheek.

And it hits me. Xan is dead. Gone. My body bends forward as my heart breaks, huge uncontrollable sobs at the loss of the one person who is always there for me. Was always there for me. I put my arms around his lifeless body, my tears soaking into his shirt as I cry for the loss of the closest friendship I've ever known. Letting the blackness take me, all noise fades into a dull hum and I allow myself to get lost in it.

The sound of running feet penetrates somehow and I vaguely hear a voice calling my name.

"Jax? Jax. Move."

The sharpness and urgency of the tone makes me lift my head from Xander's chest and sit up. When my vision clears, I see Emelia kneeling at the other side of him. I frown in dazed confusion. She can't be here, she's in New York, I think stupidly.

"Emelia?" My voice is barely a whisper as my head spins with everything that's going on.

"Move your hands, Jax," she orders and for some reason, I do as she says without question.

Her spine straightens as she closes her eyes, moving her hands forward to hover over Xander's lifeless form. When she opens them, it isn't to look at me. She stares blankly into space and I watch numbly. Her hair starts to move as though blown by a breeze that is only around her, and when I look in her eyes, I see them flash white.

"What the—" I begin to say but am stopped from finishing the words by matching gasps from Mathim and Sallas.

She moves one hand to his forehead and the wind I can't feel blows harder through her red hair, making it move more noticeably. I look to Mathim dumbfoundedly for an explanation, but his stare is on her too.

Beads of sweat appear on her skin and I know that whatever she's doing is taking a lot from her. Her hands begin to tremble in the air and her breathing quickens.

"I- I almost have him," she says shakily, and I hear the exhaustion in her voice. "I just can't get him. It's taking so much."

14

I jump to my feet and run around to her side. I reach out to place a hand on the tree beside me and grasp her shoulder with the other. I don't know what makes me do it, it just feels right. And as soon as my skin touches the bark of the trunk, I feel it. The tingling in my palm that starts to travel into my wrist and up my arm, infusing every cell with life as it passes.

"Pull, Jax," says Lizzie's little voice in my head. "It'll help him."

I nod in answer and focus on the sensation spreading into me. I pull it into me, feeling it build inside stronger than ever before, until I am almost humming with its energy. Using myself as a conduit, I send it flowing down the other arm and out into Emelia. When I hear her draw a sharp breath, I know it's working and force myself to concentrate to keep it going.

I open my eyes and see the world in beautiful, vivid colours but when I turn my head to look at Emelia, I see she's surrounded by an aura of the brightest white light I've ever seen. She frowns in concentration before taking a deeper breath and pushing it out deliberately, forcing herself to relax. Her expression softens into pure serenity and she moves her hands closer to Xander's body. When she touches his brow, I see the aura meet his skin first, seeming to sink into its surface before her fingers come to rest there. When she places her other hand on his chest, my legs almost give way beneath me as somehow, she manages to draw on the energy that I'm giving her, pulling it through me faster.

As the feeling becomes almost too much to bear and blackness threatens at the edges of my vision, I hear two voices speak at once.

"Stay with me, Jax," she orders, as I hear Lizzie at the same time.

"You can do it, Jax. Stay awake. You have to."

I bite down hard on my bottom lip, the pain sparking me back into full consciousness and clearing my vision. My eyes widen when I see the light from her beginning to surround Xan. No, I realise. It isn't her light that surrounds him. Before my eyes, I see a different aura starting to envelop him. It seeps out from different places of his pale skin, more and more as each second passes and as it grows stronger, I realise that this light has a purple hue to it. As I watch, it appears and spreads until it completely covers him.

"Get ready, Jax," Emelia warns. "One last push, okay?"

I steel myself for what's coming, forcing more life from the tree and from the grass beneath my feet in preparation.

"Always ready," I say through gritted teeth, just before it hits. I feel the energy being sucked through and out of me but force myself to stay focused on the body of my friend. As the last gap in the cocoon that covers him is filled, I hold my breath and pray.

For a second, nothing happens but then I'm forced to look away as the aura completes itself with a dazzling flash so bright it hurts my eyes. And then I hear it. A noise I wished so hard for that I think I might have imagined it. I stare at Xander's chest, longing for it to be true, and when I see it rise with the next deep breath I hear, I cry out in relief.

"Wait," Emelia warns. "We need to break this properly."

I force myself to remain still as she closes the connection between us, waiting until I see her give a brief nod before I drop to my knees on the ground beside her.

"Xan?" I ask. "Xan, can you hear me?"

His eyelids begin to flutter, then open fully.

"Oh my God. You're alive!" I can't stop the tears of joy and relief from falling as I see him looking back at me and smiling weakly.

"Wait, let me see if I can help you."

I look to Eremiel, who is staring in shock at what he has just witnessed.

"It won't hurt him, will it?" I ask.

"No, I do not think so, Jax. You could try. Xander, if you feel anything but good effects, you must say so immediately. Do you understand?" he says.

"Don't try to speak yet, Xan," I warn. "Just lift your hand if you need me to stop, okay?"

His eyes meet mine and he nods. I move to the tree and rest against it, threading one hand into the grass and reaching for Xander's with the other. He grasps it and I smile before closing my eyes to focus. Again, I let it fill me with life and slowly I release it into my friend. Not wanting to overwhelm him, I maintain a steady flow, opening my eyes when I know it is set. And for the first time, I see what I have only ever heard of until now. The others have told me how fast the effects of nature are on me, but now I get to see for myself. While I watch entranced, I see the colour begin to return to Xan's face, light beginning to shine in his eyes again and his smile

18

widening as he feels it working.

"Okay, Jax. I think that'll do for now," he says. "I don't want you wearing yourself out."

I look at him closely before agreeing and letting the pull slow to its normal tingle.

"How do you feel, Xan?" asks Emelia.

"Well, I'm alive. That's really all that matters. But yes, I feel good. Thank you. Both of you." He looks from her to me and his expression turns sad. "Jax, I nearly left you. I'm sorry. I can't even imagine what that must have done to you."

I cut off his words by pulling him into a hug.

"You're back. That's all that matters, Xan. And why are you apologising?" I laugh. "It wasn't your fault!"

"Well, umm, I don't know, really," he chuckles. "I just hate that you went through that."

I shake my head at his words. Only Xander could be killed and then come back and apologise. Killed. He really was dead. So how is he here?

"Emelia? How the hell did you do that?" I ask her, still amazed at what we've just witnessed. At what I've just been a part of.

"It's a long story, Jax. I'll tell you it all later but for now, here's the short version. We've discovered that I have certain gifts that aren't exactly human. We were working on them when you went missing. I figured one or two out on my own, with Sal there to help me if I needed it. When we got here and I saw Xan lying there, after I got over the shock of it, I mean, I just knew what to do. I know that will make zero sense," she finishes with a wry smile.

"Actually, it kinda does," I say, earning a raised eyebrow and surprised expression from her. "When I saw you fading, I just knew I needed to help you. I knew that I could do that because it was almost what Mathim and Eremiel did to me to help me the first time."

"Speaking of them," she says, looking around, "where is Sal? Oh, there you are. What's wrong? You look, well, I dunno, weird."

I turn my head to see what she's talking about and see a strange look on his face. Shock and sadness mixed into one, perhaps. I look to Mathim to see what he thinks but see the same expression from him. He recovers and looks at me with a small smile.

"He is fine. You just brought back some memories for both of us," he explains. "I too will explain later. Now, if Xander is ready to move, perhaps we can return home."

"Home? Is it safe to move him?" I ask in concern. "I mean, he just came back. Shouldn't we wait and let him recover a little first?"

"Hey, I'm right here, you know. And I don't feel too bad. I'm pretty sure I can stand up. Let's start with that and see how we get on," he suggests, beginning to move to his feet.

I jump to mine, my arms out ready to steady him in case he falls.

"Okay, Xan? How do you feel?"

"Fine. I'm good, Jax, really." He looks at me and starts to laugh. "Is this really what you had to deal with for all that time?"

"Huh? Well, no, obviously. Astaroth tortured me but he never actually killed me. I kinda feel I got off lightly," I answer, my eyes still trained on his face for any sign of pain.

"Not what I meant," he chuckles. "I meant from Lee and I. Fussing around you like you're doing to me now. It must have driven you crazy. I really am okay, Jax, I promise."

"Still, Jax may be right. A long journey is not what you need," says Mathim. "Scirlin?"

I can't hear him respond so I turn back to Xan and catch him grinning at me.

"What?" I ask.

"I'm just wondering if we tell Lee what happened. She'd go after Jay on her own if she could. Can you imagine?"

And as much as I know how upset she'll be, the image of an angry Lee makes me laugh too.

"He wouldn't know what hit him," I agree.

"The doorway Scirlin created for Xan and I will be open again in a moment," Mathim tells us. "As for Lee, as much as I would save her the pain of finding out how close she came to losing Xander, I think everyone needs to know everything."

As Xan and I both nod in agreement, Xan's phone rings.

"Speak of the devil," he says. "Are you sure you're the psychic one, Jax?"

I laugh and shrug my shoulders as he swipes the screen to answer.

"Hey, little chica. Woah, slow down. Yes, we have Jax and she's fine. We're coming home now. Oh, and we have visitors so make the coffee, sweetie. Yes, I promise we're all okay. We'll be on our way in a minute and you can see for yourself. Okay, Lee, see you soon."

He raises his eyebrows at me when he ends the call.

"Nope, no need," I say, "I got it from your side. She's worried."

"I'm a little worried too," he replies. "You realise how much she's gonna fuss over me, right?"

I laugh at the mock terror on his face and nudge him.

"Yeah, well, next time, just don't get dead." I stop and take his hands in mine. "Seriously though, Xan, I mean it. You scared the crap outta me."

"Me too, Jax. Me too." He drops his hands and wraps his arms around me in a hug. "Now, come on. Let's go home."

3

First Meeting

I blink to refocus my eyes to the dim light of the Throne Room as I step forward into it. Turning to see Jay follow me through only seconds behind, I watch as he does the same. The human realm is so vivid in colour compared to our home that, once away from here, it can take some adjustment upon returning.

"Well met, Astaroth. It is good to see you home once more. Although I do not know how long your stay will be," greets Lucifer from his seat in the corner. "Come, bring him forward."

I stride across the room, hearing Jay's footsteps matching my own, and drop to one knee before my Master.

"My Lord, it is good to be back. No matter the length of my stay. There is no news of the final child as yet, I take it?" I ask.

"There is not. The mists remain around my offspring. But no matter, we have a victory to celebrate, do we not?" He looks at me with a broad smile before turning to his son. "Welcome, Jay. You made a wise choice in coming to the side of your father. A very wise choice

indeed."

"Thank you, Father," Jay answers, without a second's pause. "I am happy to be here. And will do whatever I can to be of help to you."

"All in good time. For now, I would hear of how exactly you came to be battling angels and traitors so soon after you made your decision. Astaroth? What happened?"

"I intercepted Jacqueline as she came to make her approach to Jay, Sire," I explain. "I knew she would attempt to sway him to the side of the angels. To keep her under control seemed the best strategy. I am unsure how they found her though. Bathin arrived with the human, Eremiel separately but at the same time." I risk a glance at him to gauge his reaction. Jacqueline was not my target. Nor was Bathin.

"Yes, very good. I imagine the angel located her. They have their ways and unfortunately also have talents that even I must acknowledge. Albeit grudgingly. Carry on." He waves his hand in encouragement.

"Yes, Master. My priority was of course the safety of your son and so I was fighting for an opportunity to get him out of harm's way.

His attack on the man proved enough of a distraction to allow us that."

"Yes, a job well done it would seem. I imagine Jacqueline will feel the sting of that for many a year to come. It is a shame the prophecy forbids harm to her until it has run its course. But patience brings its own rewards. For now, let her suffer the loss of her friend. It will be punishment enough for the meantime. For the moment though, we must remain focused on the task at hand." He stands and descends the steps to come face to face with Jay. "And so, my son, it is time that you discovered your destiny."

"Yes, Father," Jay agrees readily, following Lucifer's steps to stand before the glass we just crossed through.

"There are three of you, your births foretold in one of the oldest prophecies in existence. It is said that the fallen son will seek revenge upon his father, wreaking havoc upon his favourite creations. Three children, borne of the son, will come into their own, and will be the deciding factor in the final outcome. No angel or demon may approach them, their decisions must be made of their own accord. Only one may have any sway, one from their own kind; the Chosen One." He pauses to arc his arm over the mirror's surface and from my position behind them, I see it cloud before it refocuses *on a busy scene in Jay's human world. He sneers as he watches them milling around. "You are so much more than them, Jay. You have always known it, have you not?"*

The sudden change of direction in conversation does not affect the boy, and he answers without hesitation.

"I've always known I was different, Father, yes. I never really connected with anyone. Apart from my mother. And even that wasn't the same way all the other children my age did when I was younger. But I respected her greatly. The man who claimed to be my father never seemed worthy of that. And now I know why. But, may I ask a question?" He turns his head to seek permission.

"Of course," Lucifer replies.

"If I knew this, deep down, I mean, how did my sister not feel the same thing? And why would she have sided with the angels and the Chosen One?"

"Because she is weak. It takes a great deal more strength to take the part of the less 'popular' choice, for want of a better word, when a decision is laid before you. Fear of judgment from others, the lack of courage to seek the one thing that all of your race desire. Power.

You admit readily that you desire it. Emelia lacked the backbone to do the same and so was easily convinced by Jacqueline that she was 'good'. She will show her true colours before the end." The surety rings in his tone, allowing no room for doubt.

"What do you mean?" Jay asks.

"She is my daughter. My blood runs through her veins as it does yours. She cannot fight the pull forever."

I wonder how long this will take. Depending upon the amount of time that passes before the next child is unveiled, we might need to speed up the process somehow. I shake my head to refocus on my Master and leave the thought for further consideration later.

"Do we need her?" Jay's question earns him a hard stare from Lucifer, making him pause suddenly. "Sorry, Father, I only meant—"

"I know what you mean, Jay. Why do you apologise? You wish to be the only one of my children raised high by my side? There is nothing wrong with that desire. But it must be tamed. If the third is to come to us, you will work with them. Once my goal is achieved, you may tear each other to pieces, if that is what you wish. I will not stop you."

A smirk appears on Jay's face for a moment, but soon disappears to be replaced with one of concern that he strives to hide. No doubt he realises that if Lucifer cares so little for the outcome of the other of his children, then he cannot care for Jay.

"I will prove myself to you, Father," he vows.

"I am sure you will," replies Lucifer. "And you will have the best help I can provide." Clearing the image from the mirror, he turns back to me.

"My Lord?"

"Until we have news of the next of my children, I task you with Jay's training. I do not mean as a normal soldier, Astaroth, that would take too long. I wish for you to make him capable of defending himself, to see what strengths he brings and to identify any weaknesses that may need further work. I can call Tezrian back from the Realms if needs be. If you need to leave before this is completed, I mean."

"Yes, my Lord." My mind begins to whirl with thoughts of Bathin and Jacqueline. If I am here, then I have no chance of getting anywhere near to them. I know the chance of discovering them

away from the protection of Jax's home is small, but I would not miss even the most miniscule of opportunities if I can help it.

"What is it?" he asks, seeing something in my expression that gives away my discontent at his order.

"I do not question your orders, Sire," I say, thinking quickly to find an excuse to return. "It is only that Jay expressed a desire to unleash some sort of punishment or revenge on people back on Earth. Perhaps this could be a part of his training? I can secure us somewhere hidden to develop his skills first, of course."

I wait, holding my breath as I wait for his decision.

"Is that so?" he says, glancing to Jay for confirmation.

"It is, Father. There are people that I would see brought low if I could," he answers, meeting his Father's stare.

"Very well, then. But, Astaroth, you will keep me informed as to his progress. And should we receive news that requires your attention, then Jay will return here before you leave to find the next."

"Of course, Sire." I see Jay smiling at me and realise that he has

mistakenly assumed that I made the request for his benefit. No matter, that could well work to my advantage too. To have the loyalty of the son of Lucifer could be very helpful indeed.

4

Long Stories

"Hi, honey, I'm home," calls Xander as we pass through the mirror side by side, making me laugh.

The office door slams open as Lee comes running through it, throwing her arms around me and hugging me tight.

"Jax! Thank God you're okay. What happened? How did you get away? Are you sure you're alright?" Her questions run one into the next and I hold my hands up in surrender when she releases me and holds me at arm's length to check for herself that I'm unharmed.

"I'm fine, Lee. I promise. I'll tell you everything once everyone is here. Want a hand with the coffee while they get here?" I placate her and usher her towards the door.

"Yeah, okay," she agrees. "But then you tell me all of it, right?"

"Right, sweetie, I swear. Xan, take everyone outside? I'll be out in a minute."

He sees the concern on my face and rolls his eyes at me.

"Okay, Jax. Go, make coffee. I got this. I'll go sit with everyone when they arrive." He smiles at me and I nod at his hinted concession to take it easy without arousing Lee's suspicions.

As I put cups on a tray, I hear Mathim's voice and the quieter ones of Sal and Emelia as they all make their way out to the garden. When we're ready, I pick it up and carry it down the path to the table at the end of the grass.

"Emelia?" says Lee. "How are you here? I mean, it's awesome to see you but how?"

Emelia looks at me, not knowing how to explain and I rescue her quickly.

"Lee, honey, give me a minute and I'll start at the beginning and fill you in on all of it. It won't make sense unless I do."

"Okay," she agrees. "But I got this, you sit."

I do as I'm told with a chuckle, gratefully taking the coffee she hands me once I'm seated on the grass. When I see her finally sitting next to Mathim and looking around curiously, I know I'm good to begin my story.

"Okay, so, I got the train to London, as you know, but when I got to the station, all the pain I used to get hit me again outta nowhere. I couldn't figure out what was happening until I heard Astaroth's gloating voice behind me. Somehow, he got control over me and took me to this old prison that's now a museum. He said he'd done something to it to make the staff have to close. Anyway, he kept me there and when I tried to call to Mathim, I couldn't. He'd managed to block whatever part of my mind creates the link between us. Honestly, I didn't know what I was gonna do.

"I sat and sat, trying to think of something and then I realised that I wasn't always able to do that, to be able to communicate with angels and demons so easily. And I remembered the first time I spoke to Ambriel was when I was meditating, so I tried that. You know how that went, but when I came back from it, he was watching me. He guessed what I'd been doing and so he filled my head with this white noise so I couldn't hear myself think, let alone try to meditate again. But it was too late really, I'd already got word to you guys.

"Anyway, he went to meet Jay, or rather to be in the right place at the right time so that Jay could approach him. That way he wasn't breaking the rules of the prophecy. The streets were busier, and it took more focus from him, which let Lizzie come through. She came to tell Eremiel where I was and that's when everyone came to get me."

I pause and flick my eyes to Xan, who takes a deep breath to steel himself for what's coming before nodding at me to continue.

"And?" asks Lee impatiently. "Please tell me someone killed him. Or at least stomped on him a bit."

"Now, you're really not gonna like this bit, Lee," I warn her. "Try to stay calm, okay?"

"Oh God, what? Just tell me," she sighs.

"Well, Mathim and Eremiel were fighting Astaroth, and Xan pulled me to my feet and pushed me in front of him to get out of the way. When we were at a safe distance, I turned to see what was happening, but Xan wasn't there. He was a little behind me and that's when, umm—" I stop, not knowing how to tell her.

"That's when Jay stabbed me," says Xan, quickly following his sentence with reassurances. "I'm fine, Lee, I promise."

"He what?" she screeches. "Where? Do you need a hospital? Why the hell are we just sitting here if you're injured?"

"Lee, calm down. I said I was fine. Look, sweetie, see?" He stands and lifts his shirt, blood dried on his skin but no wound in sight.

"How? How are you 'fine', Xan? You were stabbed. Or not. I don't understand. Jax, what's going on?" She looks at me in bewilderment and I smile ruefully at her.

"I know, chick. It doesn't make sense. Hell, I don't understand it and I was there." I turn to the only one who can explain the rest. "Emelia, your turn, honey."

"Yeah, your turn, Emelia," agrees Lee. "And don't leave out the part where you suddenly turn up from New York."

"I won't, Lee, I'll get to it," she says, running her hands through her hair and sitting back in her seat. "You know that Sal and Malaphar came to help me learn to protect myself from Astaroth, I'll start from there.

"When they came through, Mal warded the house somehow while Sal began to talk me through some ways of blocking anything that Astaroth might try to put on me. Like building a wall in my mind?" She looks to Lee and seeing her nod, she continues. "And putting a bubble around me too."

"Oh, we do that on hunts," says Lee.

"Yeah, so, we did that but when Sal saw me do it, he noticed something in my eyes that made him think I could do a little more than protect myself. He spoke with Mathim and I don't know who else, and they thought it was a good idea to figure out what I can do and teach me how to use it properly as well as how to control it." She pauses for breath and glances at Sal. "Have I missed anything so far?"

"No, you are telling it well, Em. Carry on," he replies.

"Wait," interrupts Lee. "What did you see, Sal?"

"Demons' emotions, as well as their abilities, are reflected in their eyes. Different colours have different meanings. The first I saw of this in Emelia was upon mention of Astaroth. Her eyes flared purple. It made me wonder just what she is capable of."

"Purple?" asks Lee. "What does purple mean?"

"Violet is the colour of war. Emelia, do you wish to finish the telling of this?" he asks.

"Sure. We worked on using that to create a sort of energy bolt and I seemed to get the hang of it okay. So, we moved onto other things. We discovered I can create fire and wind but didn't have time to try with water before Scirlin came for us. Oh, and I can use the earth too. A little like Jax, but not as powerfully.

"While we were working on this stuff, I started to get a feel for how it all works and I tried a few things on my own, knowing Sal was there if I needed help. I managed to create a link like Scirlin does, after Sal said he wished he could speak to Malaphar. I tried to reach Jax, but I guess Astaroth had her too well blocked.

"When we arrived to help Jax and I saw Xander fall, after the shock of it that is, I ran over to them and somehow I knew what to do. I felt this massive wave of peace settle over me and wanted to at least try to help him. I didn't think I was gonna be able to manage it until Jax zapped me," she adds with a grin.

"You 'zapped' her? With what? Oh, you mean like Eremiel and

Mathim did to you?" asks Lee.

"Yeah, like that," I say, taking back over the story. "I saw Emelia's eyes turn white and knew what she was trying to do but she seemed to be fading. So, I did what I could to help. I don't know how I knew; I just did. Lizzie was there too, encouraging me. But when I heard Xan take a breath—" I pause, the near loss of him still raw enough to stop me talking for a second. Swallowing the lump in my throat, I continue. "I've never heard a better sound in my life."

He reaches down from his chair to squeeze my shoulder and I look up at him and smile.

"Wow. That's a helluva lot to take in," Lee says. "So, Emelia has superpowers that make her eyes like a mood ring, Jax can heal people using nature, and this Jay just joined Astaroth at the top of my hate list. Is that everything?"

"I think so, sweetie." I smile at her and shake my head at how matter-of-factly she sums it all up.

"Good. Sorry, Jax, can I move you for a minute?" She waves me away from where I sit at Xan's feet and jumps up from her chair. Crossing the distance between them, she sits on his lap and puts her arms around him in a tight hug.

"Please, please, please, don't ever leave us again, Xan. I know you couldn't help it, but we need you here. Like forever." I hear the emotion in her voice and my eyes fill with tears.

"Amen to that," I mutter.

"I promise, Lee," he agrees.

"Thank you. But I guess I'd better stop squishing you, huh?" she laughs, standing up to take her own seat once more.

"That's not quite everything," says Emelia. "Mathim, you said you'd explain why you and Sal both freaked out so bad."

"Yeah, I saw that too. You both looked like, well, I dunno what you looked like," I agree.

Mathim looks off into the distance and huffs out a deep breath.

"You all have heard us speak of Lilim?" He looks at Emelia in particular and when he sees her brief nod, glances quickly at Sal before he goes on. "Lilim was the gentlest soul I ever met. Lee, you remind me so much of her, sometimes it takes my breath away. Lilim had powers like all other demons, but she had the rare ability to choose between the darkness of destruction and violence and the light of healing. She chose the light. When she did this, her eyes would shine white and she would look like peace itself. I never thought I'd see it again and so it brought back memories and took my breath away. Sal, I'm guessing that it was the same for you?"

"Yes. Beautiful memories but painful ones," he agrees quietly. "I miss them both more than I ever thought possible."

A quiet settles over the group, none of us wanting to disturb it until the demons have time to compose themselves. A gentle breeze brushes my skin, making me shiver as it passes, and I look to Mathim to see if he's ready to talk again. I stifle a gasp at the golden aura I see around him, its glow brightening and fading gently. I've seen it before with him but only a very dim light until now and only when speaking of Sabnak. I know where his thoughts lie at the minute and so turn my head to look at Emelia.

"Emelia, how long can you stay?" I ask softly, not wanting to disturb Mathim or Sal as they remember their friends.

She drops her concerned gaze from Sal to answer me.

"I hadn't thought about it yet, Jax. I'm supposed to be working tomorrow. Not sure what I'm expected to do while they sort out the mess from the fire, but I think I need to show my face, at least," she says.

"Can you guys both cross back through the mirror?" Lee's question makes Emelia turn back to Sal who nods.

"Yes, the mirror will be fine," he replies, seemingly recovered. "But we can stay for a while yet."

"Good, cos we all need to figure out what we're doing next, and the more ideas we can come up with, the better," Lee says decisively. "Mathim?"

She looks for his opinion and seeing him still preoccupied, looks worriedly at me. I shrug my shoulders and shake my head. I don't know whether I should disturb him or not, but Lee saves me the decision.

"Hey, big guy, you with us?" she asks, nudging him with her elbow.

"Huh? Oh, I am sorry, Lee. My thoughts took me away with them. What did you say?" he answers apologetically.

"You okay, Mathim?" Lee drops her voice to ask this, but I still hear her.

"I am, little one. I was distracted. But now you have my full attention once more."

He smiles at her, but it doesn't quite reach his eyes, clouded with sadness as they are.

"Hmm, okay. I don't believe you, but I'll let you get away with it. For now. I was saying that we need to figure out what our plan is. While we wait for the next vision, I mean."

"I think we must simply pass the time as well as we can until the day arrives when we can find the third child. That is a job for the three of you; you know I am happy to go along with whatever you decide. I will go and see if Scirlin is free."

And before we can respond, he stands and walks to the house. Lee jumps to her feet to follow him but when I see Sal raise a hand to stop her, I place mine on her arm.

"Maybe give him a few minutes, Lee?" I suggest, looking to Sal for backup. "I know you hate to see him hurting, sweetie. I do too."

"He has been through a lot. We all have. He will talk when he's ready," explains Sal.

"I hope it's soon," she sighs.

"Me too, honey. Me too."

5

Possibilities

"So, Jay, what do you think of your temporary home?" I ask, watching his face as he takes in his surroundings and waiting for his response.

"Yeah, it's fine. Where we sleep isn't really important. I learned that growing up. Doesn't matter where you lay your head, it's what you work towards that counts." He looks off into the distance as he says this and for a moment I wonder at his past.

"That's right. And we work towards the ultimate success of your Father. There can be no greater aim than that. It is late though. Perhaps you should sleep. We start your training in the morning, you should rest while you can. We may not have long to accomplish all that you, and my Master, would wish."

I lead him down the passage, pushing open the first door we come to and ushering him inside. He sees the bed in the corner and crosses the room to sit on the edge.

"Goodnight, Astaroth," he says. "And thank you."

"For what?" I ask, surprised.

"For bringing me here. For training me. For helping me become the man my Father needs me to be. I don't feel gratitude easily, but with you it's impossible not to."

I consider his words and nod.

"Goodnight, Jay."

I close the door, leaving him to his thoughts and to sleep, and return to the fireplace in the main room. Taking a seat next to it, I stare at the flames, allowing the sight and sound of them to wash over me and lull my mind into an easy flow of thoughts. I close my eyes and see the events at the cathedral play out once more. The look of surprise on Xander's face, the look of horror and then utter desolation on Jax's. But above all else, the face that I see the most is that of the traitor. Bathin.

I growl in frustration and attempt to clear his image from my head. I need to concentrate on Jay's training tomorrow. I cannot allow my mind to be clouded in these few quiet hours I have. Breathing deeply, I try again.

Sallas and Malaphar are here somewhere, working to the orders of Lucifer. I need not worry about them. Sargatanas seems to be making progress in gaining their trust. He will inform me of anything of importance happening with them. He may be growing in character, but he will always answer to me. Which leaves Jacqueline and her now diminished group of comrades.

Emelia will undoubtedly do whatever she can to aid Jax and the angels. But according to my Father, the bond between them will eventually win out. Perhaps I can hurry that process along, if necessary. For now though, I do not think it necessary. I will have enough to do with one of Lucifer's children for the next few days. Or weeks. I huff out a breath. Waiting for action is one of the things I abhor most of all. But wait I must. At least I have Jay to distract me.

I take a moment to consider Jay. His reaction to killing Xander was a surprise, albeit a welcome one. He does seem to have a natural affinity for the darker things. I hadn't thought him a natural warrior or adequate soldier for Lucifer's ranks, but following the conflict, I begin to see his worth a little more easily.

I force my thoughts back to Jacqueline, wondering briefly at the disorganised way my mind is working this evening. I put it down to seeing Bathin and the angels and leave it there. The next vision approaches. I will build on my success with Jay and secure the third

to the side of my Master. And should our paths cross again, I will not

hesitate to do whatever is necessary to drag Bathin back to Hell to

face his punishment. I roll my eyes at my inability to focus properly

and stand up, pushing the chair back as I do. And being apparently

unable to concentrate tonight, I stride down the hall to the room at

the end and lie on the bed in the corner. Closing my eyes, I know I

will sort all of this out tomorrow.

***

"Good, Jay. Again," I order.

The boy's skill at fighting has surprised me somewhat. I expected to

have to begin teaching him the very basics of combat but find him

to be more than capable of defending himself. But defending oneself

against humans is very different from being attacked by angels or

other demons.

He moves as though preparing himself to swing a fist at my head,

but quickly switches to aim the other at my ribs. I move easily out of

his way and nod in approval. His breathing is under control, despite

his exertions and he jumps quickly when he sees my foot move

towards him in an attempt to sweep his legs from under him.

"Very good," I murmur. "I'm beginning to think your reflexes are a little more than human, Jay. Let's try it again."

And as we work through the morning, I see I am right. With every attack I aim at him, his defences become quicker, his movements faster and earlier each time. Before midday arrives, I'm astounded to see each move I make, parried and blocked almost before I make it.

"You need food," I say. "You may be the child of Lucifer, and have gifts that may be demon-like, but you are still using energy and that needs to be replaced."

I gesture to the door into the house and watch him as he enters it. Sitting down on the wall of the garden, I shake my head in wonder. The more time I have spent working with him this morning, the more he seems to be connecting with the demon side of his blood. A seed of a thought begins to grow in my mind, and I allow it to settle and work itself through without bothering at it for a result until it is ready. I stand up and begin to walk around the small area of grass, my mind taken away from my surroundings.

If Jay is so easily led into these physical gifts, then what else might he be capable of? Is it possible that this human has been blessed *with other talents by the blood of my Father? Deciding upon my next course of action, I cross the small distance to the house and as I pass the room in which Jay stands eating a hurried meal, I wave my hand across the doorway to silence the conversation I am about to have. I come to a halt when I stand in front of the glass, for now holding only my reflection.*

"Sire?" I say, not knowing if I will get a response. The mirror clouds and then clears to show Lucifer looking at me curiously.

"Yes, Astaroth? What do you need?" he asks.

"I need your instruction on Jay's training, Master. He has shown more talents than are human and I am wondering if there may be other undiscovered gifts," I explain.

"Like what?"

"I began basic soldiers' training, and was surprised to find that once we began, it was not really necessary. His reactions got faster, as though just waiting for an opportunity to be worked. He fights as well as any demon in close combat now, my Lord. Further work on this is not necessary." I pause, allowing him time to take that in before I ask my next question. "Sire, do you think it is possible that

he could have any other of our strengths? He has not mentioned anything like this, but I wondered if he'd even know of them if he does have them. He seemed as surprised as I was at how well he did this morning."

"Demon powers, you mean?" he asks. A frown wrinkles his brow as he considers this. "It is possible, I suppose. They are passed to you all by me when I make you or turn you. Perhaps as I made Jay, he could have received them too. But by blood rather than intention."

"Do you wish me to continue and to find out, Master?"

"Yes, Astaroth." His tone seems distracted as he replies, and I wait for him to elaborate, prompting him gently when he remains silent.

"My Lord?"

"Report back to me as soon as you find out. In fact, no. I'll have Scirlin monitor your training until we have the answer. Astaroth, if he does have gifts, you do know what that means?"

"If Jay has demon powers, then so does Emelia," I say.

"Indeed, my Grand Duke. So does Emelia. Go, Astaroth. Discover the *truth."*

"Yes, Sire."

The glass clears back to the normal reflection of the room and I turn away from it.

"Jay," I call. "Come on. It's time to see what the children of Lucifer can really do."

6

Painful Memories

"Hey, sweetie," I say, as I walk past Lee's desk towards the kitchen. "I need caffeinating, you want one?"

"No, I'm good," she answers quietly. She sits back in her seat and pulls her hair back from her face, dragging her fingers through it and sighing loudly.

"Something wrong?" I ask. "You know I'm here if you need to talk, right? About anything."

I frown at how stressed out she looks. It's not like Lee at all, so I move to perch on the edge of her desk, waiting for her to meet my concerned gaze.

"I'm okay, Jax. Honestly. It's not me. It's Mathim. Have you seen him this morning? He looks terrible." Seeing me answer with a shake of my head, she goes on. "It's been a week since the Jay thing. I thought he'd pull around out of it, but it really hit him hard. Seeing Emelia do her thing, I mean. I guess he meant it when he said it brought back memories."

"I know, Lee. I'm worried about him too. But I can't force him to talk to me. I don't wanna push him if he's not ready. I just don't know what to do." I squeeze her shoulder as I return to the coffee machine.

"Me either. I don't want to hurt him either, Jax. But we can't leave him suffering like this for much longer. It's breaking my heart to see him like this."

"I know, sweetie. Trust me, I know."

A heavy silence settles on us and I try to busy myself throughout the morning, but my mind keeps returning to the demon who saved me from Hell. He did that literally, maybe it's my turn to do it figuratively.

"Lee? Got a minute?" I call.

"Sure, boss," she replies, a minute before she appears in the doorway. "What's up?"

"You're right. We can't leave Mathim like this. We have to do something. Any ideas? Like I said, I can't force him to talk to me."

"No, you're right," she agrees. "But maybe Mrs C could."

She looks as though she's expecting me to tell her off for suggesting it, but I smile in relief.

"Of course, why didn't I think of Joanna? You can't help but talk things over with her as soon as she looks at you. She really knows how to work the empath thing. So, all of us or just Mathim and I?"

Joanna Chapman, or Mrs C, has become such a close friend to all of us since Xan saw Rose Hill Farm from the road and went to see if we could do a ghost hunt there. Always ready to listen and offer advice and support, it's no wonder we all love her so much.

"All of us. Like a catch up. We did it after we got Emelia, why wouldn't we do it after Jay? It won't seem weird that way," she suggests.

"I'll call her and see if she's free. Can you find Xan and Mathim?" She nods and heads towards the door as I reach for the phone.

I hear her talking to someone a moment later while I wait for an answer from the Chapman's home. I can't help but smile when I hear someone pick up.

"Rose Hill Farm," says Joanna.

"Hey, Mrs C, it's Jax."

"Hello, Jax. It's good to hear from you. How is everything?" she asks.

"It's good to talk to you too. Things are quiet at the moment. We're okay, well, most of us. That's kinda why I'm calling," I begin.

"What do you need? What's wrong?"

"It's Mathim. I think he's struggling at the minute. I know you talked to him before and it seemed to help. I wondered if you'd mind trying again. We could visit and say it's to catch you up on everything." I wait for her answer, my knee bouncing up and down under the desk, the concern for my friend showing through.

"Of course, Jax. Bring him here. Are you coming right away?" she replies quickly. "I know how much pain he carries in his heart. When I spoke to him alone like you mentioned, we didn't talk of her though. He tried to but it was too difficult for him. Maybe today will be different. If you hang up the phone, I can call you back to invite you, if it'll help."

"Thanks, Joanna. I don't know what we'd do without you. I'll end the call now and wait for you ringing back. Give it five or ten minutes so I can have him in the room when you do. Is that okay?" My gratitude to this amazing lady knows no bounds.

"Okay, Jax. I'll speak to you in ten minutes."

Putting the phone down, I sit back in my chair and wait for Lee to bring Xan and Mathim. I don't have to wait long before she appears with Xander in tow.

"Hey, Jax. What's up?" asks Xan. "Lee said you wanna discuss work stuff. We have bookings?"

I open my mouth to answer him but am interrupted by a ringing.

"Hello," answers Lee, beating me to the call and sticking her tongue out at me while she listens. "Umm, sure. Hang on, I'll pass you over."

"Who is it?" I ask, seeing her cover the handset as she passes it to me.

"Greg," she says. "He sounds kinda weird."

I frown as I take it from her. Greg's last contact with us did not end well. Being possessed by a demon is not something easy to cover up, and I wrack my brains for a way to explain it away.

"Hi, Greg," I say, still scrabbling for something to tell him. "How are you?"

"Hi, Jax. I'm okay, I guess. This is a business call though, not a personal one. Although I do have questions for you once that's out of the way." His voice shakes a little as he gets to the end of his sentence.

"Of course, Greg. Whatever you need. But first, business?"

"My employers wish to have you do a full hunt here. Whenever is convenient for you. They are anxious to build the working relationship between the castle and your company."

Give Greg his due, he manages to force professionalism into his tone, keeping his voice steady.

"Of course, we'd be delighted. Let me just get the diary up on my screen so we can work out a date." By the time I finish my sentence, Lee spins my laptop around to face me, and I see the schedule loaded already. Giving her a quick grin, I drop my eyes back to the screen and scan over it. "Actually, Greg, we're quiet at the minute. How soon do you want us?"

"Umm, not sure. Give me a minute." I hear him tapping on his keyboard in the brief pause. "Hmm, they're away tomorrow and Friday. I don't suppose you're free on Saturday? They want to be on site, although it'll be me you deal with again. You'll have the whole ground floor, as well as access to all of the rooms the public are allowed into. The family suite is off limits, as it was before."

"Sure, that's fine with us. So, if we're meeting with you, is Saturday the hunt at night or a meeting through the day? I'm not quite sure what you're asking."

"Oh, sorry. I think we got past the discussion stages before. No need to repeat them. Saturday night."

"Are you staying with us?" I ask, hearing a sharp intake of breath in response.

"Yes, I'll be there. But first I need to talk to you about what happened last time you were here."

I close my eyes and wonder what the hell I'm meant to tell him. That he was taken over by an earth-bound demon, hellbent on capturing Mathim and returning him to Lucifer?

"Of course, Greg."

"I don't really remember much," he starts. "I'd been feeling unwell that day, almost like the beginnings of a migraine. It felt like a pressure building over and around me."

I wait out the silence that hangs after these words, not wanting to interrupt him.

"Oh, for God's sake," he says. "Jax, we'll have to leave this until I can call you back. Unfortunately, I have to go. Duty calls. I'll ring you tomorrow? It's a quieter day here tomorrow. Is that okay?"

I have to stop an audible sigh of relief escaping. Tomorrow gives me time to figure out what to tell him.

"No problem, Greg. I'll be around all day, just call when you're free."

He says goodbye and ends the call just as Mathim walks into the office through the doorway to the house. I've only just put down the phone when it rings again.

"Hello?" I say.

"Hi, Jax."

"Oh, hi, Mrs C. How are you?" I answer, as though I haven't spoken to her today.

"I'm well, thank you. I was calling to catch up on things."

"Catch up? Yeah, there's kinda a lot happened since we saw you last. Where do I start?" Knowing it's safe as Mrs C is playing her role well, I reach and press the button on speaker. "I've put you on speakerphone so everyone can help make sure I don't miss anything."

"Hi, everyone," she says. "Look, if you're not busy, you can all come here. We can talk properly over a coffee?"

I look around the room to see the reactions of everyone. Xan smiles, while Lee claps her hands happily, eliciting a chuckle from Mathim.

"Guys? We're not busy, wanna go?" I ask.

They all agree quickly, and I grin at Lee's excitement.

"That's a yes, then. Okay, Joanna, we'll be there in half an hour if you're sure you're not busy."

"Of course I'm sure. I wouldn't have invited you otherwise. See you soon."

***

"Oh my, Xander, and you're alright now?" I see the concern on Joanna's face as we finish telling her the story of recent events.

"I'm fine, Mrs C. Honestly. As soon as Jax and Emelia did their thing, I was recovered. It was crazy." He shakes his head. "I'm just glad Emelia figured out the healing thing."

This is what I've been waiting for and I nudge Joanna's elbow gently from my seat beside her. If anything is going to set off Mathim's thoughts down whatever path they've been going down lately, it's this.

"Yes, that's quite a gift. Jax," she says, turning to me, "have you tried healing anyone else?"

I wonder at her attention to me when she knows she needs to help Mathim but trust to her instincts and go with the conversation.

"No, I never even thought about it until then. Well, even then, I didn't think about it. I just knew Emelia needed help. Why?"

"Just a thought. I don't sense a healing energy around you. I can usually pick that up quite easily. I think perhaps it was a combination of events that allowed you to do it, so please don't any of you put yourselves in more danger thinking that Jax will always be able to help or save you." She looks sternly at all of us until we all nod in agreement. "Good. Now, Mathim, your turn."

He starts a little, her sudden focus on him catching him off guard.

"My turn?" he asks, a puzzled look on his face.

"Yes, my boy. Your turn." Her affectionate name for him makes him smile. "You are lost from us a little, I feel."

He opens his mouth to reply but stops himself before he starts, sighing deeply instead. Lifting his eyes to the ceiling, he seems to take a moment to gather his thoughts before meeting her eyes again.

"I know better than to try to lie to you, Joanna. Or the rest of you. I know you have been worried about me. Especially you, Lee. I am sorry. My thoughts have been pulled in one direction only of late."

"It helps to talk, Mathim," Joanna encourages. "We cannot change the past, but we would share your pain."

"I do not think I can," he says quietly.

"Try," she replies.

"All of it?" he asks. "It is not a pretty story. Some of it is the stuff of nightmares."

His eyes have come to rest on Lee, and I smile sadly realising he wants to protect her from what he's seen and suffered.

"All of it," says Lee firmly, putting her hand over his.

"Very well, I will try." He takes a deep breath and begins his story. "I was Captain of one of Hell's armies, respected by most and loved by a few. There were six of us. Sallas, Tezrian, and Scirlin some of you have met. But the two you never got chance to were Lilim and Sabnak. We were more than friends, we became like family. No matter where we were sent or for how long, we always came back to each other.

"Until we didn't. Astaroth was jealous of me and of the regard in which Lucifer held me. He worked against me in any way he could. When nothing worked, he turned his attention to those I loved most in the world."

He looks around as he pauses and sees encouraging nods from Lee and Joanna. As always, Lee cannot help herself.

"Tell us about them, what were they like?"

Seeing the smile tug at the corners of his mouth as he remembers them, I give Lee a mental pat on the back for this interruption.

"They were so different, but so close. Lilim was the most gentle soul. She was born to Samael, hell's torturer, and Lilith, Lucifer's most ardent follower. She was forced to witness such horrors as a child, that when her powers became apparent and she had both the ability to heal as well as to harm, she chose the path of light. She was caring and kind and the best healer I had ever seen. The only time I ever saw her other side show was in her defence of those she loved. And that was her undoing.

"Sal was kidnapped by the angels and held captive and beaten. Kushiel's blade almost killed him, but Lil healed him when we got him back to Hell. Astaroth was determined to wake him early. Lilim knew I needed to speak to him first and refused Astaroth, her eyes betraying her darker side. Her standing up to him was her downfall though. He accused her of conversing with angels, of treachery to Lucifer."

Everyone is silent, not risking stopping him with questions as we can all see how difficult it is for him to tell us.

"We defended her, of course, and I used whatever sway I had with Lucifer to plead for leniency. And so, he did not kill her. He made her work with her father in his torture chambers. It almost destroyed her but somehow, she found the strength to deal with what she was forced to endure. But still Astaroth was not satisfied. He told his underling, Sargatanas, to accuse Sabnak of betrayal too, while they were in the Realms. Lucifer was furious. He ordered Lil to torture her, but she refused. She stood up to him and defied her

Master. Her powers betrayed her once more. He killed her."

7

New Skills

"But how, Astaroth?" Jay asks, his frustration evident in his tone and expression. "I don't know what you mean."

I am somewhat disappointed in the boy. I had thought that he would have no difficulty in this, considering how quickly he developed in his fighting.

"You must focus, Jay. Focus your mind. Think of everything that has ever stopped you from getting what you want, of anyone who has hurt you or got in your way. Feel the hatred grow inside you like a ball of fire. And when it can build no more, then release it from your mind." I keep my voice even and calm, putting pressure on him now will not help him.

I watch him, looking for any sign of the gifts I suspect he may have. He narrows his eyes at his target, a small tree in the corner of the garden, and I see him frown with the effort he puts into his thoughts. But to no avail.

"Why?" he growls. "Why can't I do this?"

And honestly, I have no answer for him. The anger is there, bubbling barely under the surface and ready to explode at a moment's notice but he cannot harness its great power.

"Come, Jay. Sit. Let us rest for a while."

He looks surprised, but crosses to the chair opposite me and huffs out a disappointed sigh as he drops into it.

"Tell me about yourself," I say, leaning back in my chair.

"What would you like to know?" he asks.

"I don't know. Just about your life before I came into it. You need to take a break and it would be preferable not to sit in silence."

He stretches his legs out in front of him and crosses his ankles, looking off into the distance for a moment before he starts.

"I was born Jason Forster and had a normal childhood, I suppose, up until I was five. I lived with my mum and dad. One night, a fire started and the man I thought was my father woke us up and sent us running outside. As he was about to follow us to safety, the stairs collapsed under him and he was stuck. He didn't get out. My mother *thought there was something wrong with me, that shock stopped me from grieving properly. But it wasn't that. I didn't really care. He meant very little to me. I think I always knew he wasn't my real father. I never had any respect for him."*

He pauses to check that I want him to continue and I nod but remain silent.

"My mother tried her best. Always. Even before the fire, I think she had doubts that her son was 'normal'. I suppose I seemed detached or isolated, but in truth, I didn't ever feel like anyone was worth my time or attention. She never said anything about it though, she just kept trying to encourage me to try new things, reassured me she'd always be there for me and that life would get better. That I could become anything I wanted if I worked for it.

"She died when I was eight. Cancer. I was sent into a care home; foster families just didn't work out and I returned to the system again and again. I focused my efforts on school, and then university, working so hard towards the job I thought I wanted. When I got there, I realised how empty it all is, how futile. You work and work to reach the targets you set yourself, but when you achieve them, it doesn't satisfy you. You work long hours for what? To buy a house? A car? To escape to somewhere else for two weeks a year, only to

return to your mundane, boring life until you can escape again. I knew I was always meant for more, I just didn't know what until now."

"And the people at the cathedral you watched so closely? Who are they to you?"

At the mention of the place we first met, the frown takes hold of his features once more and his words are spit through gritted teeth.

"They are hypocrites. All of them. So judgemental and pious, yet all with their dirty little secrets. They go there once or twice a week, sometimes more, to make themselves feel better, looking down on everyone else." Seeing me regarding him closely, he shrugs. "They are nothing to me personally. I would just like to see them, and those like them, brought low."

I nod slowly, wondering how best to use all of this to encourage him, while at the same time, filing it away in my mind in case I can ever use it to my advantage at a later time.

"Hmm, very well, Jay. If you can master these things that I am trying to help you to learn, then your 'punishment' as you call it, will be far more spectacular than if you don't. So, shall we try again?"

I gesture to the tree, and he sets his jaw determinedly as he stands and walks back to his original position. But a few moments later, his expression is as frustrated as it was before.

"Keep trying, Jay. I will be back in a moment."

I walk into the house and do not stop until I face my own reflection.

"Sire?"

"Yes, Astaroth?" Lucifer replies, appearing in the glass almost immediately.

"Master, I asked you once before about how far I could push your children. Is your answer still the same?"

"It is. Do what you will. We must discover the truth of their abilities."

"Yes, my Lord." I bow my head as his image fades, waiting until it has completely gone before walking back outside.

"Still nothing?" I ask. "Hmm, perhaps I was wrong."

"No. I can do it. I know I can," he argues, turning away from me for another failed attempt.

"Really, Jay, I just do not think you have it. You can fight well, but that must be all you're capable of. No matter, perhaps when we turn your sister from the angels, these gifts that your Father so wishes to have under his command may still be available to us. Emelia did seem a little more intuitive than you, after all."

I shrug my shoulders dismissively, and as I do, I see the sight I've been waiting for. Although not the colour I had thought. Instead of the violet flash, red sparks light his eyes. Bloodlust. I strain not to smile triumphantly, keeping my expression neutral, unlike Jay, whose face twists into a snarl of rage as he whirls away from me and zeroes in on his target. Without any sign of him doing anything, it explodes into splinters that fly out so fast that I do not have time to put up any kind of barrier against them. Jay spins to face me, a challenge in his stare, and I smirk at him. He does not even realise that he has been struck by one of the airborne results of his work, blood trickling down from his cheekbone, as he waits for my reaction.

"Easy, Jay. One tree does not make you ready to take me on," I warn. "You needed motivation."

He scowls for a second at the realisation of my having manipulated him so successfully, but it soon clears into a proud grin.

"Thank you, Astaroth. Now I know how to do it, I think I'll be able to apply it to anything else you might ask me to do. What's next?"

"Again. Let us make sure you have mastery of this before we move on."

Working his way around the garden, destroying plant after shrub, each explosion takes less and less effort and his actions become more fluid. When he reaches the end of his circuit of destruction, he looks at me expectantly.

"Like I said, Astaroth, what's next?"

For hours we work, until the daylight begins to fade around us, the fires Jay has created the only light we have. In one afternoon, he has gained full control over the gifts of destruction, fire and wind.

"It is getting late, Jay. We have done enough for one day. We will start again tomorrow." Seeing the disappointed slump of his shoulders, I shake my head in amused regard. "You need to rest. As demon-like as you have proven yourself thus far, your body is still a *human one. Tomorrow will be harder than today, you will need all the strength you can muster."*

"Why?" he asks eagerly. "What are we doing tomorrow?"

"You have shown great skill today at using your natural talents on inanimate objects. Tomorrow we will test your skills on things that have at least some say over what you're doing to them."

His eyes light up at my words and I know for certain that this child of my Master has an inner darkness so obviously missing from his sister.

"You mean—"

"Yes, Jay, in the morning we will start teaching you how to give out the punishment you desire."

8

Discoveries

"Oh, Mathim," says Lee, her voice cracking a little, "I am so sorry."

"Thank you, little one. Lilim's death hit us all so hard but we did not have time to grieve for her before we had another nightmarish situation to deal with. Immediately following her death, Sabnak was taken to Samael and tortured."

He stops and closes his eyes, pain written all over his face.

"Mathim, if it's too hard—" I begin but am cut off by his eyes opening and snapping to mine.

"I have started now, Jax. I think if I stop before I reach the end, I won't be able to ever have this conversation again."

I smile and reach for his hand.

"Take your time."

Taking a deep breath and squaring his shoulders, he continues.

"Hours. For hours, she was tortured. Every kind of pain imaginable and all done as I was forced to watch next to Lucifer through the mirror in his throne room." A gasp from Lee makes him pause for a second and he reaches for her hand when he sees the tears appearing and falling from her eyes at what he had to go through. "I am sorry, Lee. I will save you the details as I do not wish to cause you further anguish. Suffice it to say, she was put through every kind of punishment that Samael could think of to try to get her to admit guilt she did not have.

"And through it all, I talked to her. Scirlin risked his life to open and maintain a link between us, allowing our final moments to still be spent together in the only way we could be. Telling her tales of better times, trying to keep her with me for as long as I could. And then I heard the words I'd been praying for all along. Samael stopped, saying that anyone would have admitted their treachery following everything he'd put her through and declaring that she must be innocent. I told Scirlin to ready all the healers he could and to have them ready for me bringing her to them. It would have been a race to try and save her, given the state she was in by now. She had already said goodbye to me as she knew she was dying. A spark of hope and for a moment I believed it. I thought we might get through it."

He straightens his spine and looks at me, and I know how much it's taking for him to speak the words that are coming next. I see the tears form and spill and my heart breaks for him.

"Lucifer crossed through the glass and cut her throat. Said she might have been innocent but being as ruined as she was, she was useless to him."

His words run out and a heavy silence drops onto us all like a blanket. Lee gets up from her seat quietly, walks behind Mathim and puts her arms around him. He places one hand on her arm, using the other to wipe away the tears from his face. Not sobbing, crying tears, instead noiseless ones he couldn't help from falling.

"My poor boy," says Joanna. "It is a wonder you were able to go on."

Clearing his throat, he chuckles.

"Sabnak would never have allowed me to give up. She made me swear to get revenge on Astaroth. To make sure that he did not succeed in his plans. I would not let her down."

"She sounds amazing, Mathim. I'd have loved to know her." A cool breeze makes me shiver as I speak but I know the raw emotion in the air contributes just as much to the goose bumps appearing on my skin.

"She would have liked you too, Jax," he says. "Your stubborn streak? You remind me of her sometimes. It makes me smile."

"I can't imagine the pain you're in, Mathim. But we are all here for you, I hope you know that." Xander's words bring a quick smile from the demon we've all come to care so much about, but it drops as quickly as it appears.

"She was more than a life partner. She was the better part of everything I am. I am just so lost without her."

The look of desolation on his face brings fresh pain to my heart that I can't help him, but a flash of gold round him distracts me for a moment as it flares brightly before fading away.

"Doing what you're doing, in helping Jax and the angels, is a huge thing, Mathim. I know your Sabnak would be proud of you. If I can do anything at all, you only have to ask. You know that goes for you too, don't you?" Mrs C's concerned gaze makes him smile.

"I know that. Thank you, Joanna. I am glad to know you. All of you."
He rubs his hands over his face. "I feel a little less burdened now
that you all know. But I would walk for a while, if that's okay?"

"Only if I get to keep you company," replies Lee. "I promise, I'll be
quiet and everything. But I don't want you to be alone."

"Of course. And you do not need to be quiet," he laughs. "Because
if you do that, then you will not be you."

They make their way outside and I smile to see Lee slide her arm
through to link Mathim's, making him look down at her fondly.

"Wow, I just can't even imagine what that's been like," says Xan.
"Carrying that around with him."

"It hurts him even more than you think. But hopefully, he has
unburdened himself a little by sharing his grief." Mrs C looks sadly
out of the window after them. "He seems to have grown close to
Lee though. That is a good thing."

"Yeah, they hit it off instantly. Her reminding him of Lilim, I guess," I
agree. "Joanna, when he spoke of Sabnak, did you see it?"

"See what?" they ask together.

"The soulmate glow thing we talked about before." Seeing Xander's confused expression, I quickly fill him in on the conversation I had before about it surrounding Lee and Marcus, watching a smile spread across his face as I describe it.

"That's beautiful, Jax. And if anyone deserves it, it's our girl," he says.

"Definitely. But Joanna, you didn't see it around Mathim?"

"I didn't, Jax. But it doesn't really surprise me. I can't imagine that a relationship like theirs is commonplace between demons. It must have been something very special though for that link to remain after her death." She looks thoughtful and I raise my eyebrows at her. "Oh, nothing. So, what next for you all?"

"Nothing planned as yet. We're stuck waiting for the next vision. Until then, we'll just do what we do, I suppose. We're back at the castle soon though. Greg called to set up another hunt. How am I meant to explain that he was possessed last time?" I look at each of them in turn. "I don't like lying to anyone if I can help it, and even if I had to, what story could I make up that would be believable, considering what he went through?"

"I'd suggest the truth, Jax. Keep it as simple as you can and go into as little detail as possible though. Xan? What is it?" Her attention has been caught by him moving to the window.

"I dunno," he murmurs. "Probably nothing. Only I thought I heard a voice calling for Jax. I thought maybe it was Lee, but there's no one there. I must have been mistaken."

"Xan, tell me what you saw when you were stabbed." Joanna's voice has taken on a curious tone and he comes back to sit at the table.

"What do you mean, Mrs C?" he asks.

"Well, Jax said you died. Do you remember anything?"

"Like a tunnel with a bright light at the end of it?" he replies with a grin, making us chuckle. "Honestly, I don't really remember anything. Just everything going black, being unable to keep my eyes open and feeling so heavy. But then, I felt kinda weightless and peaceful. Eventually I heard Jax's voice, and I tried to find her in the darkness. And then, this warmth spread through me and Jax got clearer until I could see her. That's when I came back, I guess."

"And since then?" Joanna encourages.

"I've been fine. I don't feel ill or anything. I feel like my old self. Well, apart from… No… It doesn't matter." He shakes his head and grins at us. "Really, I'm good."

"Apart from what?" I ask quickly. He hasn't mentioned anything to me about feeling anything less than normal and his abrupt stop in his sentence worries me. "Xan, if you're not a hundred percent, we need to get you fixed."

"Relax, Jacqueline. I'm fairly sure that's not what Xan meant. Am I right, Xan?" Joanna says calmly.

He sighs in defeat and shakes his head with a smile.

"I'm not gonna be able to just change the subject, am I? Okay, so I've thought I've heard things, maybe seen some stuff too. Only here today though. And only just now. Like that voice? I could have sworn I heard Lee calling to you. And for a moment, when we arrived, I thought I saw someone in the window of the old house. But I just put it down to the light reflecting. What's going on, Mrs C?

Why do I get the feeling you know something?"

"I don't, for certain. I think though that when you crossed over, no matter how briefly, it may have opened you up a little. Don't be surprised if you have one or two extra perceptions, that's all. It's nothing to worry about." She laughs and rolls her eyes. "I really don't need to tell you that, given what you do though, do I?"

"No, I know its not a problem. In fact, I kinda like the idea."

I see excitement in his eyes at the possibility of sensing spirit and honestly, I can't blame him. I've always loved what we do, ghost-hunting and the like, but the actual interaction with those passed fills me with such a sense of wonder that I don't think it'll ever get old.

"Maybe you can test it all out next time we work, Xan," I suggest. "We have the castle to visit. That should be a good start for you to get a handle on whatever new stuff you find you can do."

"Oh, yeah. That'll be perfect," he agrees happily, a second before his head snaps to the right, his attention grabbed by something I missed. "There it is again. Did you hear it?"

"No," I say. "I didn't."

"I have a better idea. I think maybe Lizzie wants some company," Joanna chuckles. "Why don't you go over and see what she wants?"

Xan leaps to his feet, almost knocking his chair over in his hurry to get there.

"Alright, Xan. Jeez," I laugh. "Chill."

"Sorry. I just wanna meet the girl who helped save you, Jax."

"It's fine, but we have loads of time. No need to destroy furniture."

We walk out of the kitchen towards the front door, leaving Joanna giggling at us both.

"What about the others?" asks Xan. "Should we get them first?"

I look around and see them sitting on the grass a distance away and shake my head.

"No, let's leave them to it. If they come back before we're done, Joanna can send them over. Plus, you'll need to concentrate, and

Lee will be way too excited to let you do that if she thinks you're suddenly some psychic superman. Why don't we figure out what's going on first?"

"Good idea. Yeah, okay, I'm good with that."

I push open the door and step into the cool air of the old building I've grown to love so much. Instead of calling out, I step aside to allow Xan to lead the way further inside.

"Ooh, you can see me too now," a little voice says ahead, just as Xander stops dead in front of me, making me walk into the back of him.

"Hi, Lizzie," I say, stepping around Xan who's still frozen in disbelief. "Give Xan a minute, you're the first person he's been able to see."

"Okay," she says happily, her nodding making the blonde ringlets bounce and catch the rays of sunlight filtering through the door. "But he knows I'm not scary or anything, doesn't he?"

I grin at her as I open my mouth to reassure her, but Xan beats me to it.

"I know you're not scary, sweetheart. I was just so surprised I could see you that it shocked me a little. It's my pleasure to meet you, Lizzie," he says.

"And mine," she replies politely.

"So, Lizzie, why did you call from the house today? You usually just come right to me. Is everything okay with you?" I wonder if the exertions from escaping Astaroth and helping with Xan have drained her energy a little.

"No, I'm fine. But the lady angel said I get to play a new game with you now. With both of you. So, I had to call from here to see if Xan could hear me. And you did. Does that mean you won the game? Or did I win cos I made you hear me?" Her little face screws up into a confused frown, making my heart melt.

"I think it means you both won, and I lost because I was the only one who didn't hear you. Did the lady angel want anything in particular, honey, or was it just so we could see if Xan could see you?" I haven't heard from Eremiel, so I wonder if perhaps Ambriel has sent Lizzie.

"Nope, just to play. Xan, can we play like Jax and I do?" she asks brightly. "I send you pictures, and you have to try and think what I'm sending."

"That sounds fun, angel," he agrees.

"And a really good way of practising all this. If Lizzie and I hadn't built such a strong link... Well, I dunno what might have happened."

"Yeah, that doesn't bear thinking about," he mutters, before turning back to her. "Lizzie, I wanted to thank you. You saved my friend. I can never repay that."

"She's my friend too," she smiles. "And I'm glad we beat that mean man. I do not like him." Her eyes narrow as she speaks of Astaroth.

"Me either, sweetie. I'm glad we have you and the rest of my friends."

"Me too," she replies, before going silent and losing focus on us, as though listening to something we can't hear. "Oh, I need to go back. I'll see you both soon. Don't forget to listen for me, Xan. You can still play too, Jax. Bye."

She skips back down the hall and fades from sight as we say our own goodbyes, leaving us standing in silence.

"Wow," breathes Xan. "Just wow."

"Yeah, I know. I felt exactly the same way when I saw her for the first time."

"She was so clear, so in focus. I don't know how I thought you see spirit, but that's not what I'd imagined. She's adorable, by the way," he adds.

"Oh, she's definitely that. What do you say we go find Lee and Mathim and head home? It's been an interesting day, but I'd like to check he's okay when there's just us around, I get the feeling he tries to shield Joanna from as much of his pain as he can. He can relax around us."

"Yeah, good idea. And he may well be in dire need of rescue from Lee by now too."

9

Amusement

"You are sure?"

"Yes, my Lord. He has shown an affinity for these things, gaining not only the knowledge of how to use the gifts we have uncovered, but also how to control them with ease. He has mastered many of the skills we demons possess. He is ready, either to return to you, or to remain here unsupervised and begin the works you have planned for him."

And as much as I am anxious to be alone once more to track the traitor before the next of Lucifer's children is unshrouded, I do not lead my Father false. Jay is indeed as ready as I say.

"Very well, Astaroth. I trust to your judgement once more. As for Jay's immediate future, you said there was something he wished to accomplish before he left Earth once more?"

"Yes, Sire," I answer. "He wishes to bring low some of those he scorns. It is not for personal vengeance. He just despises those of his own kind who paint themselves as better than they are."

"On this occasion, I will permit it. It will allow me to observe his progress in what you have taught him. Make your plans, my Grand Duke, and inform Scirlin before you begin. I am very interested to see my son at work. After that, I will decide on if he should stay where he is or return here."

"Of course, Sire." I bow my head as his image fades and turn my step to find Jay.

"Good morning," I greet him as he comes out of the doorway from his room. "I have some interesting news from your Father."

I see him strain to keep his eagerness from his face and am impressed when he does not prompt me to carry on.

"I have told him that you are ready, that you have learned and mastered all I have shown you. He agrees that it is time we reward your work with the opportunity you requested."

This time his calm mask slips and he grins openly.

"Really?" he asks.

"Yes, Jay, really. I have no doubt that you have spent some time

thinking of how you would accomplish all that you would wish to,

but I will ask, do you need help to plan this? Or to make it as

fulfilling as you would like it to be." I see him start to answer but

then pause before he speaks and so continue. "There is no shame in

requesting help, Jay. I will think no less of you for it. In fact, I am

always happy to bring sorrow to this race and would enjoy the

distraction of assisting you."

"Yes, Astaroth. Please. I have ideas but am unsure of how to carry

them out. Your expertise would be most appreciated."

I nod and begin to turn from him, impressed once more at how

easily he comes under my influence.

"Very well. Come, let us sit and plan our strategy. This will be

another valuable lesson. You can never be too prepared."

I don't look back or listen to check he follows me, I already know he

will. And so, with a smirk, I take my seat and get ready to help the

son of Lucifer make his first real impact on the world.

*** *

As we walk towards the huge cathedral, I shake my head in wonder that this human has mastered one of the most difficult skills given to

any demons. As he explained his idea to me, it became apparent

that he would need to have it in order to be able to carry out what

he wished. I had thought there would be a need to postpone his

plan, and so began the journey here instructing him on the way. But

to my surprise, it came easily to him and so no further delay was

necessary.

"Umm, Astaroth, there is one thing I hadn't thought of. You can't

enter, am I right?"

I had wondered how long it would take him to realise this,

deliberately leaving it unsaid to test him on his strategic thinking.

"I cannot," I agree.

"So, then, how do we do this?" he asks, panic appearing for a

moment before he forces it away.

"Well done, Jay. Your ability to calm your mind to think is improved

vastly. Perhaps a walk while you work it out to its conclusion?" I

gesture to the grassy corner where we first talked.

"Yes, I need a moment." He walks ahead of me, head bowed in

thought and he begins to pace back and forth between the trees.

I stand and watch him, offering no help until he asks. If he asks. This son of my Master is not one to request advice unless absolutely necessary.

"You taught me the power of visualisation. I think I have it," he says. "No, actually, I know I do. I know how to fix this."

The determination and surety in his tone makes me chuckle and I still cannot quite believe the change in him in just a few short days.

"Very well then, Jay. If you are ready?" I encourage.

"You don't need to know what I'm doing?" he asks, surprised.

"I do not. Unless you would wish me to check over every detail of your plan?"

"No. I mean, I just thought..." His sentence trails off as he straightens his spine and squares his shoulders. "Thank you for your faith in me, Astaroth."

He turns back to the cathedral and strides to stand in its shadow.

Positioning himself at the entrance, I watch as he closes his eyes and settles his breathing. I can feel the energy building around him even from the distance at which I stand.

"Astaroth, the door if you wouldn't mind. I would prefer you to secure the building from this side while I do this, as well as when we enter."

I walk to the door and getting as close as I can to it, before the dim white glow protecting it stops me, I wave my hand over it, preventing anyone from being able to leave. Stepping backwards, I move behind Jay once more to observe his actions.

"It is done, Jay," I say quietly, seeing him nod in response.

The air around us begins to charge and I can feel static in it. I look to the building and see it unharmed so far. The white aura is whole, the angelic shield still intact, but as I begin to look back to Jay, something stops me. A faint pulsing of the light it emanates, hardly noticeable at first, but growing more apparent with each passing moment. My eyes widen at what I'm seeing as the pulsing turns into a flashing before I hear a crack and then a noise almost like the rending of metal upon metal. A fissure of red appears down its centre, eating its way down from the top, and growing brighter as it progresses. Almost like a bolt of lightning in appearance, it does not stop until it hits the ground, a shuddering in the air around us when it is complete.

I snap my head to Jay in disbelief, masking my expression when he turns to face me.

"It is done," he says simply, but I notice the beads of sweat that betray how much it took to accomplish.

"You are ready then?" I ask evenly.

"Yes, Astaroth. And as this building is now unconsecrated, you will be free to enter." A wry chuckle escapes him, and I raise an eyebrow in question. "It just seems fitting that now this place is as unholy as those inside it."

No one pays any attention to us as we enter the dark, previously sanctified space and I nod to Jay as he gestures to the door. Repeating my actions from a few moments ago, I seal the entrance and take up position in the shadows. I nod to Jay and see him take a deep breath to steady himself, before moving silently down the side of the pews until he reaches the front.

"Our God is mighty," the priest declares with vigour. "And He is good. We have been told that our place with Him is secured if we live our lives without sin."

I scan those in the congregation, some looking bored but some with expressions of awe and adoration on their faces. Adoration in which this "holy man" revels, almost preening under their gazes with pride. Jay catches my attention and rolls his eyes as the sermon continues.

"And this is what we must do. Be ever on our guard for evil thoughts and actions tempting us, fight against those who would lead us from this path of righteousness, be ever vigilant for their approach."

The irony of his words does not escape me, and I have to stifle a laugh at the timing of them. Jay begins to move slowly towards the stairs of the pulpit, and I see a shimmer as he creates the glamour that I showed him yesterday with ease. I smirk at his success, no one noticing his approach but me.

He looks at me, eyebrows raised in question and I nod in answer. It is time for the show to begin.

10

Next Steps

"Hey," I say, nudging Mathim's foot with mine. "You okay?"

"Yes, Jax, I am. For the first time in a long time, I feel better. I have carried those images with me for so long that it felt as though I were drowning in them. Sharing them with you all seems to have lightened the load a little. It does not hurt any less, but it does not quite torture me as much as it did somehow."

His eyes lift to mine as he says this, and I smile at him. I lean back on my arms, stretching my legs out in front of me, and my smile widens as I feel the energy tickle my palms. He looks down at me from his seat at the table and shakes his head with an amused expression.

"What?" I ask.

"You could not look any more at peace if you tried," he says. "I have never seen such a connection with nature as yours."

The sound of Lee's voice makes us both turn to watch her and Xan making their way towards us, Xan rolling his eyes as he approaches.

"Honestly, Lee, there's not much to tell. Before I died, I couldn't see or hear spirit at all. And now I can. That's it."

"But how?" she asks.

"Mrs C said it was because I'd 'crossed the veil'. I guess that's why." Hearing her sigh, he shrugs apologetically. "I'm sorry, kid. I dunno what else to tell you."

"Hmm, well, yeah. I guess it is as simple as that," she concedes.

Xan takes the seat across the table from Mathim, turning his chair to face me, as Lee flops on the grass beside me.

"As much as I'd like to just chill out with you, Jax, business first. Greg called. He'll meet us at the castle, ready to set up at eight. But he asked that we meet him an hour earlier." She looks briefly at the notepad in her hand.

"Yeah, that's fine, sweetie."

"I knew it would be, so I just agreed. We have a few queries about hunts, one wants to use the big house though, Xan. Think we can find a weekend when your parents aren't around?"

"Sure, chica. Gimme a minute." He pulls his phone from his pocket and taps on the screen. "There's three you can choose from, I'll send you them. Find the one that fits the best for us, and just let me know so I can give everyone the time off."

She nods as she ticks the page, reaching for her tablet and checking she has what she needs.

"The other suggested locations are normal ones, apart from a group that wants somewhere 'really spooky'." She makes air quotes as she says this, making me chuckle. "I wondered if Mrs C would let us use Rose Hill Farm. Or are we keeping that private for now?"

I frown at the idea of allowing anyone else into the beautiful old house and, looking around the group, see that my distaste is mirrored by Xan and Mathim.

"No," I say, "I'd rather keep it for us for the time being. Public hunts are a long way down the line there, I think. Maybe the castle, if tomorrow goes well."

"Ooh, yeah. That's a much better idea. And the owners seemed really keen for them to start." She scribbles on the paper and then puts the pad aside. "Okay, we're all caught up, I think."

"Looks like that could be perfect timing," says Mathim, nodding behind me unnecessarily, the cool breeze ruffling my hair telling me of the angel's arrival.

"Hey, Eremiel. Nice to see you. Is this a social call?"

A sudden laugh from Xan makes us all turn to look at him and he shakes his head.

"Lizzie. She sent trucks," he says in explanation.

"Hi, Jax," Lizzie says in my head. "I have to send boys things cos Xan is a boy." Her grumbling tone makes me smile.

"I'm sure you can send anything you like, sweetie," I send back.

"Okay," she says happily. "I have to go but we'll play later. The lady angel says it'll be good for us. Bye, Jax."

"Bye, sweetheart."

I realise everyone is waiting for me and sit up straight.

"Sorry, guys. She popped in to complain at having to use boys' toys to talk to Xan. I said she can send anything though, so be prepared for teddy bears." Turning to Eremiel, I continue. "She seems to get on well with Ambriel."

A look of complete confusion appears for a second before it clears, and he nods.

"Yes, she does. But to answer your previous question, Jax, this isn't a social visit. The next child has been unveiled. Do you need time to prepare?"

I puzzle over his reaction, but quickly dismiss the thought and focus on what he's just said.

"Nope, I'm good. Ready whenever you are, although Lee might need a few minutes."

"Yes," she states firmly. "I'm not having you scare me ever again. Five minutes, Eremiel? Just so I can make coffee and have the sugary stuff for when she's done?"

"That's fine, Lee. We will wait for you before we start." He sits down on the wall behind the table. "Xander, you look much better than the last time we met. How are you feeling?"

"I'm fine, thank you." He glances quickly at me and I nod in answer to his unspoken question. "I did however gain a few new skills. It seems that my brush with death left me with some new abilities."

"Really? Well, I suppose I should not be surprised. It does happen sometimes. What can you do?" he asks curiously.

"I can see and hear spirit. That's all. Well, as far as we know."

"Very good."

Lee's return ends the conversation and we wait until she finishes what she's doing and sits back on the grass opposite me, reaching for her pen and notebook and crossing her legs.

"Okay, I'm ready whenever you are."

"Mathim?"

"Yes, Eremiel, I am ready too."

"Very well then. Jax?"

"Yup, hit me." I settle back, threading my fingers into the long grass and kicking off my shoes so I can do the same with my feet.

They take their places at either side of me and place a hand on my shoulders. And in an instant, I'm astounded by the beauty of the scene before me, but I force myself to close my eyes and focus. Reaching out with my mind, I concentrate on the pinprick of light in the darkness, moving towards it through the mists.

"This is different," I murmur. "It's darker."

I push my way forward, straining to see anything. Sighing in frustration, I know I need to do something to be able to see clearly. I focus on the feeling in my hands and feet and, as I did to save Xan, I pull on the energy from the earth. The darkness recedes a little and I huff out a relieved breath when I see the figure I'm searching for.

"Okay, I've got her."

Drawing nearer, I see a small, thin girl, with blonde hair and dark clothes. As I look around for other clues, a name echoes in my head.

"Aurora."

As I speak her name, she turns towards me and I hear faint music in the air. Even as I notice it, I see she's standing on a stage, the spotlight making her seem even smaller somehow. But when I look at her, something makes me gasp. A shadow approaches from behind her, growing bigger as it gets closer until finally it wraps itself around her and she disappears into the darkness, leaving only a final image of a map with a route plotted across it hovering in my mind.

My eyes snap open and I look straight at Lee.

"Music. I think she's touring. But there's something wrong," I say quickly.

"What is it, Jax?" asks Xan.

I turn to answer him, barely noticing the white aura around him.

"I dunno. There was a shadow behind her. It got closer and closer, then it kinda swallowed her up. What can that mean?"

"I do not know, Jax," answers Eremiel, as I take the chocolate being shoved at me by Lee.

"She can't be lost already, though. Right? I mean, we get these visions at the same time as Astaroth, if not before?" I ask. "Okay, Lee, I'm eating it."

I wait for an answer while I replenish my energy, smiling gratefully as Lee passes me a coffee.

"That is correct, he cannot have her already. But I am at a loss as to what the shadow can signify," Eremiel says.

We all sit in silence for a few minutes, but no one comes up with an answer.

"Okay, let me see what I can find. I'm not sure where to start though, we don't have a location this time." A frown mars Lee's normally happy expression. "Just a map."

"It looked like Australia at first, then crossed the ocean. Maybe start there?" I suggest. "Sorry, sweetie, I wish I could have got more for you to work with."

"It's fine, I'll get it. What did she look like? If she's a singer, then she'll be on the promo stuff online."

"She's small, blonde and had really dark eye makeup."

"Right, let's start with that. I dunno how long this will take though, so if you have anything else to do, I'm fine to do this bit on my own. But I'm gonna do it at my desk." She jumps up and jogs down the path in her hurry to get started.

Xan frowns after her, turning to me with raised eyebrows when she goes inside.

"In other words, she wants peace and quiet to think," I grin.

"Ah, yeah," he chuckles. "She's just too polite to say it. So, what now?"

"I think I need to return home. I have other things to keep an eye on. Let me know if you need me," Eremiel says shortly before disappearing from sight.

"Oh, okay, bye," I say. "Anyone else think he was a bit weird today?"

Xan and Mathim shrug in unison and so I push the thought to one side.

"If we are at a loss for something to do, perhaps I could see if Sallas is free to talk? Or Scirlin? They may have news," suggests Mathim.

"Ooh, yes. You do that and I'll call Emelia. We need to keep in touch with everyone. Might as well be now," I agree.

I jump up from the grass, Xan falling in step beside me and putting an arm around my shoulders as we all head towards the house.

"I love seeing you all fit and healthy, by the way. It makes me smile."

"Me too," I agree, walking into the office and picking up my phone. "Let's see how Emelia's doing, shall we?"

She answers after two rings, her sleepy voice making me wonder if I've calculated the time difference wrong.

"Hey, Emelia, did I wake you? What time is it there?" I ask.

"Hi, Jax. No, you didn't mess up time zones if that's what you're thinking. I'm just a still a little tired from the other day. It kinda took it out of me. I'm fine though, apart from that. What's up?"

I hear her moving around as she speaks and grin when I hear the unmistakable sound of coffee being made. It's no wonder she fits in so well with us.

"We found the third. Your sister, so to speak. Lee's working on tracking her down, but she just started, and we don't have a lot to go on. So, we thought we'd check in with you. How are you, apart from tired? No sign of Astaroth or anything?"

"Oh wow, who is she? Wait, ignore that, you said you don't know yet. I'm good, I promise, and no, no sign of anything remotely demon-y. It's a little quiet here. I can't go into work until they fix the damage from the fire. Umm, speaking of which—" She pauses for a moment as though uneasy about what she's about to say.

"Go on, Emelia. Whatever it is, we can't help unless we know what's happening," I prompt.

"No, I don't need help. It's just that the insurance is paying out for the work I lost, and the gallery has given me time off while they refurbish. So, I was wondering if maybe I could visit? I'd like to do more than just sit here waiting for something to happen. It won't be right away, I need the money from the insurance first, but I thought I'd mention it now, while I have you on the phone." The doubt in her voice as she asks this makes me frown.

"Of course!" I exclaim. "We'd be thrilled to have you here. Even without all this stuff going on. You'll always be welcome here, Emelia. I thought you knew that. But, yes, I'd much rather have you with us here than at the other side of the world when whatever's gonna happen finally lands on us."

"Really? Awesome! I'll let you know as soon as I do. Thank you, Jax." Emotion makes her voice crack a little. "You've all become like family to me already. It's crazy."

"I know, but what else could it be with everything we have going on?" I ask, making her giggle. "You just make the arrangements whenever you can and let us know when you're coming over, okay?"

"Okay. Let me know when you find out any more about the next one?"

"Sure, Em—"

My words are cut off by a shout that floats through the door from the main office.

"Jax, I got her."

"Emelia," I begin.

"I heard," she laughs. "Go, before Lee spontaneously combusts. I'll catch up with you later."

"Okay, honey. Talk soon."

I end the call and walk through to Lee's desk, grinning at the excited expression on her face.

"Success?" I ask.

"Definitely," she says. "Did you ever doubt me?"

"Never," I reply with a chuckle. "So?"

"Aurora Jackson, or as she's more commonly known, Rory. She fronts the band, Darkened Dreams, who are currently touring Australia but are due to leave there tomorrow to fly to the States.

They have two weeks in LA before they start travelling again. If we're gonna get her, that would be the best time, I'd guess. This is her, right?" She turns the monitor to face me and I nod as soon as I see the image on the screen.

Blonde hair with faded bubble gum pink at the ends, her dark eyes greet me but it's the almost haunted expression that hits me hardest.

"This kid's got a story, Lee. I can see it. Can you try and get past the publicity?"

"Sure, boss lady. That might be harder than just finding her though."

"Yeah, I know, sweetie. Just do what you can."

"Where is she now, Lee?" asks Mathim suddenly, from behind me.

"Sydney. Hold on, I've just seen the tour schedule. Let me write the venue down. They're not quite big enough for the opera house yet." She reaches for a pen but stops and looks at Mathim. "Wait, you need a visual, don't you?"

"If you can," he replies.

She grabs the pen, scribbles down an address and types quickly. Bringing up the image of the building, she presses a button and the printer behind us comes to life.

"Right, you have a picture and a real-life street address so shoo," she orders. "You go do your thing and let me do mine."

"Ooh, bossy Lee today," teases Xan, earning a fake glare from her. "I think we'd better do what she says, she scares me when she's angry."

Avoiding the screwed-up ball of paper she aims at his head, he opens the door to my office, laughing hard.

"Agreed. Let's find Rory."

11

Fulfilment

I observe Jay as he climbs the steps of the pulpit to take his place unseen at the shoulder of the priest. Seeing him inhale deeply and force his breathing to slow, I know he is about to begin his work.

He leans in closer and begins to whisper in the ear of this holy man.

"Our God is good." The priest frowns and turns his head in Jay's direction but, seeing nothing, turns back to his congregation. "He is good, and we must be good in return. We must turn away from sin. Who here denies evil at every approach it makes?"

He looks around at those seated before him, awaiting a response. Surprised at the unusual interaction rather than just being preached at, a few people look at each other uncertainly.

"Come now, I asked a question. How many of us can say that they refuse temptation, that they live good, honest lives?"

Still no one answers, but a quiet murmuring begins. It would seem that his questioning is making them a little uneasy.

"No one? Not one person here in this most beautiful house of God can say that they lead a sin free life? I'm not talking about having that one piece of cake, that one pint of beer. I mean real sin."

Jay moves back a step to allow the priest to move and he climbs down from his perch, approaching his flock in their seats. Some cower back a little, his expression changing from piety to mania in an instant, making them wary as he nears them.

"No one." He shakes his head. "I am disappointed. So, by admission, then, you are all sinners? Even you, Mr Clarke? You pray here almost daily. You dig deep into your pockets each time the collection plate is passed around."

The man he speaks to breathes a sigh of relief, obviously feeling that he is somehow immune from whatever is to come. But his imagined reprieve is a short one.

"I do what I can," he says in fake humility.

"You do what you can. Indeed. We all do what we can. Although we do not all do it for the right reasons. Perhaps you do this in some vain hope that it will make up for the years of embezzlement from your company."

Shocked gasps echo around the church, its acoustics making the sound louder than it should be.

"What? How dare you?" the man shouts, but the priest has already left him.

"And what of you, Ms Claybourne. The flowers here so beautifully arranged, and your time so freely given. Is that because you wish to atone for the cruel way in which you treat the mother you're supposed to be caring for, when no one is around?"

The woman accused cries out in shock and covers her mouth, guilty tears springing to her eyes. The murmuring of the people so far unscathed grows in volume and they begin to shuffle in their seats.

"Maybe we should leave," I hear one say and, getting a nod of agreement from their companion, they begin to rise from their seats, hoping to get to the door unseen. Even as they reach it, the priest turns on them.

"Ah yes, let us not forget the young Mr Shelby. So respectable with his good job and new car. Never mind that he uses it to pick up young, vulnerable girls. Or perhaps, Miss Thomson, who looks so shocked at her friend's indiscretions yet sneaks around behind her

fiancé's back to sleep with his brother."

"For God's sake, man, stop!" yells a man to his right, making him spin to confront him.

Taking their chance, the young pair just accused pull at the door to no avail, sealed as it was when we came in.

One by one, the priest faces his followers, reputations destroyed in a moment after a lifetime of their owners creating them. Only when every person has been addressed, each sin more heinous than the last, does the priest stop his barrage of abuse.

"But, my friends, do not despair. I am not without sin either. And yet I cast the first stone. You think I believe the nonsense I spout to you every Sunday? Every day? No. I say what I need to, what I'm supposed to tell you. I look around at the world and I despair. What kind of God can see all this suffering, man turning upon his brother, children starving, and yet do nothing? And so, I turned from my path a long time ago. I stole from the church, I have broken my vow of celibacy using the money you give so willingly. I stay here because of the life it affords me. But no more."

He looks around at the shocked faces and in some cases, broken spirits, so terrible were the acts he accused them of, and sits heavily on the altar steps.

"I am done," he says, putting his head in his hands.

I look quickly to Jay and he nods silently. I wave my hand over the door, earning puzzled looks from those clamouring to escape. They cry gladly when it opens and rush out into the daylight. Jay walks towards me, a smug look on his face, triumph in his eyes.

"So, your plan went smoothly. But now it is done, I have a question. Why so small? You could have destroyed a city, had some innocent kill thousands of others, and yet you chose to destroy the good opinion of a score of people. This is not the impact I would have thought you would have liked to make." I have not raised this until now as I know how important it is for him to make his own mistakes and to learn from them. But when his eyes meet mine, I do not see regret in them at all.

"Up there is the surveillance system. And in here," he says, reaching into his jacket pocket, "is the recording device. Those images will be leaked into the public domain later today and this little record of events is going to be my next story. My Father wishes for humanity to despair? Then what better way to start than a holy man

destroying his flock. Besides, the day's adventure may be over for us, but not for him. Are you ready to leave? I just need five minutes to get what I need."

He dashes through a door at the back of the church, reappearing quickly and going outside. I follow him, amused that he had left out these final details. Saving the best for last. It would seem that Jay has his Father's sense of timing. A sudden cry makes me rush back inside, and when I do, I skid to a halt in sheer surprise. There at the altar, stood with arms spread and being devoured by flame, stands the priest. His cries turn to screams before they stop as he crashes to the ground, flames from his body spreading to the cloth as he brushes it on his way to the floor.

I shake my head in amazement that Jay has been able to make this man succumb to his will so fully as I turn my step to join him once more.

"You wish to watch it burn?" I ask, when I reach him on the grass in the corner.

"No, I just didn't know how long you'd be. I thought I'd get out of people's way. I don't need to see it play out, I know what will happen. I made it that way. We can leave," he replies casually. "I'm *ready whenever you are."*

"Before we go, I will congratulate you, Jay. It seems you thought of everything."

"Thank you, Astaroth. Oh, even better," he says, waving a hand over the face of an onlooker, one I recognise from being inside a few moments ago. Taking the phone out of the man's hand unseen, he presses a few buttons, checks his own, and with a brief nod of his head, taps the screen again before placing it back in the man's hand. At my questioning look, he grins. "Well, there may have been questions asked about how I got the security footage from a burning building. He filmed it on his phone. After his indiscretions were aired, obviously. I sent that to mine and deleted it from his. Now, I have an exclusive and all because I happened to be in the right place at the right time."

The ease at which he clouds the human's mind and holds the control as he completes his task speaks volumes for his capabilities. And with such a small act, I know that my Master is right in all he plans. With children such as Jay, there is no way we can fail. We just need the other two. And I will not stop until I have them.

12

Living in Shadow

"How the hell did you find her anyway, Lee?" I ask. "I mean, I know you're brilliant, which is one of the many reasons you are completely indispensable, but you had so little to go on."

Torn between the need for quiet and the intrigue of this new child of Lucifer, curiosity won out and she joined me in my vigil in front of the mirror, still working on finding out anything else she can from my office.

"Well, to be honest, I can't decide if it was a brilliant moment of out of the box thinking, or sheer luck. I searched Aurora and music but there were too many hits. I realised that the best place to start would be social media. If a band wants to make it, they need a huge online presence, right? So, I went to Twitter and searched in there, but there was still too much clutter. I tried every combination of her name, music, tour and everything else I could think of. I still got nothing though." She looks up from her tablet screen to make sure I'm keeping up. "But that shadow that you saw kept popping into my head, so I tried adding that in. And any other similar word. As soon as I typed Aurora, music, tour, and dark, I finally found her."

"Nice job, kid," praises Xan, from his position behind my desk. "Okay, ladies, if you don't need me, I'm gonna head up to the big house."

He stands and stretches, before coming around the desk and ruffling Lee's hair as he passes.

"Nope, you're good," I say, over Lee's protestations. "If anything comes up and we need you, I'll call."

"Perfect. I'll be back later."

He leaves us in silence which, after a while, makes Lee groan in boredom.

"Ugh, it's too quiet. Let's see what she sounds like, shall we?"

Guitars fill the quiet room a few seconds later and I'm about to ask Lee to skip to a different song when I'm stopped by the most beautifully haunting voice I've ever heard. Even against the backdrop of such loud accompaniment, the emotion in her tone is plain for everyone to hear.

"Wow," Lee breathes. "She's awesome."

"Yeah, she really is," I agree. My skin pebbles into goose bumps as the song builds slowly, Rory's voice getting stronger as it does.

"There, Jax. There they are. You need me to call for Mathim?"

"No need, little one. I am here. Ah, perfect." He stands in front of the glass, watching the blonde and pink hair sway as Rory walks into the building in front of her. "I'll take it from here if you want a break, Jax."

"Yeah, good idea. I'm seizing up. Feels like I've been sitting here for hours. Hmm, coffee or cigarette first?" I ponder.

"You go smoke, I'll bring coffee. I could do with moving too. Mathim, you want coffee?" asks Lee.

"Yes, please," he answers, resting against my desk and crossing his arms over his chest.

I walk out into early evening air, lighting my cigarette once I'm far enough away from the door, and look up at the stars beginning to appear. The world truly is beautiful if you take the time to look.

"Hey, boss lady. Stargazing?" She hands me a cup and looks up too.

"It really is gonna be a lovely night. Cold though, so I brought you a jacket."

Laughing, I hand my coffee back over to her, slip my arms into the hoodie she gives me and then take back my cup.

"Thank you, Lee. So, while we have a moment to chill out here, how are things with you? Everything okay?"

"Yeah, I'm good. I have an awesome job and a perfect boyfriend. Although, if you tell him I said that, I might have to hurt you," she threatens.

"I won't, I promise. I'm glad things are working out for you, Lee. You deserve it, sweetie."

"Thank you," she says quietly.

"Lee?" Mathim calls from inside.

"Coming," she answers and smiling at me, she goes back inside.

I finish smoking and follow her, but I see something move out of the corner of my eye. I turn to try and figure out what it was, but seeing nothing, I shrug to myself and head indoors.

When I get inside, I see Lee and Mathim so close to the glass they're almost touching it with their noses.

"What are you doing?" I laugh.

"Ugh, why can't this thing have a zoom feature?" Lee grumbles and I take my place beside them.

"What are we looking for?" I ask, intrigued.

"She has a tattoo. On her stomach but to the right. It's writing. We're trying to see what it says. She keeps making sure it's covered though, for some reason," explains Mathim.

I watch her delicate figure move across the stage, helping where she can to set up their equipment.

"Guys, does this seem weird to you?" I ask.

"What?" Lee's eyes never leave Rory as she replies to my question.

"Where's the joking? The camaraderie? Isn't that what being in a band is all about, apart from the music, obviously." Just as I finish my question, a tall, dark-haired man scowls at Rory, making her shrink even more under his angry glare.

"Hmm, yeah, I see what you mean. But maybe they just had a fight," Lee suggests.

Looking for somewhere away from her band members, Rory moves towards us, and takes a moment to regard her reflection in the mirror we're using as a conduit. She lifts her hand to smooth her hair and as she does, the bottom of her t-shirt lifts too with the movement.

"There!" exclaims Lee. "It's a date. 10-12-09. Wonder what it means. Must be important if she's had it inked."

"No idea, honey. Maybe you can add it to your list of things to find out?" I suggest.

"Yup, will do. Speaking of which, I'd better get back on with that."

She crosses to the doorway into her office, picking up her tablet as she passes the table.

I watch as Rory is ordered around, snapped at and generally treated badly by all of those around her, yet still she hurries to follow any orders barked in her direction. Shaking my head, I turn away with a sigh.

"I hate seeing people treated like this," I growl.

"I know, Jax. But for now, we can only watch. We will help her. When we bring her to our side, we can make sure she's okay," reassures Mathim.

I try unsuccessfully to stifle a yawn and check my watch.

"Lee," I call, "it's way past your working hours. Why didn't you say?"

Time has slipped past me again, so determined to find Rory as we have been.

"It's fine. Marcus had to work late to cover until his friend could get there, so I thought I'd just stay here. He's picking me up any minute," she calls back, just as I hear a cheery knock and the front door opening.

131

"Hi, everyone," Marcus greets as he walks into the room. "I hear there's a beautiful young lady in need of escorting home."

Lee giggles and swats at his arm, before he puts it around her shoulders and kisses her cheek.

"Hi, Marcus," I laugh. "Everything good with you?"

"Awesome, as always, Jax. You?"

"Hectic. As always." I grin at him and he rolls his eyes in return.

"You pretend to complain but you wouldn't have it any other way. You'd be bored."

"That's probably very true," I admit. "But a quiet day every now and again might be nice. Anyway, go, you two. Enjoy what's left of the evening."

They chat for a few more minutes and then leave for home. When I yawn again, Mathim orders me to sleep and I agree with a tired smile, my heavy eyes closing thankfully as soon as my head hits the pillow.

Watching the mirror over the rim of my cup, I see that nothing has changed in the way Rory's companions treat her, even after a night's sleep. According to Mathim, the show went well, without fault as far as he could tell. Having packed up their equipment this morning, I see them leaving the arena and, from their schedule, know they're on their way to the airport.

"We can do no more," he says, as they file out silently. "Not until they reach their next destination. Once they are there, I will follow their steps to wherever they are staying. Then we can begin the visits. Dreams to start with again?"

"Yeah, I guess so. And then a flight to LA. Ugh," I complain, eliciting a chuckle from Mathim. "Don't laugh. It's alright for you, you can just jump through a mirror."

"Well, if we had a way to create the doorway on Rory's side, then so could you. But as it is, we can't. I'm sorry, Jax. I really can't fix that for you."

"No, but I could," says a voice behind me, making me jump. "Sorry, Jax, that was a little close for me to appear from. Forgive me."

"No, Eremiel, it's fine. You just startled me. However, if you tell me you can make a doorway that makes it unnecessary for me to fly again, you can manifest on my lap, if it makes you happy."

He laughs and shakes his head.

"That will not happen, I promise. But yes, if you have a visual image, I can go to wherever it is and make the connection between the mirrors, making flights completely unnecessary."

"Oh, that's awesome. Hold on, why didn't you tell me that before? When we went to see Emelia?" I ask, narrowing my eyes.

"You did not ask, there was no immediate hurry, and up until now, I did not realise it troubled you." His matter-of-fact tone makes me frown, but I shrug it off.

"Oh well, that's done with now, I suppose. But you've arrived when we're at a bit of a standstill," I tell him.

"A good time for you to fill me in on what you have discovered then. I admit, I have been a little distracted of late and for that I apologise."

"No worries, I know you have more on your hands than the fate of the world as we know it."

His eyes snap to mine, but seeing me smirk, he relaxes and laughs in response.

"So, who is she?"

"Her name is Aurora, but she's known as Rory. She's the lead singer in a band called Darkened Dreams. She's treated badly by those around her, as far as we've seen. She seems so downtrodden, almost beaten. I really do feel for her. Also, I'm not sure how she's gonna take the news we have to give her. And, God forbid, Astaroth gets there first. No pun intended, by the way. But she'll have no chance against him."

Mathim nods in agreement as he walks over to join us at the table.

"True. She is no match for him. So, we must get there first." He places a hand on mine. "Don't worry, Jax. We will get there first."

"I hope so, Mathim." Turning back to the angel, I go on. "That's really all we know, so far. Lee is trying to find out more."

Eremiel opens his mouth to speak but Mathim beats him to it.

"Speaking of Lee, shouldn't she be here by now?"

I look up at the clock and see that he's right. She's an hour late and I hadn't realised. It's not like her to not call if there's a problem. Just as I'm about to get my phone, I hear the front door open and her voice calling through as she comes in.

"Sorry, Jax."

"God, Lee, you sound terrible."

The face that appears in the doorway looks worse than she sounds. Pale skin and dark circles under her eyes show how ill she is.

"I feel it. Like I got hit by a truck. But I'm too nosy to stay home, so I dragged myself here in case I missed anything."

I huff a laugh but stand up and usher her to the sofa in the main office.

"Okay, but no work. Sleep or just rest, we'll tell you if anything happens. But she's travelling today, remember?"

"Ah hell, I forgot about that. Well, Marcus didn't want me to be on my own anyway, so I guess I'll just do as you say and sleep here." She lies down and shuffles to get comfortable.

"Here, little one," says Mathim gently, covering her in a fleece blanket he must have retrieved from what is now his room. "Stay warm."

She smiles gratefully and closes her eyes.

"As it appears we have spare time today, is there anything you would have me tell you, Jax?" asks Eremiel. "Anything that has cropped up that we have not had chance to discuss?"

"No, I don't think so. Only, why now? Why these children? Mathim said Lucifer has had other kids before now, why Emelia, Jay, and Rory? Are they more special?"

"Hmm, that requires a little history," he says.

"Ooh, yay, a story before I sleep," Lee murmurs happily, making me laugh.

"Yes, child. A story. You know of the great betrayal, of course?"

Seeing a frown on Lee's face, he purses his lips in thought. "Very well, from the beginning, but you'll have to forgive me telling you anything you may already know. Lucifer was the favoured one, he was the Son of the Morning, but he grew tired of our Father's regard for humans. He became desiring of His power and was thrown from Heaven. And so, the Lucifer prophecies came into being. And with them, a covenant.

"It is said that the fallen son will seek revenge upon his father, wreaking havoc upon his favourite creations. Three children, borne of the son, will come into their own, and will be the deciding factor in the final outcome. No angel or demon may approach them, their decisions must be made of their own accord. Only one may have any sway, one from their own kind; the Chosen One."

"Ooh, Jax, you're famous," coos Lee, this time making us all laugh.

"Indeed. Lucifer has three attempts to raise himself from Hell. He has already failed twice, the children at the time not willing or not able to fulfil the prophecy. Which leaves Emelia, Jay and Rory. For without them breaking the binds placed on him by our Father, he cannot leave his prison."

"Wait, he's stuck there?" I ask.

"He is. He created demons to do his bidding as he is tied to Hell. There is some ritual that must be performed but as yet, we have not found the details. However, it requires two out of the three to be on his side. Which leads us back to Rory. We must have her working with us. We cannot lose another to Astaroth."

"Well," says Lee, struggling to sit up and breaking the silence that has settled over us, "you'd better pass my iPad so I can figure this out, huh?"

13

First Impressions

"My son surprised you, did he not, Astaroth?" Lucifer's question does not catch me off guard, I have been expecting something like it since Jay's successful mission.

"He did, Sire. Or maybe impressed is a better word. I knew him capable or I would not have suggested he undertake such a task, but I admit I did not think him that capable. To be able to break the sanctity of such a place as that was beyond my expectation."

"I agree. These children of mine have powers that exceed any expectation I may have had. His plan went according to his wishes, nothing went wrong?" he asks, watching me closely.

"No, nothing went wrong. He made a slight change at the end, but it was an improvement not anything he had forgotten or done wrong. I believe he is ready, Master."

He looks thoughtful and takes a moment to consider before answering me.

"You would have him return here?"

"No, my Lord. Not if you do not need him. He is fully capable of defending himself against anything that might approach him, at least until he can summon help. I know he is anxious to start your work here. May I make a suggestion?" I wait for a nod before I continue. "As he can look after himself here, both physically and mentally, I suggest we leave him to do what you need him to. He has the record of today's events and wishes to begin to report the story to the world, to plant the first seeds of despair into the minds of whomever he can reach. If you change your mind, you can always get Scirlin to bring him back."

"Hmm, you may be right. After all, the sooner we can make the humans suffer, the better. Yes, Astaroth, I agree. Jay will stay on Earth to do as you say. But to do so independently. He cannot rely on you being there to support him, it is time my son stands on his own two feet, to use a human saying," he says. "And now, Astaroth, I have news of my own. The third has been unshrouded. A girl. Aurora. She walks in shadow, which means she is half ours already."

"Sire?" I ask, not sure what he means.

"It is just as I say, the visions show her as walking with a shadow looming over her. That can only mean that she already sways towards the path of shade. She will be no match for you, I am sure, my Grand Duke. As we speak, she crosses the ocean, I will inform you when we have a view of her."

"Yes, my Lord. I will await your orders. And send Jay on his way with his."

The mirror clears, leaving me looking at myself, my attention drawn to the door as Jay appears in it.

"Was that my Father?" he asks.

"It was. He is very happy with your actions. So happy in fact, that he has decided that you do not require further training and will return to your home and your job, in order to begin the second part of your plan." His face falls a little and I frown at him. "You are not ready for this, Jay?"

"No, I am. Really. It's just I thought perhaps my Father would wish me to return to him first."

"Our Father has more on his mind than you or I, Jay. He will call you home when it is time. Until then, you have the honour of putting his schemes into action. And you are the first to do so, your sister having turned away from her duties as she did."

I watch my words have the desired effect. Jay's spine straightens and he squares his shoulders.

"I will not disappoint him," he vows. "Or you, Astaroth. Thank you for all you have shown and taught me."

I simply nod in answer, before turning back to the mirror and arcing my arm across it. Jay's home swims into view.

"Well? Are you ready?" I ask.

"I am." He steps through and I follow him, glancing around out of habit more than anything. I would have sensed any angel presence even through the glass.

"I will bid you farewell for now, Jay. If you should need any help, just wave your arm across the surface of any mirror as you have now seen me do countless times and focus your mind upon whom you wish to speak."

"Okay," he says. "Goodbye, Astaroth."

"Goodbye, Jay. I have no doubt that you will continue to make your Father proud."

I step back through the glass, clearing the connection once I reach the other side. I settle in the armchair nearby, knowing that all I can do now is wait. She walks in shadow, my Master said. Can it really be as simple as already being susceptible to my approach to her? I search for another explanation but being unable to find one, I force myself to relax and await the call of Lucifer.

***

"Astaroth." My Master's voice booms through the mirror, echoing in the sparsely furnished room.

"Sire," I reply, clearing the block I placed upon it while I slept.

"You do well to rest while you can," he says, as his image appears before me. "But that time is over, for now, at least. She has arrived and we have her location."

I watch him move to one side, creating a separate image in the other half of the glass. A uniformly decorated room, her belongings in a case on the bed, all of these things are there for me to observe, but my eyes are trained on the small frame sitting in the chair in the corner. Blonde hair pulled back from her pale face, I notice the dark circles under her eyes.

"She does not appear to have the strength of Emelia. Not the determination of Jay," I say. "She already looks defeated."

"And so I thought, Astaroth. I do not think it will take much to bring her to us. It will have to be fast though. I do not think Jax and the angels will waste time in their approach. Not even I can block them."

I look past him as I think of how best to gain any advantage.

"Sire, I do not ask for help in anything I do. But I feel that this must be the exception." As much as it pains me to speak the words, I know that I cannot be in two places at once.

"What do you need?" he asks immediately.

"A distraction. And as I cannot approach this Aurora until she sleeps, I have time to explain."

And so, working out the details as I go, I make my request. Once *agreed, my Father leaves to set things in motion and I return to my place, only this time, instead of clearing the mirror, I allow the image of her room to fill the glass.*

Aurora moves listlessly, finding places to store her clothes and muttering to herself as she does. With a huff of breath when she completes her task, she sits on the bed and drops her head into her hands, rubbing her eyes, apparently forgetting she has darkened them. Seeing the smudges on her hands when she drops them from her face, she shakes her head at herself and crosses to the bathroom. Emerging a few moments later, she looks like a much younger girl. Her face is devoid of any artifice, her hair allowed to fall freely, and she looks exactly what she is. A small child left alone.

Crawling under the covers, she lies her head on the pillow, but then throws back the sheets and lifts her shirt to look at some marking on the skin above her hip. I cannot see what it says, but when she runs a finger across it, she begins to cry. I watch as the tears run unchecked down her face, soaking into the material her head rests upon. Eventually they subside as she falls asleep, her small frame curled up into an even smaller ball in the middle of the large bed.

I stand and approach the mirror, only pausing to form a link with Scirlin. The red-haired youth appears before me, and I barely look at

147

him as I speak.

"Is it done?" I ask him.

"It is," he replies.

"Good."

I refocus upon Aurora, stepping silently into her room, and wondering as I do, what has broken her so badly that she cries herself to sleep? Or more importantly, whatever it is, how can I exploit it in order to get what I want?

14

Surprises

"Holy crap!" Lee's exclamation has me running back through into the office where she's sitting propped up on the sofa.

"What?" I ask, having to repeat after she removes her earbuds when she sees me. "What's wrong?"

"I think I found it," she says cryptically.

"Not helpful, sweetie. Found what?"

"All of it. The shadow, the date, all of it. Here, sit." She pats the seat next to her as she moves her feet to make room. "It's kinda complicated though, so you'll have to bear with me. Ready?"

I hold up a finger in the air and pour us a coffee, handing Lee hers as I sit.

"Ready."

"Okay. I tried to search the date that Rory has tattooed, once I realised that cos she's American, the month and date are back-to-front, alongside her name, but found nothing." She looks at me and shakes her head with a frown. "No, it doesn't matter what I did that didn't work. I'll cut to the chase."

"Good idea," I agree with a grin.

"I was listening to her music while I searched. Listen to this." She unplugs her earbuds from her iPad, and taps on the screen, making music fill the air. "Let me try and cue up the part that made me realise."

I wait patiently as she scans the track for the section she wants. She taps again and it pauses.

"Got it?" I ask.

"Yeah."

A much quieter song than the others I've heard from her band so far begins to play and after a few seconds, Rory's haunting voice joins in.

"That was when I lost the light,

Trapped forever in the shade,

My heart is held by the shadow of you."

Lee makes it stop and I look at her, eyes wide in surprise.

"Wait. The shadow is someone she lost?"

"That's how I took it, so I looked deeper into her personal life as much as I could. I didn't find anything on social media obviously, but I took a stab in the dark and tried obituaries from her home town around that time and added her surname to the search. Gabriel Jackson, taken tragically, much loved son and brother."

"She lost her brother? Oh wow, I can't even imagine what that must have been like. Did it say how old he was?"

"That's the thing, Jax. I found a brief mention of the accident in an article too. He wasn't just her brother, he was her twin. They were thirteen when he died."

The look on Lee's face says it all. To lose a brother is bad enough, but to lose a twin? But then the full realisation hits me, and I sit open-mouthed for a second before I pull myself together enough to speak.

"Lee? You know what this means, right?"

"Huh? Yeah, that we figured out the shadow from your vision," she says, giving me a "well, duh" look.

"No. Well, yes, but something else. Lee, if Gabriel was her twin, then Lucifer has—"

"Four children this time!" she interrupts.

"I gotta get Mathim. And Eremiel. And Xan." I jump up and run to the hallway. "Mathim!"

"Slow down, Jax, you can't do all three at once. I'll call Xan, you call to Eremiel." She reaches for her phone but stops before she even unlocks the screen. "Hold on."

I open my eyes, having just started my thoughts of the angel.

"What?" I ask.

"So she had a brother. But he's dead now. And if he's dead, then he can't be that important, right?"

Incredulously, I look at her. When she looks innocently back at me, I drop my eyes to stare pointedly at her "ghost hunter in training" top I bought her last year and wait for the penny to drop.

"What?" she asks, glancing down. "Did I spill lunch on me again?... Ohhhh... Yeah, you'd better call him."

Shaking my head with a low chuckle, I fill my thoughts with Eremiel and call to him. When I open my eyes, Mathim is standing in front of me, a concerned look on his face.

"Xan? We need you back here. We have a situation."

I hear him agree so I move into my office, waiting for everyone to arrive, and moving the chairs around the table. It's not too long until I hear Xan's running footsteps approaching on the gravel path. Just as he comes through the door, Eremiel appears at the other side of the room.

"Mathim, Lee, we have everyone now," I call.

I wait until everyone is seated and look at each of them in turn.

"We have a problem. The shadow in the vision of Rory? It's her brother. Her twin brother."

This time I don't have to explain any further, the realisation showing on their faces as soon as the words leave my mouth. They all start to speak at once and then stop suddenly.

"Eremiel?" I ask. "You first."

"We need to find him. If he is in Heaven, then we can keep him safe. If, however, he is in Hell, then Astaroth has a huge card to play in his approach to Rory. We cannot allow him to have them both on his side. A fourth child has a huge impact on the balance of things. Even if we have two, then we are tied with Lucifer. I do not know how that will work in relation to the covenant." I see worry lines marring the normal serene look he wears.

"Mathim? Any ideas?"

"I will talk to Scirlin. He knows all demons, he will find him if he is there."

I nod and turn to my friends.

"Lee? Xan?"

Lee shrugs in response while Xan drags his hands through his hair.

"I dunno, Jax. There's not really anything we can do until we know where he is. Let's let the guys find that out and go from there."

"Yeah, I guess that's all we can do. We can't make any move on Rory until we find her at the venue tomorrow either. Okay, Eremiel, can you find out if Gabriel is with you guys? Mathim, can you do the same? We'll regroup when you both know."

I push my seat back from the table and stand up to stretch.

"What about us?" asks Lee, and I realise how poorly she looks. I've definitely allowed her to push herself too far today. I look outside and an idea forms in my mind.

"We see what we can do to fix you, while we wait. Come on kid, let's test out this healing thing."

***

"Damn it!" I exclaim. "Why isn't this working?"

Try as I might, I've been unable to channel the energy I draw from the earth. I've been over and over everything I did for Xan but can't think of anything else to try.

"Hey, it's okay. I'm not dying or anything, I'll be fine. I appreciate you trying, boss." Lee stands up a little shakily and heads back to the house. "Maybe it's an Emelia thing."

"Yeah, maybe," I agree. "I just wanted you feeling better, sweetie. And as I can't fix you, then the least I can do is make sure you rest until Marcus comes to pick you up. So, boss lady's orders, sofa and sleep. No arguing."

"Okay, okay," she laughs, her hands held up in mock surrender.

"Maybe what's an Emelia thing?" asks Mathim as we enter the office.

"I tried my nature stuff on Lee. It didn't work. We're thinking it was more to do with Emelia than me."

"Yeah, but Emelia brought me back, you were the only one healing me once I returned," points out Xan.

"Oh, yeah. Hmm, I dunno then." I try to make my mind work

through the problem but then realise Mathim isn't talking to Scirlin as he should be. "Mathim? News from Scirlin?"

"He does not think that he is in Hell but is checking as we speak," he explains.

"Okay. Another waiting game then."

Just as I finish speaking, Xander's phone rings noisily, startling me for a second.

"Hi, Mum. Wait, slow down, I can't understand you... What? I'm on my way... I'll be right there." He ends the call and looks at me. "Jax, can I borrow Vinni? The house is on fire."

"I'll drive," I say, not wasting any time as I run to the door.

When we speed up the drive to the big house, I see the flashing lights of fire engines and the shocked faces of everyone outside. I jump out of the car and run to Xan's parents, only a few steps behind him.

"Mum, are you okay?" he asks, putting his arms around her. "Is Dad here? Did everyone get out?"

His questions run one into the next in his panic as his mum collapses against him.

"Everyone's out," she answers. "Your father is talking to the fireman, helping him with the layout. Oh, Xander, our beautiful home."

She breaks into sobs, unable to say anything else, and he hugs her tight, looking over her head at me.

"I'll go and check on your Dad," I offer, and he nods in answer.

I walk towards the small group of people I see surrounding Xan's father. I'm about to reach them when suddenly the world explodes around me. A huge booming noise, accompanied by a change in the atmosphere around me as the air itself gets hot, carrying slivers of glass on it, and the force of it knocks me onto my knees.

My ears are ringing as I stand slowly, careful until I know I'm unharmed. Looking around, I check on everyone I see, breathing a sigh of relief when I realise no one is injured.

"What was that?" I ask the nearest person I see in uniform.

"Looks like a gas leak. Won't know until we get the fire out and investigate," he says. "Can you help me get everyone further back? All of our crews are in there."

"Of course."

And for the next hour or so, I do what I can to keep everyone calm, sending the ones who look the most affected to the ambulances to be checked over. Once everyone has been cleared to leave, I join an exhausted-looking Xan and his parents.

"Hey, Jax. Thanks for staying," he says.

"No problem at all, honey. You want me to go and leave you guys to it?" My question is as much to Xan's mum as to him, I know she's not my biggest fan.

"No, Jacqueline," she answers. "You don't need to go. Now the fire's finally out, I suppose we need to find somewhere to stay."

"Why don't you come back to the office?" I offer, surprising myself. "Lee can make any arrangements you need, and I can make you a cup of tea and feed you while we wait. I can run you to the whichever hotel you decide on."

Xan looks at me in amazement, and I have to force a grin from my face.

"That's very kind, Jax," says his dad, walking towards us from the short distance at which he's been standing. "I already booked us a room and there's a taxi on the way. Xan, I didn't book one for you, but there's one on standby if you want it. I thought you might prefer to stay with Jax."

"You know you're welcome," I say unnecessarily.

"Yeah, if that's okay. I'll need to be close for the investigation." He gives me a pointed look and I know he isn't just talking about the fire.

"Sure. We'll wait with you until your taxi gets here though," I say to them. "Here."

I slip out of the hoody I'm wearing and put it around Xan's mum's shoulders when I see her shivering.

"Again, Jacqueline, thank you." She reaches for my hand and holds it for a moment.

"Of course," I say with a smile.

We don't have to wait long until the taxi arrives, taking them to their new temporary home and leaving Xan and I alone in the driveway.

"Ready then, Xan?" I ask, slipping my hand in his.

"Yeah, I suppose so. There's nothing I can do here." He starts to turn towards Vinni but stops and looks back at his home. "I hope it's not as bad as it looks."

"Me too, sweetie. Did they say anything to you?"

"No, not really. Some of the ceilings fell as they got control of the fires in different rooms. They won't know the structural damage until they come back and check it all out properly." He lets out a huge sigh. "I'm just glad no one was hurt. It's a miracle, really."

"One of the guys said it looked like a gas leak?" I ask.

"Apparently. Although the fire was already spreading before the explosion." He pulls my hand to turn me to face him and looks into my eyes. "Would you think I was paranoid if I said my thoughts turned straight to Astaroth?"

"Not at all. I wondered that myself. But surely he has no reason for this. He's got to be busy with Rory, right?"

"Hmm, maybe. Ugh, I can't even think. Let's go back."

***

"Xan! Are you okay?" asks Lee, jumping up from the sofa to hug him. "Are your parents alright? And everyone else?"

"Hey, chica," he replies, in a tired voice. "We're all okay but the house is a mess. We won't know how bad it is for a few days though."

"Come on, sit," she says, pulling him towards a chair. "I'll make coffee."

"Xander, I am sorry to hear of your home." Mathim appears from the other room.

"Thank you, Mathim."

"I would not wish to distract you all from that, but I have news if you are ready to hear it," he offers.

"We might not be ready for it, but we don't really have the luxury of time. Go on, Mathim," I reply.

"Gabriel is not in Hell. Scirlin is quite certain."

I breathe a sigh of relief.

"Hold that thought," says Eremiel from behind me. "We do not have him either."

"What?" I exclaim. "Well, if neither of you have him, then where the hell is he?"

"There is only one other place he can be, although how that is possible after ten years, I have no idea," he answers, looking at Mathim with raised eyebrows.

Mathim shrugs and shakes his head.

"Where?" I ask, looking from the angel to the demon for an answer and seeing Mathim open his mouth to provide it.

"He is in the Realms."

15

Making an Impression

"Hello, Aurora."

I watch her as she spins to face me, the voice she hears in the darkened room of her dreams.

"H-hello," she stammers. "Who are you? And where am I?"

"Which would you have me answer first?"

"Where am I?" she asks. "And why is it dark?"

"It is dark because I have not decided where I should take you or what it is that I need to show you yet. And so, for now, you are here. With me, in the void."

She nods as though she understands, her simple acceptance of what I tell her demonstrating her submissive nature.

"And who are you?" she prompts.

"My name is Astaroth. Who I am is irrelevant for now. I merely wished to make an introduction."

I allow the darkness to brighten a little so that she can see me properly, but deliberately leave the surroundings devoid of any detail to ensure her full attention is on me.

"An introduction? Why? I don't understand?"

The difference between this child and the others is staggering to say they share parentage. No sign at all of the challenging personality of Jay, or even the curious intelligence of Emelia. This should make Aurora easier prey, but for now I am unsure of how best to turn her to the side of my Master. No matter though, I have a plan to give me all the time I need. The fire in the house near Jax should have distracted them all. I would have preferred it to be in her home but obviously that was not possible given the angelic protection around it.

"I will tell you briefly some of what is to come. You are destined to fulfil a role of great power and influence. In time."

"Me?" she asks before laughing. "No, you definitely have the wrong person."

"Trust me, child. I am not mistaken. You will see."

All amusement disappears from her face to be replaced with worry lines as her shoulders slump and she turns back into the shell of a girl she is.

"And if I don't want to see?" she asks, looking up at me as though awaiting admonishment for the question.

"You have no choice, Aurora. Fate cannot be altered."

"Yeah, tell me about it," she mutters scornfully.

"I will leave you to rest for now. I will return to talk more to you soon. This is not something to be feared or avoided. It has many rewards. But before I leave you, one small thing."

I approach her slowly, towering over her delicate frame and lift my hand towards her head, making her flinch.

"Aurora, I am about to help you, not harm you." My tone leaves no room for argument and she nods slightly although her eyes never leave mine, almost frozen as she is.

I lift my hand once more and place it on her brow. When I have completed my act, I drop my hand and take a few steps back.

"What did you do?" she asks. "I didn't feel anything."

"See? I told you I would not harm you," I answer, deliberately avoiding her question. "And now, I will leave you to your rest, Aurora. You have busy days approaching."

I step back into the darkness, watching as she fades back into a dreamless sleep and allow the dream to fade. Standing once more at the side of her bed, I see a serene look on her pale face. I frown for a moment. If this child has no ambition, no drive, if she is in fact as insecure and shy as she appears, how am I to tempt her to join Lucifer? There must be something I can persuade her with.

Mulling this over, I step back through the mirror and take my seat in front of it, dozing as I wait for her day to start.

***

"Jesus, Rory!" the youth with the long dark hair yells, making her jump as she stands at the front of the stage. "We've been over this a million times!"

"I-I'm sorry," she stammers. "I just can't get the jump up to the bridge. It's the key change, it's a little awkward."

"If you can't sing it, why the hell did you write it?" he growls. "Maybe you should stick to looking pitiful in the spotlight."

Her eyes fill with tears and she drops her head to allow her hair to fall around her face, hiding her.

"Come on, Corey. Ease up," says an older man, appearing from the side of the stage and handing Aurora a bottle of water. "She'll get it, right?"

His words are kind, but his look doesn't match it as he glares at her.

"Yes. Yes, I think I've got it now," she reassures him uncertainly.

"Do not forget how far we've brought you, Rory," he says quietly enough so that only she hears him. "We've all worked our asses of to get you here. You'd have none of this if not for me. For us."

"I know, Ted. I do. And you know how much I appreciate all you've done. I just, umm, I didn't sleep very well."

"Nightmares? Again?" he asks, but there is no concern in his voice. "You have a photo shoot in the morning. We can't have you looking like shit when you turn up there. Make sure your makeup covers the dark circles."

And with this final hissed order, he spins on his heel and walks away from her.

"Okay," she says to his back as he moves.

"Again!" he shouts as he leaves the stage. "Get it right this time, Rory."

She sighs and takes a sip from the bottle he handed her before taking a deep breath and returning to the microphone.

"Right, guys, I'm ready."

She closes her eyes when the song begins, swaying gently with the music. She tenses a little when the part that was giving her trouble comes up, but a small smile crosses her lips as she succeeds. When the song reaches its end, she turns happily to her companions, opening her mouth to speak but is cut off.

"About time," Corey spits. "Now you've finally managed that, do you think we can run through the set?"

His sarcasm kills any happiness she was feeling, and she slumps once more into the little dormouse. *Is she really worthy of my Master?*

I clear the image from the glass and sit forward, resting my head on my hands as I think. *This child is going to need a very different approach.*

"Astaroth?" My Master's voice echoes around the room and I stand to face him.

"Sire?"

"You are as disappointed in the third as I am, I feel," he says.

"I regret that I am, my Lord. She shows none of the traits so apparent in the others. In fact, I cannot see anything admirable in her at all," I admit.

"That is my thinking too, Astaroth. However, no matter how insignificant she may seem at present, her destiny for greatness *does not change. We will simply have to mould her into what we want her to become. From what I have seen, that will not prove difficult. However, we do not have long to do this. Have you considered how you will win her over?"*

I puzzle at how to answer this, as my plan is only really a seed of a thought.

"I have had an idea, Master. I have not thought it out fully though. I do not think that the block on her talents will do anything other than cause problems for her, making her even more difficult to engage with. Nor does she have any ambition that I can exploit, as far as I can tell. I think perhaps, the guise of kindness and care may be the best way forward," I suggest.

"As much as I loathe artifice in this task, I cannot think of an alternative either," he agrees.

"I think perhaps, I was not clear in what I meant, Sire. I meant only that I can use such arts of deceit in order to gain some of her trust. Once that is done, I will bend her to my will."

Yes, this will be the easiest way. To make her dependent on me as one she can trust, will make the turn into obedience a smooth one.

When I see a malicious smirk appear on Lucifer's face, I know he approves before he even speaks.

"Very good, Astaroth. Yes, I can see that being very successful. But, are you sure you can manage to be that 'nice' for that long?" he laughs.

"I will cope, my Lord. Somehow," I reply, making his amusement grow even further.

"Before I leave you to your work, I have news of my own. Jay's attempt to take the life of Jacqueline's companion was unsuccessful, it would seem."

"What? I checked back and saw him—" I stop and reconsider what I was about to say. "Actually, no, I didn't. I saw him on the ground and Jax looking destroyed. I assumed he was dead."

"No matter, Astaroth. He was not a target, merely a casualty. You will inform Jay? He will be disappointed."

"He will indeed, my Lord. Yes, I will tell him," I say.

"Good. You may also tell him that any disappointment I may have *felt was avoided by his actions at the cathedral. In that, he far surpassed my expectations."*

"I will, Sire," I agree.

"Then I will leave you to your task."

He fades from sight, and my mind begins to turn these new events over and over. Yes, Jay will be disappointed. I, however, I am not. For now, as our success draws near, I am able to achieve a personal aim too. I can once again be the cause of Jaqueline's greatest possible pain.

16

The Plan

"He's where?" asks Lee.

"The Realms," says Mathim. "It's where spirits go when they aren't completely 'good' enough for Heaven, nor 'bad' enough for Hell. They prove themselves one way or another in the Realms and are taken from there."

She opens her mouth to question him more but is interrupted by Eremiel.

"But how is it possible to remain there for so long? It is unheard of." His words are spoken to Mathim, who shakes his head in response.

"I have no idea. It is not somewhere that anyone would want to stay. And for ten years? Unthinkable."

"What do you mean?" Lee takes advantage of the pause to voice her curiosity. "How do they prove themselves? What happens when they do? And why couldn't he stay there?"

With a sigh, Eremiel turns to her.

"I am sorry, child. I forget that you do not know all that we do. The Realms are a barren place where souls go to have their fates decided if it is not immediately apparent where they belong. Demons are sent by Lucifer to tempt them to descend to Hell by creating battles between them. With each act of violence they commit, they lose some of their humanity and become wilder. When they have transformed enough, they are taken to Hell. If they do all they can to avoid it, then we bring them to Heaven. Needless to say, Hell takes more from there than we do. It is not easy to retain goodness there. Nor is it a place in which you would wish, or even be able to, stay for long."

"That doesn't sound like somewhere I'd want to stay," she agrees.

"It is not."

"So," I say, drawing their attention, "never mind about how he's still there, can we get him out?"

They look at each other for a moment before Mathim speaks.

"I think it would be possible. I could not transport him from there though. I would have to travel to find him, then it would be down to Eremiel to bring him back. Could you do that?"

"Yes, once he is located. You will need help though, when searching for him. You know better than to travel there alone, I'm sure."

"Indeed. I will talk to Scirlin and see if we can arrange for Tezrian to meet me. She knows the Realms better than any other." He stands as though to move back to the mirror.

"Wait." Lee's sudden panicked tone halts his step and he turns to her, resting his hands on the back of the chair. "Won't they find you? You're number one on the Devil's most wanted list. Surely you can't go there without risking being caught."

"We have no choice, little one. We must secure the brother. Do not worry, I will be careful."

He crosses to stand in front of the glass and calls to Scirlin, but it is Tezrian that appears.

"Well met, Mathim. It has been some time. What do you need? Shall I send to Scirlin?" she asks hurriedly.

"No, there is no hurry for him to join us, as it is you that I was about to ask for anyway. Are you needed elsewhere soon, or would you have time to talk?"

She breaks into a smile.

"I will make time, Mathim. It has been too long. Now I know that it is not an emergency, I can relax somewhat. What can I help you with?"

Mathim briefly fills her in on the whole situation and she nods as he tells her, showing she understands. When he reaches the part about the Realms, she interrupts.

"He's been there for that long?" she exclaims. "Why would he do that?"

"I do not know, Tez. And so it seems that I must go and bring him—"

"No!" she interrupts. "Mathim, no. You know you cannot."

"I have no choice, Tez. We need to find him before Lucifer learns of his existence, if he doesn't know already."

"Mathim, no, I mean it. I will find him and send word to you. You cannot enter the Realms. You will be captured as soon as you set foot there. Lucifer has more and more demons there with every passing day." Her expression tells me that there is no room for argument, but still Mathim disagrees with her.

"You cannot hope to do that unseen, Tez. You know that your missions there are observed. I need you to keep all demons there at the time away from me. It is the only way," he states firmly.

They stare each other down, neither one of them willing to give an inch, and I'm relieved when Scirlin appears in the side of the glass, breaking the tension that's descended as they argue.

"What's happening?" he asks, seeing his friends in an apparent standoff. "What's wrong?"

"Well?" says Tez. "Would you like to explain your idea, or would you like me to tell him how you're planning to walk right back into Lucifer's grasp. After all you've done, all we've done, to keep you free from him."

With a sigh, Mathim explains quickly to Scirlin, being interrupted at exactly the same point by him as he was by Tez.

"I agree with Tez. There is no way you will not be caught. Think of all we have gone through, Mathim. You cannot throw all of that away."

"And as I was trying to make clear to Tezrian just as you arrived, there is no other choice," he says wearily.

"That may not actually be the case," Eremiel offers, his voice sounding unsure, as though he is mulling things over as he speaks them. "There could be another solution."

He glances at me and looks back to Mathim.

"No," he answers flatly. "Just no."

"What?" I ask.

"No, Eremiel. I will not risk her."

"Hold on a minute. Before you start fighting over what I can and can't do, I'd like to hear what it is you're both thinking. I can decide for myself." I meet Mathim's gaze and don't allow mine to drop until he huffs out a frustrated breath and gestures to Eremiel with his hand.

"Fine, tell her. But I will not allow her to travel to the Realms without me. She is tough, but still needs protection."

"The Realms? Me? How?" I ask.

"You have travelled further than there in the not-so-distant past, Jacqueline. Your journey to Hell, not to mention the dream realm, shows that you are capable of such things. In fact," he adds, looking at Xan, "as you have both been beyond the veil, it may be possible for you both to journey there."

I look at Xan, the shock on his face mirroring my own.

"Are you sure?" I ask.

"I am as certain as I can be," he replies.

"Xander, I know you would do anything to keep her safe, but she still needs more protection than you can offer her. I am sorry, I do not wish to offend you, but I do not know how else to say it."

"No offence taken, Mathim," Xan chuckles. "I know what you mean, my friend."

Mathim smiles at him, obviously relieved at Xan's understanding.

"What about Sal?" asks Lee. "He sneaked away before. And if any demons saw him there, they'd just assume he was there under orders, wouldn't they?"

I look quickly to the mirror and see Tez and Scirlin nodding in agreement.

"So, what if Xan and I go, Sal meets us there, and Tez keeps everyone distracted?" I ask. "Mathim, you can't go. You have to see that. This is the best plan we have. You know Sal will take care of us."

He lets out a frustrated sigh as he slumps a little in defeat.

"Fine. Yes, I can see how dangerous it is for me to go to the Realms, but I would save you such a journey, Jax. It is not a place for anyone, especially not you two. But if it is the only option we have, then I cannot fight it. I am not used to being on the outside of such missions," he complains.

"You're not. While we're away, you'll be concentrating on the other side of it. You need to make the approach to Rory. Tomorrow we'll have her location, it's vital that you make the first contact. We need her on our side," I remind him.

"Very well. I will work on Rory while you go to find Gabriel. Astaroth cannot be allowed to succeed with her." He shakes his head and looks at me. "This does not mean I'm happy with you going though."

"I know, Mathim. We'll be careful, I promise."

"I don't like it either, boss lady, but if anyone can do it, you can," says Lee. "Just don't feel like you have to kick demon butt. Hiding is fine."

I laugh and hug her.

"Like I said, sweetie, we'll be extra careful."

"I would offer help, if I may," says Eremiel. "I will send someone to you when you arrive there."

"Okay," I say. "When do we leave?"

"Tomorrow. You need to rest and build your energies if you are to travel to the Realms," he advises.

"Tomorrow? Fair enough. I guess that's everything sorted until then?" I ask.

"Yes," says Scirlin. "I will arrange for Sallas to accompany you. For now, I suggest you do as Eremiel says. You will need your strength."

"We will. Thank you, Scirlin. And you, Tez. Oh, how will you know where we are and where you have to keep everyone away from?"

"Scirlin will be the communication between us all," she says.

"Right. That works, I guess." I look around at everyone in turn and seeing agreement, albeit dubious, I smile. "Don't worry guys, we've got this."

"I wish I had your confidence, Jax," says Mathim.

"We will leave you to your rest," says Scirlin. "Call to me in the morning when you are ready. I will have the gateway prepared for you."

Their images fade and I turn to Eremiel.

"You too?" I ask.

"Yes, I too have things to prepare. And like Scirlin, just call to me when you are ready."

Even as I nod in answer, he is fading from view, leaving the four of us in silence.

"So, what now?" asks Lee.

"Now we rest, like they said. And you can let Marcus know that you're ready to be picked up whenever he's free. We're gonna have an early start in the morning, if you can manage it? I know you'll want to be here with Mathim while we're gone."

"Definitely," she says. "I'll be watching as much of all of this as I can. You know I'll be stressing until you come back through there."

She points to the mirror, and I notice her hand trembling a little as she speaks.

"We'll be fine, sweetie. I swear."

She nods silently and reaches for her phone.

"I'm gonna go ring Marcus," she says, walking back through to her desk.

"I need to check on my parents, Jax. I'll go outside though, so you guys can talk."

Xan heads out into the garden, leaving Mathim and I in the quiet.

"Mathim, I'm sorry. There's just no other way to do this," I say, putting my hand on his arm.

"I know, Jax. That does not mean I like it though." He runs a hand through his hair and sighs. "I have lost so much already, I will not lose any more friends."

"That won't happen, Mathim. Sal will take care of us. And whichever kickass angel Eremiel sends."

My words get a small smile from him and I'm happy to see even the tiniest sign of humour on his face.

"Yes, I wonder who he'll send," he muses. "Oh well, I suppose you'll find out soon enough. And, as much as it pains me to say this, no matter who it is, angels can always hold their own in battle."

"Here you go, Jax" says Lee, handing me a coffee. "Charging up?"

I grin up at her from my place on the grass.

"Something like that," I say. "Xan coming out?"

"Yeah, he's just finishing up the call with the fire people. It doesn't sound good," she replies.

"Ugh, poor Xan. All of that to deal with on top of everything else we have going on. The timing couldn't have been worse."

I see him come out of the office and walk towards us, a smile ready despite everything. And even though I'd never want to put him in harm's way again, I'm glad he's coming with me today. As we've both been beyond the veil... A thought occurs to me, and I pat the grass beside me.

"Xan, come here, I have an idea."

He drops to the ground to join me and frowns in curiosity.

"What's up, Jax? What are you thinking?" he asks.

"You know how I zapped you, but it wouldn't work on Lee?" I ask.

"Yeah, I still dunno how that happened," he replies.

"Well, I wondered if it's the whole beyond the veil thing. Want me to try?"

"Ooh," says Lee. "I wanna see it work."

"Wait, Jax," he interrupts. "Won't it take your energy to do this? You need your strength for the Realms, remember?"

"Actually, no, I don't think so. I think the only reason it took it out of me before was because Emelia was pulling it through me and then through her to you, that it was just too fast. Cos when I did it after that on my own, I didn't feel any drain on me at all. So, wanna try?"

"Sure," he agrees, happy enough with my reasoning.

"Okay." I reach for his hand and hold it in mine. "Ready?"

"Ready," he agrees.

I make the connection with the grass with my free hand and focus on the tingling in my palm, pulling on it as I've learned to do, and feeling it climb up my arm and through my body. When I hear a sharp intake of breath, I know it's working, but when Lee gasps, the sound confirms it.

"Wow, I can almost see it," she whispers, before clearing her throat. "Honestly, guys, this is awesome. Xan looks better already."

"What do you mean, better already?" he asks. "Are you trying to say I looked anything less than perfect before?"

We all laugh together, and a feeling of contentment passes through me. I open my eyes and look at them both in turn.

"Okay, Xan?" I check.

"Yes, Jax. Thank you," he says, letting go of my hand.

"No problem," I answer, enjoying the time just sitting with my friends.

A moment later, Mathim appears in the doorway.

"Eremiel just got here," he says. "And Scirlin is waiting too. It is time."

I stand up, pulling Xan up after me.

"We ready for this, Jax?" he asks.

I look at Lee and wink.

"Always ready," we reply in unison.

-17-

Preparations

"You mean I failed?"

Jay's face shows his disappointment in hearing the news of Xander's wellbeing.

"You did not fail, Jay. You created the distraction which allowed me to get you to safety. That was the most important thing. He was never meant to be killed. Well, not yet, anyway. In your first real task, you were most successful. Your Father was very impressed," I say, watching as his eyes light up at my words.

"He was? He saw it?" he asks, a beaming grin replacing the downcast look from the moment before.

"Of course. You are his son, he would not miss your first impact being made on the world. Now, speaking of that, how goes the next part of your plan?"

"I have the story written. I spoke to my editor as I left work today and outlined it. He was loathe to publish it, as he said it was

hearsay, until I told him I had proof. I have a meeting with him in the morning to show him, and then it will go out in the morning's edition. It is all under control," he says confidently.

"Excellent, Jay. I may have another story for you soon. An exclusive, as it were. You are in the best possible position to be able to spread the word of your Father."

I see curiosity spark in him but am pleased when he does not push me for any further details. He is definitely under my control.

"Of course, Astaroth. I look forward to helping any way I can. Until then, is there anything else you need me to do?"

"No, not at present. Publish your news, Jay. The downfall of the priest and destruction of the cathedral will be a shock to many. And will suffice for now."

He nods and I clear his image. Resting my elbows on the table I sit at, I clasp my hands and rest my chin on them as I think. Another small piece of the plan to recruit the girl to her Father's side has just fallen into place, almost of its own volition. I narrow my eyes as I try to pad it out, but realising the time, I stand to approach the glass, bringing Aurora into view.

Again, I find her downcast and downtrodden, this time being shouted at by the older man I take to be an employer of some kind.

"I'm not managing you for the fun of it, Rory," he says, confirming my thoughts. "I do this to make money. The kindness I show you is only because I'm a nice guy."

Her eyes flit to him as he says this, but she manages to keep her expression neutral.

"I know, Ted. And I appreciate it, I really do. But this publicity schedule you have me on is so busy. I won't have any time for myself for two weeks," she explains cautiously. "Can't some of the guys do some?"

"Time to yourself? What do you need that for? It's not like you have friends to hang out with. Or family," he adds, watching as any further argument is destroyed by his words.

She seems to shrink in front of him, retreating into herself and I wonder which of his cruel words have had such an impact.

"Fine," she agrees, her voice even and free of any emotion. "I'll be there. Are we done?"

"Yes, Rory," he says with an exaggerated sigh. "We are done. You have thirty minutes before rehearsal. The car will pick you up right after that. Interview then photo shoot."

She nods mutely and leaves the room. It is frustrating to watch her move so listlessly, to see her so easily defeated, given what I know she can become. I clear the mirror once more, knowing that for the rest of the day, no approach can be made by Jax or Mathim. They will be limited to dreams as I am, unlikely as it is that they will travel halfway across the world so soon after Xander's home has been destroyed.

"Sargatanas?" I say, sitting to wait for his response, but surprised when he appears almost instantly to answer me.

"Yes, my Lord?" he answers.

"That was quick. Was my timing so convenient that you happened to be next to a safe place to speak?" I ask.

"No, Sire. We were called back home this morning. The plans our Father had for our human target have been achieved. He has met with the one as dangerous as he is. They have formed an alliance, albeit an uneasy one. And so, our mission is complete."

I really am amazed by the transformation in him from this one mission on Earth. He stands taller, does not shy away from eye contact and somehow just holds himself like more of a soldier than he has ever been.

"And you were going to inform me? When?" I ask sharply. As improved as he is, he still needs a reminder of his place.

"I was about to call to you, Sire, but Lucifer demanded we all attend Bufas for our debrief. I had just left there to come and tell you everything when you called me." His hurried speech and dropped gaze tell me that my reminder has worked and so I relax a little with him.

"Very good. What of the others?" I ask. "Sallas and Malaphar? Are they still working together?"

"No, Lucifer has left them on Earth for a few days more in order to observe the new partnership."

This explains why Sargatanas was required by Bufas. He would not normally be the one to tell of their mission.

"That will keep them out of harm's way for now, I suppose. And

you? What does our Master have planned for you next?" I ask curiously, wondering just how far the mission has raised him in Lucifer's opinion.

"I am to go to the Realms soon. He has been building demon presence there, I hear. I do not know why though."

"It is not our place to question, Sargatanas, only to serve."

Of course, I know why Lucifer sends more and more of his soldiers there. He wishes to swell our armies' numbers in preparation for his move on Earth and then on Heaven.

"Of course, Sire," he agrees humbly. "Is there anything you wish of me?"

"No, not at present. Just listen for any interesting or useful information as always. Tezrian is in the Realms, I take it?"

"She is, my Lord."

"Good. Well, now I know where everyone is, I can concentrate on my own task. Thank you, Sargatanas. Let me know when you leave to join her."

He half-bows and I replace his figure with my own reflection. Sallas and Malaphar on Earth but busy, Tezrian in the Realms, and Lucifer leaving his most important tasks to me, as usual.

My mind returns to Aurora. Not only do I need to bring her into her Father's fold, I also need to instil in her all she needs to become what she is destined to. That may take more time than we have, if left until her birthday. I wonder if I can expedite her decision as I did Jay's. I may need to use those around her to help my plan.

I bring the "manager" into view and smile to see him sleeping on the sofa. Perfect. I step through into the room, waving a hand towards the door, sealing it and ensuring no one can interrupt.

Crouching by his head, I place my hand on his brow, making sure he cannot wake.

"She needs pushing harder. She is letting down her comrades, holding them back. And while she does this, you are being made to look weak and foolish. She does not deserve sympathy or kindness. You must drive her forward. For without her, you will have nothing. Everything you have worked for, the money and fame you so desire. All to fade away unless you take action."

"Mmm … action…" he murmurs.

I remove the seal from the door and the hold over his consciousness as I cross back over, turning to see him wake. Sitting up and stretching, he frowns as though trying to remember something important.

"I needed to do something. What was it?" he asks the empty room. "Oh, yes. That was it. Rory."

He stands and strides purposefully to the door. And I know my work was successful. She will come to me soon, I will ensure it.

18

The Realms

I stare in disbelief at the scene I see in the glass.

"I cannot emphasise enough how careful you must be here, Jax," warns Scirlin, after he opens the doorway. "The Realms are dangerous enough for demons and angels, never mind humans."

"I know, Scirlin. We'll take care. And we have Sal and whoever Eremiel sends to watch out for us too."

"Do you have a fix on him?" Mathim asks.

"I cannot find him. We have no connection to him, and I assume neither will the angels. I am unsure of how best they can begin the search."

We spend a moment looking at each other until it hits me.

"Wait, why didn't we think of this? I have details of all of Lucifer's children, right? Let me find him," I say. "I can link to him, I'm sure."

"Do we need to go back outside?" asks Xan. "And call to Eremiel?"

"There is no need to call, Xander. I am here," Eremiel says as he appears in the corner of the room.

"Are you going to have time to do this, Jax? You'll need to recover before you go through there." Lee nods towards the mirror, a look of worry on her face.

I look to Mathim and he nods.

"You do not need to leave immediately. And it will save you valuable time if you can find out where he is."

"Very well, let us get Jacqueline prepared. Lee, if you would like to do your own preparations for when she is done while we settle outside?" Eremiel suggests, prompting Lee to jump up from her seat and start hurrying to the kitchen area.

Once we're ready, I close my eyes and wait for the contact from both angel and demon, not wasting a moment to admire the world, but instead searching for Gabriel as soon as I feel the energy hit me.

I scan the strange world, my mind straining to see in the dim light.

Suddenly, I see a small flash in the distance and focus on travelling towards it, watching it grow from a pinprick as I near it. When I reach the glow, I see it surrounds a young man with blonde hair, looking around cautiously before moving to a nearby rock formation and hiding behind it. I take note of the exact shape of the cover he is using and then scan the area for reference points.

"Got him," I say. "Lee, before I come back, can you get me a pencil and paper please?"

I vaguely hear her move from her seat, and refocus on the scene I need to remember. I scan the area once more, noting the big stone outcrop overshadowing the area, and what looks like the shape of a doorway etched into it.

"Okay, guys," I say, opening my eyes and taking the drawing pad from Lee. "It looks like he's moving. But for now, he's hiding behind a formation that looks like this. And in the background, there's a big outcrop of rock that looks as though there's been a door carved into it, but just the outline. It's not much to go on, I know."

I draw as I speak, getting as close an idea of what I saw down on paper before it fades in my mind. When I'm done, I hand it to Mathim, who looks at it and passes it to Eremiel.

"It is more than we had ten minutes ago, Jax," says Mathim. "I know this outcrop you speak of, but I am unsure of Gabriel's location around it. Let's hope Sallas has a better memory than I do."

I sit for a few minutes, allowing the cool grass to reinfuse me with the energy I just used, and stand slowly. Taking the coffee Lee offers me, I walk back to the office, hurriedly eating chocolate as I go. Stopping in front of the mirror, I tilt the cup to my lips and wait for Scirlin to speak.

"Sallas is awaiting you in the Realms. Would you like to speak to him before they cross, Mathim?" he asks.

"Yes, please. And thank you, Scirlin, I know how difficult this is for you."

Sallas appears in the glass, his quick grin putting me at my ease.

"Hello, Jax. Ready for a real adventure?" he asks jovially.

"I think so," I say, returning his smile. "Xan, you ready?"

"I am. Hey, Sal, good to see you again," he greets.

"And you, Xander. I am glad to see you well. What's that?" He points to the pad in Mathim's hand and regards it closely when Mathim turns it for him to see.

"This is the only hint we have at Gabriel's location. I recognise this," he says, pointing at the larger stone formation, "but he could be anywhere around it."

"No, he can't. See that doorway? I made that. It's a cell. I know which side he is on."

Mathim looks relieved, but a word catches my attention.

"Cell?"

"For the converts." Seeing my confusion, he chuckles. "I'll tell you on the way. Now, if that's everything?"

"It is," Mathim concedes. "Take care of them, Sal."

"I will, friend. Do not worry, I'll have them back to you safely in no time."

"Well, here goes nothing," I say, stepping through the glass and turn to watch Xander arrive behind me. Looking at Mathim through the glass, I realise this is the first time since escaping Hell that I won't have him by my side for part of our mission. "Go get her, Mathim."

"I will. You be careful. I really am not happy to have you both there without me." Worry lines deepen on his brow as I smile reassuringly.

"I know. I'd rather you were here with us too. But we can't help that. And this way, we can deal with both kids at once. We'll be fine. And we'll see you soon."

With a cheery wave from Sallas, we turn away and begin our journey into the Realms.

* * *

"The problem we have is that if I transport us to the place we know he's hiding, we do not know what may be waiting there for us. I don't suppose you'd wish to arrive in the middle of a fight?" Sal asks.

"No," I answer, "that's definitely not a good idea. Is there somewhere you know of nearby that may be safe? Or is it really that far away from where we are now?"

"It is not too far. But even making the trek has its dangers. We will be out in the open a lot. As you can see, there's not a lot of cover."

He gestures to the open space that stretches out before us and I take a moment to fully take in our surroundings. Dry cracked earth under a strange orange sky, the only thing for miles being rocks and cliffs.

"Really, Sallas?" Tezrian's voice says in my head, startling me. I didn't realise any connection had been made.

I look at Xan and see no reaction.

"Hey, how come Xan isn't hearing you?" I ask.

"Remember when you were first in Hell, Jax?" asks Scirlin. "You had to clear your mind and you knew what we were trying to do. I know your friend has new abilities, I am not sure this will be one of them."

"Oh, okay. Want me to teach him?" I ask.

"Not now," he replies quickly. "You have company. Demons will approach your location shortly, you need to move."

"Hands, Jax. Xan," Sal orders aloud.

We take his hands and the world around us blurs for a second, my ears popping as we arrive on the very top of the rocks we were heading for.

"Nice job, Sal," praises Tez. "No one will be up there. There is not enough space for a battle."

"That's what I thought," he replies. "Now, Jax, this will be easier if Xander can talk as we are. Safer too, if no one needs speak aloud."

I nod at him and turn to Xan, keeping my voice low as he blinks to clear the disorientation he feels.

"Xan. We have a link with the others. We need you to join it, in here." I tap the side of my head and he frowns.

"How?"

"Close your eyes and focus on calming your mind. Then concentrate on me."

He does as I ask and before too long, I hear him.

"Jax?"

"Yes, Xan," I think back. "Everyone else?"

They all speak as I watch him nod in acknowledgement at each voice.

"Excellent, Xander," says Tez. "Now, I'm about to call for all demons near you to come instigate a battle here instead. That should give you time to start looking for your target. But it will require all my concentration, so I will be a little quiet while I do this. If you need me, just call through the link, I will keep it open."

"Okay, Tez. Thank you." I turn to Sal. "Will the angel be able to find us?"

"They will. They have their own version of Scirlin, I imagine," he answers, grinning when he hears Scirlin laugh.

"So, what now? We get down from here and work our way to

where we think he is until they turn up?" I ask them both.

"Yes, Jax. Time to start walking," Sal answers, taking the lead.

We make our way down the steep slope of the outcropping, trying to avoid loosening the small stones as we walk. When we finally reach the bottom, we take a moment to figure out where we are before we start. I see the door-shaped mark and gesture to it.

"Oh, yes," says Sal. "When the spirits are too few to do battle, we capture them and hold them in cells until we have enough. That's one I made. It's secure though, don't worry."

"Not worried. A little unhappy at the thought maybe, but not worried. To be sealed in there until you release them to fight? That's horrible."

"I never said it was pleasant, Jax. You sometimes forget what we are, I think. We're demons, supposed to be doing Lucifer's work." He looks at me as he says this, and I sigh.

"Yeah, I know. But you're not like the rest," I argue.

"I was. We all were. Until Lucifer killed Lil and Sab, pushing us over the edge. Mathim especially."

"He's a cool guy," says Xander. "I can't imagine going through what he did and still having the strength to go on."

"Me either," I agree.

Sal stops dead in front of us, holding a hand up to warn us to do the same. I listen carefully and hear the sound of someone or something trying to move quietly. I point to myself and then in one direction, followed by at Sal and then in the other. He frowns as though he wants to argue, but before he can even begin to speak in my head, I start to move in the direction I pointed. I grin to myself as I hear him huff out a resigned breath and begin to move the other way. Coming around the side of the large stone as Sal comes around the other, I hold my breath as I exit into the open, not knowing what to expect to see.

"Lizzie!" I exclaim.

"What?" says Xan, running around to join us.

"Hey, Jax. Hey, Xan," she answers simply, as we stare at her open-mouthed.

"Sweetie, what are you doing here? It's way too dangerous for you." I glance at Xan and see he's as worried as I am. "You can't be here, honey. I'm not even sure how you got here."

"No, Jax. It's okay. I can run home really fast. Faster than any of you. And she said you would need me," she says.

"Who said?" I ask. "The lady angel?"

"Yeah, she said that there was someone you need to talk to, but that when he sees you, he'll run. She said he won't run from me, so I had to come and be his friend." She pauses and looks around. "It's weird here, isn't it? The sky's a funny colour and there's no trees or anything."

"Yes, sweetheart, it's very weird." I look to Xan and Sal in turn, changing to the link to speak to them. "Really? Eremiel sends a little girl? Wait until I see him next."

"Focus, Jax," answers Sal. "She might be right. If he sees three human-looking adults, he'll think we're going to attack. Lizzie might be the only way we have to get him to stay in one place."

I wrack my brains for another solution so that we can send Lizzie home where it's safe, but I can't. When Xan meets my look, he shrugs his shoulders.

"Fine. But I hate this," I state. Turning back to Lizzie, I smile at her. "Okay, angel, but let's make this quick, shall we? Then we can get back home."

"Yes," she says, smiling back at me. "Where is he?"

"He's around here somewhere, kid," says Sal. "But we have to be really quiet. Can you talk in your head with us? Like you do with Jax?"

"Sure," she says through the link. "I like it better this way anyway. It's like a secret."

Despite everything, her enthusiasm has me grinning as I turn to scour the area for sign of Gabriel. Something seems out of place in the shadow of the cliff, and I narrow my focus onto the area.

"There," I say, pointing at a tiny movement, hardly visible in the darkness.

Sal stares to where I point, and I see his eyes flit between points in the path between us and where I gestured.

"Okay, so we should be able to get close by using the rocks as cover. Once we know it's him, we can let Lizzie go and talk to him. Follow me."

He steps out and makes his way to the next large group of stones, while I watch the shadows for any sign of him being seen. Doing this for all of us, we repeat it until we're close enough for me to make out the shape of the boy in the shadows.

"It's him," I send to the others. "Okay, Lizzie. You ready to make a friend?"

"Yes, Jax. I'll come and get you when he's ready, okay?"

"Okay, honey," I agree with a heavy heart, watching as she leaves the safety of our group and steps out into the open. It's possibly the strangest thing I've ever seen, this little girl so full of life and vibrancy skipping her way over the barren ground towards the boy as he hides.

"Hi," I hear her say cheerily. "I'm Lizzie. Who are you?"

"Hush," he warns, not unkindly. "Come here and hide, quick."

"Sorry," she replies in a quieter voice, still making it loud enough for us to hear.

"It's okay. But how are you here? And who are you?" he asks.

"I told you already, silly. I'm Lizzie. And I came to say hello."

19

The Importance of Family

"What is wrong with me?" she asks herself as she closes the door and leans back against it. "Why do I keep making everyone so mad at me?"

I have watched her as she dragged her way through another difficult day. One by one, those around her picked fault, shouted and lost their tempers with her, without really understanding why. Aurora herself had no idea of what was causing it either, simply ducking her head and apologising for things she hadn't done. And now she is alone, she allows herself to react to the pressure of the day.

She sits in front of the mirrored dresser, looking closely at her reflection. Unshed tears shine in her eyes as she tries to breathe calmly, somehow managing to centre herself. I had expected a total collapse once behind closed doors. I am somewhat impressed she has fought it off.

"Why?" she asks simply. Getting no answer from herself, she sighs and begins to clean off the makeup from the day, leaving the young, *fresh face looking back when she is finished. Her stomach begins to growl, and she crosses the room and picks up the phone. Sitting cross-legged on the bed, she presses a button and waits to speak.*

"Hi, I'd like to order room service, please. Room 107. Yes, I'd like the cheeseburger with fries and—" She stops as though interrupted, sighing heavily before she starts again. "Ted did? Okay, well, I guess I'll have the salad, the fruit selection and bottled water then, please. Thank you."

She ends the call and drops the phone back in its place.

"Dietary requirements, pfft."

I watch as she flicks through the pages of a magazine, hurrying past the pictures of herself. Before too long, her food arrives and she eats it without any sign of even noticing the taste, let alone enjoying it. When she's done, she moves the plates onto the table and climbs into bed, pulling the covers over her.

"Imagine how different things could have been," she whispers as though talking to someone other than herself. "God, I miss you. Especially on days like this."

The tears she stopped earlier begin to fall silently, once more unchecked until she falls into an exhausted sleep.

Those three words echo in my mind, over and over as I realise that I have found the key to her choosing her Father. Quickly, I run through the possibilities before making my decision and crossing into her room. Pulling up the nearby chair to the side of her bed, I close my eyes and bring her into my newly-created world.

"Hello, Aurora," I say.

"Oh, it's you. Astaroth, you said, right?" She shows no fear. In fact, she shows no reaction at all.

"I did, child. You have had a difficult day?"

"Yeah, you could say that. How did you know?" she asks.

"I can see it in your face. You know such suffering is not necessary? These people who treat you so badly are insignificant in the grand scheme of things. You doubted me when last we spoke. Not that I can blame you. But I spoke the truth, Aurora. You are destined for better than this."

"And like I said before, you must have the wrong person. I'm not destined for anything. And as for everyone around me, I'm kinda stuck. They've all worked so hard to get me where I am, doing what I love," she says.

"And do you?"

"Do I what?" Her question is accompanied by a puzzled look.

"Love what you do? Because it does not appear to be bringing you much happiness. Nor do those you speak of. You could have so much more, Aurora. So very much. What is it you desire? What would make you happy?" I watch as her passive mask melts away to be replaced with a pained expression of raw emotion as her eyes fill once more.

"No one can give me what I want." Such hopelessness is in her voice as it cracks with sadness.

"Imagine," I say, lifting my hand as I create a new scene.

Aurora walks in a green field, white and yellow flowers dotting it in the bright sunlight. She carries her shoes in her hand as she walks barefoot, looking as though she doesn't have a care in the world.

Hearing a voice in the distance, she hurries her step a little and I hear her humming happily to herself as she rounds the bend in the foot-worn path through the grass. When her eyes alight on the tall thin frame of the young man her mind has created ahead, she raises her arm to wave. When he stands to wave back, I hear a gasp from the real girl beside me. We both watch as she runs towards him, jumping into his open arms, giggling when he spins her around.

"This, perhaps, this would make you happy?"

"It would," she says, swallowing the lump in her throat to get the words to come out. "But it's not possible."

"Tell me about him, Aurora. Who is he?" I ask.

"I can't," she sobs. "I just can't."

"Try."

"He was my brother. He took care of me when my mom was at her craziest. And then he died. I was thirteen. Mom got worse, until I couldn't take any more. I ran away from home and lived on the streets for a while, singing for spare change. That's when Ted found me. He took me in and put me in the band. He saved me."

"He used you, child. Surely, you can see that?"

I give her time to recover herself while I take in the new information. Her home life was terrible, that much is obvious, but to lose the brother who protected her for so long? It explains a lot. And now a dependence on her supposed "saviour". It is high time this child had someone to really look up to.

"Well?" I ask. "Do you see how he took you in only to better himself?"

She looks up at me and nods sadly.

"I've always known, I think. I just didn't want to admit it."

"There is a way out of this, Aurora. If you choose it. A life worth so much more. With a family to support you."

"How?" she asks.

"You will wake from this and think it was all a cruel dream borne of grief. Someone offering you the protection and care of a family. And you would be correct, in part. You are sleeping and this is the dream world but remember this name and you will find the man it belongs to is real enough. He will be telling the world through its media of the sad demise of a man of faith. His name is Jay Forrest and he is in England. You will find him and know I speak the truth. If you decide to look for him, I will take it as a sign you wish to escape this life you live at present and are ready for a much better one. I will return to you with an idea of how you can do this. If you dismiss all of this, then I will leave you. How does that sound?"

In this, I lie. If she decides not to follow the lead I've given her, I will return and wipe it from her memory, trying a different approach the next time. Like Jay, if she approaches me, then I break no covenant.

"It sounds like you could be my guardian angel," she laughs.

The mention of that word makes me think of another thing I need to do.

"As you have not dismissed the idea so far, then there is something else I should tell you. There are others who would try to gain your trust. Much like this Ted, they will tell you whatever they think you need to hear to get you to go with them," I warn. "You trust me, do you not, Aurora?"

"Yes, I trust you, Astaroth. I haven't ever told anyone else except

Ted about my past. But who are these others?" she asks. "And why would they want me? I'm just me."

"You still doubt your potential, child. I see that. But these people know what I do, what you are destined for. And they would stop you from achieving it. I know you do not care for the idea of being fated for greatness, but it also secures your happiness, your family. Do not allow them to take that away from you. You have lost too much already."

She nods solemnly at my words, taking a moment before she speaks.

"I will do as you say, Astaroth. If anyone should approach me in any way, I'll send them away."

"Very good. Now, I will leave you to a peaceful sleep. Remember the name I told you."

"Jay Forrest," she says without missing a beat. "Look for the story about the priest in the UK press."

"I will return, Aurora. Now, sleep."

At my words, the background fades into darkness and we are returned to her room. I look down at her as I stand, seeing a small smile on her face as she rests.

"Sleep well, child. Tomorrow, you find your new brother."

20

New Friends

"Nice to meet you, Lizzie," Gabriel says. "But how are you here all alone?"

"Well, I'm not exactly alone. But I'm not one of those horrible things and neither are my friends." She must see a look of panic on his face as she quickly starts to reassure him. "Just listen, okay? Don't run away. I promise no one is trying to get you or to scare you."

Her serious tone in such a young voice makes me smile and I hear Gabriel chuckle in matching amusement.

"Well, you don't look scary. But I don't wanna be tricked by anyone either. How about you tell me what you want to and if I think I need to go, I'll go?"

There's a pause as she thinks about it, and I see her hair move as she nods in agreement.

"Okay. I live in Heaven with my mummy, but I help the angels and my friends. Jax lives on Earth with Xander and they're trying to stop the mean man from winning. He's really horrible. He hurt Jax and I had to rescue her. We need to take you back with us to help stop him too. Will you come?"

I wonder how the hell he's meant to decipher that and look at Xan who shrugs in response.

"Wait a minute. I didn't really understand half of that," Gabriel replies. "You want to take me back to Earth? Not Heaven or Hell? Earth?"

"Yes, Earth. We need you to help us to stop Asta-, to stop the bad man. With Jax and Xan. Oh, and Lee. I like her too, but she can't see me. We need to stop him getting your sister."

"Aura? What about her?" His sharp tone silences Lizzie for a second and he changes it quickly. "I'm sorry, Lizzie. What do you know about Aura?"

"Well," she starts slowly, "I don't know a lot about her, but my friends do."

"Well played, Lizzie," murmurs Sal with a grin.

"Okay, can you call them? And I'm sorry I snapped at you."

"It's alright, Gabriel. I'll get them."

I see her head appear out of the shadows as she waves us over. I hold up my hand showing three fingers and point to us. She nods and turns back to him as we approach.

"There are three of them so don't panic, okay?"

"Okay, Lizzie. Thank you for the warning." He looks at us warily as we get nearer.

"Good job, sweetheart," I say, as we join them. "Hi, Gabriel. Nice to meet you. I'm Jax, this is Xander and Sallas. "

"What about Aura?" he asks bluntly.

"I'm not gonna lie to you, Gabriel. She's in danger. Shall we sit?" I sink down onto the ground, my legs grateful for the rest as I see the others do the same. "I'll start from the beginning, so bear with me. This will be easier for you to accept than it was for the others, cos you've already seen the angels, demons and afterlife."

"Go on," he prompts.

"I'll keep watch," says Sal, stepping out when I nod.

"You've seen the demons? And the angels?" I ask.

"Yeah, I've seen them. Seen the flame and the flash too, taking everyone out of this place. I stayed until Aura gets here. I left her once, I'm not doing it again."

"Right. So you get that if demons are real then so is Lucifer. He plans to destroy humanity as revenge against his Father, but he needs his children to allow him to come to Earth. You and your sister are two of those children. I can't think of any way to break that news easier," I apologise.

"Mom was right," he breathes. "Wow. We thought she was crazy."

"What?" I ask incredulously. "Your mum knew?"

"Apparently. But we can come back to that. Just take it that I accept everything you're saying and get to the part about Aura."

"He sent one of his best demons to find and recruit the three offspring to his side, that's Astaroth."

"The mean man," interrupts Lizzie solemnly.

"That's right, angel. Thank you." I turn back to Gabriel and see him looking fondly at her before refocusing on me. "He cannot approach any of you directly but can influence dreams and the like to persuade you all to go with him. There's a covenant though. It says that only the Chosen One can speak to the children, the one human able to stop him. That's me, by the way. So far, Astaroth has Jay and we have Emelia."

"I thought you said three? With me and Aura, that'll be four."

"The prophecy speaks of the three having to make their decisions by their twenty third birthday. You technically aren't there to do that. But we don't know what you still being around will do to the situation. Your sister seems to be a little vulnerable, and I know from experience how evil Astaroth can be in order to get what he wants. We need you, Gabriel, to help us protect her from him. And to stop him coming to Earth and destroying everything. Will you come with us?"

"Of course. I need to make sure she's safe. When do we leave? And how do I even get back there?" he asks, standing as though to leave this instant.

"You might not like this bit," I warn.

"Go on," he says suspiciously.

"Sal, out there, is in fact a demon. He's helping us and you have nothing to fear from him. In the same way, the angels are helping too. I need to call to them to help get you back. Is that okay?" I watch his face, waiting for his reaction. Having faced countless days trying to avoid contact with either race, I wouldn't blame him if he ran. "Gabriel?"

"It's for Aura. Call who you need to," he says firmly.

"Thank you," I reply.

Closing my eyes, I picture Eremiel, opening them to see him in front of me.

"Well done, Jacqueline," he says. "You found him faster than I thought. I am pleased to meet you, Gabriel."

"Hi, Eremiel," says Lizzie cheerfully.

"Hello, Lizzie. You have done very well, little one," he answers, while I narrow my eyes at him.

"We'll discuss that particular idea later, Eremiel," I warn him. "For now though, how do we get Gabriel home?"

"It will not be an easy crossing. Much like the flare that takes the redeemed to Heaven, you must walk through fire to reach your desired destination. It will not hurt, but you must focus on the realm you wish to arrive in. No one can help you to find your way there, you must be strong enough to find it on your own. I suggest you use the pull of your bond with your sister to help you."

I look at Gabriel and see nothing but determination in his face as he nods in agreement.

"Okay, I'm ready," he says.

"A little room, please, Jax."

I step back at Eremiel's words and watch a purple flame spring up where I stood a second before. Eremiel's eyes meet Gabriel's and he smiles encouragingly.

"See you soon, I guess," he says, stepping forward and allowing himself to be wrapped in the purple fire before he disappears completely from sight, taking the flame with him.

"Just like that?" I ask. "Where will he end up? How will he get to us?"

"Don't worry, Jax. I'm gonna get him. Once he passes through, then I'll go show him how to find you," says Lizzie.

"You can do that?" I ask.

"Of course. The lady angel taught me. Plus, I'm a big girl now. I can do all sorts of things."

"Yes, you are. I'm very glad you're my friend, Lizzie." I glare at Eremiel. How can he involve such a young child so heavily in all of this? "And us? We return the way we came?"

"Yes, Jax. Sallas can transport you back to where you crossed."

"Good. This place just feels so off. Come on, you two. I'm ready for home."

I leave the shadows and step out to join Sal and Xan, holding hands with them and feeling the air shift around me. When I open them, I see the doorway rise out of the murky water and hear Scirlin in my head.

"Good job, all of you."

"Thanks, Scirlin," I reply, stepping through into my office, glad that I stay dry. "Where's Mathim?"

"Gimme a minute, I'm making coffee," yells Lee, hearing my question from the other room. "Mathim is waiting for you outside. I'll be there in a minute, don't start without me."

"Okay, honey. Thank you."

I blink in the bright sunlight, seeming even more dazzling after being in the strange light of the Realms, and walk towards Mathim. As my eyes adjust, I see the expression on his face, and I know there's a problem.

"What? What's wrong?" I ask immediately.

"First, sit. Recharge. The time there has taken a toll on you," he orders.

"Yeah, actually, as Mathim mentioned it I noticed it myself. You don't look good, Jax," says Xan.

"I feel a little tired, that's all."

"There is no natural life in the Realms," says Eremiel, as he walks towards us. "I am not surprised you were affected like this."

"I'll be fine. But a heads up might've been a good idea. In case we were there for any length of time. I'd have been no good to the tiny child spirit you sent in there, if I was wiped out, would I? Honestly, Eremiel, what were you thinking?" I ask him angrily.

"I know what you must think of me, Jax, but had I sent one of the angels in my company, it would have drawn the attention of demons and ferals alike. Also, having Lizzie there meant that Gabriel took less convincing than if not." He eyes me warily, waiting for another outburst. "She has her own protection too, in case you hadn't guessed."

"The lady angel?" I say.

"Indeed. Now, can we move on to more pressing matters than you shouting at me?"

I laugh, despite my anger, and nod for him to continue but instead he looks to Mathim.

"Yeah. Mathim, what about Rory? Have you made contact?"

"Hey, I said wait for me," complains Lee, as she joins us.

"Sorry, kid. I'll catch you up in a minute," I promise. "Mathim?"

"Somehow, he has blocked her," he says through his teeth. "Try as I might, I cannot enter her dreams."

"Shit! Really? Gimme a break. How did he get to her before we did?"

"Hell has more eyes on her than we do, it seems, although I myself am not sure how," says Eremiel.

"So, what now?" asks Xan.

"We'll have to do it in person, that's all. Eremiel said he could create a real-world door. I guess that's the only way we have left," I reply. "And we have Gabriel, so that's a bonus too. It should help pull her out of whatever hold Astaroth has on her."

Sensing a lull in the conversation, Lee asks for details from the Realms and while I drink my coffee, I tell her all of what happened, giggling at the glare she gives Eremiel at the mention of his sending Lizzie.

"Can I ask a question?" she says, once I've finished.

"Of course, sweetie," I answer.

"What happens next? I mean once they've decided whose side they're on?"

I frown and look at Eremiel. We've been so focused on Lucifer's children, that I haven't had time to think about what comes after that.

"Exactly what happens is not written or predicted. The prophecies are vague in their description of events," he explains.

"Typical," I laugh. "Here, go save the world, but we're not sure how."

He looks quickly to me but seeing my grin, he relaxes.

"I am sorry I cannot shed any further light on this, Jax."

"It's fine, I think we're all used to being in the dark by now, right?"

"Exactly," he agrees with a chuckle.

"I guess we go talk to Rory next then, huh?" I ask, looking at Mathim.

"It looks that way, Jax," he says.

I reach up from my normal seat on the floor to put my cup on the table and then stand to go check on what Rory is doing.

"Well, no time like the—"

A blinding flash in my head takes away my vision and I close my eyes and fall to my knees.

"Jax? Jax!" I hear Lee cry and feel her hands touch my shoulders, but I can't answer her.

Flash after flash burns into my mind, each one bringing a different image.

"Wait. Visions," I manage to utter, feeling her pull back when she realises what's happening.

Like a picture book that turns itself into a moving scene when you flick the pages fast enough, I watch as the events play out in my mind. Calming my breathing now I've realised what's happening, I watch as three figures draw close to each other and sit on the ground around a strange symbol. Their lips moving in sync with each other, they join hands and the marking in the middle of their circle begins to glow. Simultaneously, their heads drop back and as they look to the sky, still chanting, the ground begins to crack and open, letting the red glow turn into a bright light. And, as suddenly as it appears, the image is gone, leaving me pulling deep breaths into me as my sight returns to normal.

"Jax?" Lee asks quietly.

"Wow. Well, that wasn't fun," I say, blinking as my eyes water.

"You said vision. What did you see?" asks Eremiel.

"More importantly, are you okay, Jax?" says Lee, giving the angel another death stare.

"I'm fine, honey. It just took me by surprise, that's all. I saw the three kids sitting around a weird symbol on the floor. They were chanting and holding hands, as cliched as that sounds. The symbol cracked open and red light came from it. I guess that's some kind of summoning ritual for Lucifer?"

"It sounds like it. Was there anything else?" Mathim watches me as I go over what I saw in my head.

"No. Well, maybe. The images came through like pictures drawn and moved through quickly to make a full scene. But the light in the background gradually got lighter until the middle, then darkened again. Mean anything to you? It might just have been my mind trying to see everything all at once though."

"Hmm, nothing springs to mind. But it might come up later, so we will make sure we remember it. Are you recovered?"

"I am," I answer, taking the hand he offers me. "Let's go get Rory."

21

Big Brother

"Well, shit," the girl exclaims, eyes widening at what she sees on the screen in front of her. "Jay Forrest, I'll be damned."

She stops muttering to herself and puts down her phone, her brow furrowing in thought as I watch from my seat in front of the mirror.

"Rory!" yells a male voice from somewhere outside the small room she sits in. "Get your ass out here."

With a sigh, she pushes her chair back as she stands.

"Coming," she calls back calmly.

I follow her progress along a dark passage and out onto the stage. But this time, I notice a subtle difference in her as she moves. Her stature isn't quite as small as she usually makes it and when she walks out into the bright lights, she does not allow her hair to hide her from the angry looks awaiting her.

"Sorry," she shrugs, and takes her place at the front. "Ready when *you are.”*

Her companions look at each other puzzled, noticing the change too.

“Finally,” one of them mutters, before counting them in.

The music starts and I wait to hear her sing before I clear the image, now that I know she is busy. I smile to myself when I hear the surety in her tone. Yes, the child is beginning to believe. With a wave of my hand the scene fades as I refocus its gaze.

“Jay?”

“Astaroth. Yes, I’m here.” He rushes in front of the mirror, smiling when he sees me waiting there.

“Ah, good. I thought perhaps you would be working. How did the story go down with the world?” I ask, allowing him to revel in his success for a moment.

“It’s been picked up by newspapers all around the world. The editor allowed the footage to be placed on our website and it’s had millions of people watching it. We asked the Church if they’d like to

respond but so far we've had no comment apart from they are shocked and saddened by the priest's actions."

"Of course not," I scoff. "What else can they say?"

"Is there any news on what I am to do next?"

His eagerness does not wear on me like that of Sargatanas. Jay's is borne of a desire to please his Father, not to merely work his way up in his estimation for personal gain. Although, I do know there is some small amount of selfish desire mixed with it. He simply hides it better.

"Not at your Father's instruction, no. But I have a task for you, if you are willing and able to do it," I say, as if I think there is the slightest possibility of him refusing.

"Of course, Astaroth. What is it?" he says without pause for thought.

"How are your acting skills?" I ask, seeing a look of confusion appear on his face.

"Umm, I'm not sure. Why?"

"You have another sister, it would seem. And while I know you would not necessarily wish to endear yourself to her, it is imperative that we get her to our side. We need to have the majority with us and not with the angels if we are to succeed in your Father's plans. She is a weak little thing, devastated ever since the loss of her brother."

His eyes have left mine, staring off into the distance as he works this through his mind, only looking back at me once he has concluded his thinking.

"You want me to take her under my wing, so to speak?" he asks.

"I do. It is vital she feels like she has another brother, another family even. At least until we have what we need from her. After that, I do not think my Master will care for her fate. Weak and dependent are not characteristics cherished in any child of Lucifer. If you were to have a hand in her coming to us however, well, I do not think I need to tell you what your Father will think of that," I say.

He watches me for a moment, as though working out if he should lie or speak the truth, before breaking out into laughter.

"You see right through me, Astaroth."

"Ruthless ambition is not a bad thing in such as us, Jay. Nor is pride, especially when warranted. You are willing to play the role then?"

"Yes, Astaroth, of course. I'll be the perfect big brother for as long as you need me to be," he agrees.

"Very well. I will allow her to contact you. Be ready."

Seeing him nod in agreement, I clear his image and sit back in my chair. Feeling confident of my success, I allow myself to imagine the look on Jacqueline's face when she realises that she cannot reach the last of my Master's children and if she does travel to meet her in person, to find her already lost to them.

"Astaroth?"

Lucifer's voice makes me approach the glass curiously.

"My Lord?"

"I have watched you with her. This is a much more difficult role for you, I imagine. But I am sure it is the right one. I am about to send Agares forward once more. This time my son will begin to make the link between all of these 'acts of nature' that the rest of the world is *too slow to find. I thought to tell you, as he will be busy over the coming weeks. You do not need him, I assume?" he asks.*

"I have, in fact, just entrusted a task to him, Sire. But it will not take long, nor will it take too much of his time. I am certain that he is up to both tasks simultaneously, if the need arises," I reply.

"Very well. Agares travels in a few days, so you have Jay's full attention until then. After that, we will test his ability to manage multiple missions at once," he agrees.

"Yes, Master. And once we have Aurora? Would you wish me to begin to test the pull of your blood in Emelia?"

The idea of stealing her from under the protection of Bathin and the angels has been playing on my mind ever since Lucifer mentioned it.

"I have not decided yet," he says. "But when I do, I will let you know. Now, I will let you get back to the third. Things are reaching a critical point it appears."

"Indeed, Master."

He disappears from the glass and I push all thoughts of Emelia, Jax,

246

and all others from my mind to focus on my current target. The music once more fills the room as I move the scene to the room in which she sat before being called out on stage. Seeing her phone on the table, I smile and step through.

After I retrieve it, I turn towards the glass I just passed through and reconnect with Jay. I ask him for the information I need, tapping the screen as he instructs. When her phone makes a noise and I see his name appear on it, I set it back in place and return to my rooms to await her reappearance.

The music stops after a while and she runs breathless through the door, breathing a sigh of relief when she sees her misplaced item where she left it.

"Thank God for that," she says to herself, picking it up. She reads the name on the screen. "How the hell...?"

She crosses to the sofa and sits down on the edge of it as she opens the message, reading it aloud.

"Hey, Rory, so pleased to find out I have a sister. Even more impressed when I find out she's a famous rock star! Gimme a call whenever you like. Jay x"

The biggest smile I've ever seen from her spreads across her face and she hugs her phone to her chest.

"Well, Jay, I dunno how you got my number, but I'm glad you did."

"Rory!" the disembodied voice calls once more. "Break's over. You think cos you managed not to screw up the first set, it gives you the right to slack off? We have the second half to get through. Time's a'tickin'."

She rolls her eyes and jumps up, jogging back to the stage and pulling her hair back, tying it in place as she walks to the microphone. This time though she smiles as she sings, her hand wrapped tight around the phone in her pocket.

22

Unwelcome Visitors

"It is done," says Eremiel from the other side of the glass. "You can cross whenever you are ready."

"Thanks, Eremiel," I reply as I step through to join him.

"Is there anything else you require of me before I leave?" he asks.

"No, we've got it from here. I'll call to you if we need you."

"Very well. Good luck."

He fades from sight and I look at Mathim.

"You ready?"

"I am," he says. "Let us hope she listens."

"Yeah. It was much easier to do this when we'd already put in the work in Emelia's dreams before we just turned up."

I start to walk towards the exit onto the street, ready to head to the music store across the road where we watched Rory prepare for her signing event earlier. Already, a small queue has formed, but it isn't as long as I worried it would be.

"Are you sure we have time for this, Mathim?" I ask, as we dodge through the people hurrying to get to their destinations.

"I think you were right, Jax. Simply turning up at her door would perhaps have resulted in her panicking. We must make time."

We take our place at the back of the line and watch her as she chats politely to the steady stream of admirers. Every now and again, she glances to the phone she's placed on the table at the side of the pile of publicity posters she signs and gives out.

"Hmm."

"What's wrong?" Mathim asks, hearing me.

"Well, she has no one, right? Her manager is over there watching her. And her band are at the back getting ready to join her." I point all of this out while I speak.

"Yes, I see them. But I still do not understand what you're getting at."

"If they're all here, then who is she waiting to hear from? We've watched her every movement as much as we've been able to, and I've never seen her get a call or a text from anyone. And yet, today, she's checking her phone every two minutes." I shake my head. "Ignore me, it's probably nothing."

"If it struck you as odd, catching your attention as it did, then it may not be nothing, Jax. Your intuition has not served you wrong so far."

I shrug as the line moves forward, and we're almost at the front when her screen lights up and her face does the same when she reads the notification.

"Yeah, that's not nothing," I agree.

She answers hurriedly before the next in line moves forward, glancing furtively to her manager to make sure he hasn't seen it, looking up at the person in front of her and giving them a beaming smile as she talks to them.

Before too long, we stand in front of her and she can't hide the surprise at how different we are to the steady stream of teenagers and younger people she's met already.

"Hi," she says brightly.

"Hi, Rory. It's a pleasure to meet you," I reply.

"Thank you. It's a pleasure to meet you too. Is it a poster you're after?" she asks. "Don't take this the wrong way, but you don't look like you'd want a signed picture for your room."

I laugh and shake my head, handing her the cd I bought instead.

"No, I'm a bit past the posters on the wall stage of my life," I agree.

"Cool," she says with a chuckle as she opens the case and pulls out the insert.

"I dunno how you do this, I have to admit." I gesture to the people behind me when she gives me a questioning look. "Smiling and talking to people all day. Don't you have days when you just don't wanna deal?"

She giggles as she hands the cd back to me.

"No. I'm really lucky to do what I do, and to have people that would want to come and meet me." Her words sound practised and I don't believe them but smile back at her.

"Thank you. And thank you for your time," says Mathim.

"No worries. Have a good rest of the day."

She looks past us to the next person approaching but her attention is taken by her phone again when it vibrates on the table. Glancing down at it, I inhale a sharp breath, making Mathim and Rory look at me curiously.

"Sorry," I say quickly. "I got cramp. Probably from standing so long. Thanks again, Rory."

I move away from the table and hurry to the exit.

"What is it?" Mathim asks when we get outside.

"The name on the screen? It was Jay."

I watch as his eyes widen at the mention of him.

"How?"

"I dunno. Let's find somewhere for a coffee and figure it out. She's only there for another hour, we might as well stay here until she's free. The sooner we make our move, the better," I point to the coffee shop a few doors down and start walking towards it. "Take one of those tables outside. I'll get drinks and be back in a minute."

My mind whirls as I walk to the counter, placing our order, paying and carrying them back to Mathim on autopilot. I light a cigarette and inhale deeply once I'm sitting down, giving myself a few extra moments before I speak.

"Looks like Astaroth got further than we thought, huh?" I say eventually.

"It certainly appears so. We carry on as planned?" he asks, giving me the chance to share what I'm thinking.

"Definitely. It just means we can't take the subtle approach any more. She obviously knows some of it. We're just gonna have to speed our plan up even more and go all out straight away. I wish we had time to do all this gently."

"Unfortunately, Astaroth has removed that possibility. I agree, Jax. We must give her all the facts and hope she will listen. Who knows how much of a hold he has over her?"

"Right." I sit back and huff out a sigh. "Well, we knew it wouldn't be easy, I guess. So, what now? We have an hour."

"Now we wait," he says, laughing at my expression. "I know this will frustrate you. Patience is not one of your strengths."

"Hey," I complain jokingly. "It's not my fault I like to get things done."

My phone rings in my pocket and I reach for it, surprised when I see Lee's face on the screen.

"Hey, chick," I greet. "What's up?"

"I checked you weren't busy in the mirror before I rang," she says quickly. "But I needed to check something. Will you be there for long? Cos we have the castle hunt tonight, I think we all forgot what day it was."

"Ah hell, yeah, it totally slipped my mind. Good catch, kid."

I see the look on Mathim's face and swap her to speaker.

"We forgot the hunt tonight," I say.

"Want me to cancel?" she asks.

I check the time and see that it's still early.

"No, we're only gonna have until she leaves for the gig anyway. By the time that's done, and she's back at the hotel, we'll be all wrapped up. Grab Xan and get him to load Vinni with all the gear. That way, we're ready to go as soon as we're home."

Mathim raises an eyebrow but then nods in agreement.

"Wow, Jax, that's a lot in one day. You sure you'll be okay?" she asks worriedly.

"Just what I was thinking, Lee," says Mathim.

"Huh? I'll be fine. It's just a long day, we've had them before and survived," I laugh.

"Jax, look," Mathim interrupts, pointing down the street. "She's finished early."

"Well, hell, something's going our way today, at least. Okay, sweetie, that's our cue. Gotta go."

"Okay, see you soon," Lee replies and I end the call.

Finishing the last of my coffee and putting my phone back in my pocket, I stand up and stretch.

"Time to see how busy Astaroth's been."

***

I hear Rory's voice from behind the door of her hotel room as we approach it, chattering happily. It only stops when I knock lightly, and I hear her say a quick goodbye as she approaches.

"Yes?" she says, as she opens the door. "Oh, it's you."

She looks at us in surprise.

"Hi, Rory. I'm sorry to just arrive at your door. I'm Jax, and this is—"

"Bathin, right?" she interrupts, and I groan inwardly as my worst fears are confirmed.

"You are half-right, Aurora. I no longer go by that name. I am Mathim. And I see by your attitude towards us that you have already at least spoken to Astaroth."

Her attempt to hide her reaction to his name fails, and I butt in quickly.

"Rory, we only want to talk. You've obviously listened to Astaroth, please, just do the same for us. That's all we want. Just for you to hear what we have to say before you make your decision."

"Decision? What decision?" she asks. "You talk of someone I've only dreamed about. How can you know that?"

Her act doesn't fool me for a minute, so I push on.

"I saw Jay's name on your phone, Rory. There's no other way you could know about him. Please, we only want to talk."

Her defiance wavers at mention of Jay for a second, but she recovers and stands straight as she looks me in the eye.

"Okay, yeah, I'm talking to Jay. And yes, Astaroth was the one that told me about him. He also told me that you'd come, promising the world if I come with you or take your side in God knows what. You want to stop me fulfilling my potential or something. I'll tell him what I told you. I'm nothing. No one. I don't have some great destiny. What I do have is a brother I never knew, and that's all that matters. Now, I've given you enough time. Please leave before I call security."

She starts to close the door on us, but a hand from Mathim stops its progress.

"And what of your real brother? Gabriel?" he asks.

"How do you know about Gabe?" she breathes, her face turning white.

"I know you won't believe this, if Astaroth hasn't told you everything, but Gabriel still exists. He may have died, but that doesn't mean he's gone. Let us talk to you and explain, Rory."

"NO!" she yells, surprising me into taking a step back. Tears shine in her eyes, despite her anger at the mention of her brother. "He said you'd lie, you'd say anything you could to make me listen. He was right. Now, go. I mean it. I'll call the police, and have you arrested."

A door further down the hall opens and a head peers out at us.

"Aurora—" begins Mathim, but she crosses her arms across her chest and stares defiantly back at him.

"I said no. Gabe is dead. That's all there is to it. And your using his name to trick me only proves that Astaroth was right about you. Jay too. Now, leave."

I look at Mathim and nod, watching as he drops the hand holding the door open, allowing Rory to slam it loudly in our faces.

"What else can we do?" I ask him. "The last thing we need is for the police to show up. Let's go home and regroup. We can call Eremiel and see if he has any ideas."

"Okay," he agrees, but then growls under his breath. "Astaroth really worked well on her."

"Yeah, he did. It's what he's good at, playing on weaknesses. Come on, let's get back."

We walk silently to the mirror we crossed through and step back into the office, meeting Lee with half-smiles as she comes in with cups for each of us.

"Thanks, honey," I say. "You saw?"

"I saw," she sympathises. "I thought maybe the mention of Gabriel would make her listen."

"Me too, little one," agrees Mathim. "If he had been with us, perhaps."

"Hmm, yeah. You could try again when he gets through, I suppose," she suggests.

"I wonder how long that takes," I muse. "We could ask Eremiel."

"I hope it's not long," says Mathim. "Time, I think, is beginning to run out."

I close my eyes and focus on thoughts of the angel, but when I open my eyes and don't see him there, I sigh.

"He must be busy."

"Speaking of busy, Jax," says Lee, "I'm sorry to do this to you, but if we're meeting Greg before the hunt, you're pushing it if you wanna recharge before we leave."

I drag myself wearily from the edge of the desk I'd been leaning on, and make my way out into the garden, kicking off my shoes as I go. Sinking gratefully onto the grass, I smile in relief at the energy from the ground.

"Mmm, how the hell did I manage before I could do this?"

***

"I was possessed, wasn't I?" asks Greg, taking me by surprise. "After it happened, I looked online for anything I could find to give me a clue what happened, and everything I read pointed me to that."

"Forgive me, Greg, but if you realised that, how are you still even working here?" I reply. "It would scare most people away."

"Honestly, I don't know. I mean, I felt okay after. A little tired for a few days, but okay. And I only half-believed it anyway. Seeing your reaction though, I guess I was right. So, tell me."

He waits expectantly while I figure out just how much I should tell him, but before I can open my mouth to begin, Mathim starts to speak.

"You have seen first hand that there is more to this world than this life, Greg. Unfortunately, you got to experience first-hand the not-so-pleasant side of what Jax and her friends do," he begins, and I notice a different tone in his voice as he speaks. "You were taken over completely, no control over anything you said or did. Luckily, we were able to free you from this hold, and I am glad to hear that you have had no ill effects since."

"No, none," Greg agrees. "It felt like I had a mild hangover, if anything. And, as for the time when I was 'taken over' as you put it, I don't remember any of that. If it hadn't been for the state of the room following your last visit, I probably wouldn't have even realised that anything went wrong. I saw that when I woke the next morning and had vague recollections of hearing what sounded like a fight, but that was all."

"Uh, yeah, about that," I start to apologise. "We'll happily compensate the owners for the damage."

"No need. I removed all signs of it. They've been making a lot of repairs and restorations. I just added it to the list of work being done by the craftsmen we have working here. As I couldn't explain what had happened, I thought it best not to even try."

I smile gratefully at him, and then shake my head with a laugh.

"You're taking all this way better than I thought you would, I have to say. I had no idea how I was meant to tell you all of this and I really didn't wanna lie to you," I admit.

"And I appreciate that, Jax. Thank you." He collects our empty cups from the table and stands up. "Now, if you're ready, I'll help you set up?"

"Yes, I think it's time we got started," Mathim agrees quickly, making me shoot him a curious glance. "We will be carrying Jax's equipment in whenever you're ready to join us."

He walks to the door, out into the hall and doesn't speak until we're outside.

"Questions, Jax?" he asks with a small grin.

"You used the whole Jedi mind trick thing on him, didn't you?" I see the confusion at my reference and reword with a chuckle. "The change in your voice. You used it on Emelia to keep her calm when you were talking to her about her father."

"I did. I thought it better to cause an easy acceptance, For him, as well as for us."

"Yeah, good plan." I pause to look back at the castle we just left. "This feel different to you?"

"It does indeed. It feels dead. I think when Abbatu used it the way he did, he may have drained it of its energy. The owners may be in for a disappointment."

"No, I don't think so. I think maybe he cleared it of active spirits, but I'm sure there'll still be enough residual stuff here for the hunts they want to work," I say. "Come on, we'd better get started or else Lee and Xan will have done everything."

"Yes, and I would not risk the wrath of Lee for anything."

His solemn tone and serious look make me giggle, and I nudge him off- balance as I walk towards my friends to start a simple night of ghost-hunting.

23

Making Choices

"It is time, Jay. Your best work is needed. Are you ready?" I ask.

"I am, Astaroth. What do you need me to do?" he replies, rubbing the sleep from his eyes.

"For now, I need you to wait. Be ready to make contact when I return and tell you."

I wait for his nod before clearing the image before me and replacing it with that of the room in which Ted is currently sleeping. Crossing silently, I bend to plant the seeds of thought in his mind, repeating my actions with everyone that Rory will work with today. Once it is done, I return to my room and wait for them all to wake. I watch as Rory begins to stir, checking her phone and sighing when she sees the screen is devoid of any news from Jay.

"Patience, child," I murmur. "He will reach out only when the time is right."

She throws back the covers and sits up, yawning and stretching before she stands to begin her day.

"Come on, Rory, today's a whole new day, it can't possibly be that bad."

I smirk at her words. She has no idea how bad it can be.

* * *

For hours, I sit and observe her. Taking the shouting, screeching admonishments from all of those around her, almost pushed to tears more times than I care to count, the silence of her phone only adding to her misery. Time after time, I hear her companions belittle and insult her, and see the confusion on her face as she tries to work out what she is doing to provoke them. She manages to hold herself together somehow, at least long enough to complete her work for the day and return to her rooms to seek refuge from the constant barrage of near-hatred they have all shown her today.

I wait until she sinks gratefully into the chair, finally able to relax, before I bring her brother into view in the other side of the mirror.

"Now, Jay," I instruct, seeing his hand reach for his phone and fingers pass over the screen.

"Done," he says. "I have a question though. What if she asks about you?"

"Then tell her what she wants to know," I reply, seeing Rory's face light up when she sees his message. "Are you ready?"

"I am." He only just gets the words out before the ringing starts.

"Jay?" Rory crosses to her bed and sits on the edge. "Is everything okay? I was worried when I didn't hear from you."

"Sorry, sis. My battery died at work and I didn't have my charger. How are you? You don't sound good."

"I'm okay. Better now I'm talking to you," she says quietly.

"Why? What's wrong?" he asks, sounding for all the world like a concerned brother as I watch both sides of the conversation through the mirror.

"Ever have one of those days when everyone hates you?" Her voice is uneven, and she swallows to try to clear the emotion from it.

"Not everyone, Rory. Come on, tell your big brother all about it."

She smiles around the tears as they begin to fall and begins her tale of woe. Jay sympathises in all of the right places, waiting patiently whenever she breaks into sobs, and I nod encouragingly when his eyes meet mine.

"Ah shit, Rory, that sounds horrendous. Why do you put up with it?" he asks gently.

"Cos I have no other option," she replies. "Where else would I go?"

"You could come to me," he suggests casually.

There's a stunned silence as her eyes widen at his words, and I see him opening his mouth to speak. I hold up a finger, making him wait though. Timing is everything in this particular conversation.

"I-I could?" she stammers, and I can almost see her trying to keep herself from reacting too quickly.

"Of course you could. You're my sister, Rory. I hate to hear you so upset. We'd be stronger together." He looks at me and points towards me with a raised eyebrow. I nod slowly in reply. "All of us."

"All of us? What do you mean?" she asks warily. "A-Astaroth? I

mean, I know he's real, he must be cos it's the only way you could've got my number. I tried not to think about it, but there's really no denying it. But I was so excited to hear from you, that I didn't wanna question it. Who is he?"

"He's the one who can bring us together, Rory. Imagine it. We'd be so happy if you were here with me. I could make sure you never have another day like today. And Astaroth and our Father would make it so you'd never have to be afraid of anything again. How's that sound? Better than what you're living now, right? Together, like a family should be."

"Like a family should be," she repeats slowly. "I never thought I'd hear that word in relation to me again. But our father?"

"It's too much to go into over the phone, sis. I could tell and show you everything if you were here. I wish I could fly you out here." He sighs dramatically down the line, rolling his eyes in my direction as he does, making me chuckle.

"Well, I have money. I could sort out my own flight," she muses, twirling a strand of hair around her finger as she thinks it through. "I don't know how I'd get away though. There always seems to be someone hanging around. Oh, I had visitors, by the way."

"Jax and Bathin?" he asks, looking at me as I sit up sharply in my chair.

"Yeah, he says he's called Mathim now. Wonder why he changed his name. I sent them away though," she finishes, pulling her mind back to the facts quickly.

"Good. They're bad news, Rory." He punctuates his speech with another sigh before continuing. "I really wish you were here. I could show you how to keep them away for good. I just wanna keep you safe."

"Keep them away how?" she asks, real curiosity coming into her voice.

"Oh, you won't believe the stuff we can do, sis. If you were here—" He stops mid-sentence as I signal for him to end the call. "Look, I don't wanna add to the pressure you're under. Tell you what, you think about it and I'll call you tonight, okay? If you need me before then though, just reach out. I won't leave you alone again, Rory, I promise."

I watch as the smile crosses her face.

"I know, Jay. And thank you."

"Okay, talk later. Love you."

He ends the call and I watch as she grins at the screen, answering as though he is still there.

"I love you too, Jay."

She sits quietly, her brow furrowed as she thinks, undoubtedly considering his words, and I turn my attention to Jay.

"Well played. You may have had a successful career on stage, if you had tried," I smirk.

"She's weak enough to believe anything I tell her so it's not a difficult job you've given me," he scoffs. "I don't deserve praise for it."

"I will return to you soon, Jay. I need to speak to your Father."

I do not have to call to him, or even to wait another moment, I realise when I see the image cloud over and be replaced with a view of the Throne Room.

"She approaches of her own volition, it seems," says Lucifer. "Well, with a little persuasion. I am impressed, Astaroth. But I am keen to hear your plan from here."

"Yes, Sire. When Aurora leaves her companions to join her brother, they will have no idea where she could have gone, being so alone in the world as she is. My plan is to have Jay make her disappearance known across the world. She has enough fame to merit this. As we train her in who she is to become, the mystery of her vanishing will grow, helped along by your son. And when you are ready for her to begin your work, then her sudden reappearance will make her message all the stronger."

I have thought all of this through while I worked upon her and am sure of success. Lucifer takes a moment to consider my words, breaking out into a wide smile when he is done.

"Perfect, Astaroth!" he exclaims. "Again, my choice to send you on this task is proven a good one. I commend you. How long do you think you will need?"

"A few days at most, Sire."

"Excellent. Carry on, my Grand Duke. I await your next

communication."

He disappears and I start to bring his children quickly back into view but change my mind at the last minute. Instead, I focus upon Ted, and project my thoughts to him before returning to make Aurora's room come alongside.

She reaches for the phone as it rings, its sudden noise in the silence making her jump a little.

"Hello?" she says.

"Rory. We need to talk. What was that complete shitshow today?"

His harsh tone would normally make her crumple, but instead I see her sit up straighter as she answers him.

"I don't know what happened today. I just couldn't seem to get anything right. Everyone was so mad at me all day. I'm sorry, Ted. I dunno what to tell you."

"Well, how about I tell you something instead? How about I remind you that you are by no means irreplaceable. I'm sure I don't need to remind you that without us you have nothing. No one to support

you or carry you like we do. No one to listen to all your 'poor me'

stories. If this carries on, you're out. Alone. Sort it out, Rory. Get

your shit together or you're done." He slams the phone down and I

wait for the reaction from this child of Lucifer.

She does not collapse in tears though. Nor does she waste any time

thinking of what she could have done to merit such a tirade. She

looks around the room for a moment, and as her attention flicks

past the mirror and I see her face, I notice a completely different

expression to anything I've seen there before. With a steely

determination, she picks up her own phone and busies herself with it

for a moment, writing on the paper next to her. She takes a deep

breath and taps again on the screen, holding it to her ear as she

waits for it to be answered.

"Okay, Jay. I'm done. Which airport am I flying to?"

24

Reinforcements

"It is no good, Jax. You see what I mean?"

I look around at the grey fog and nod to Mathim.

"Yeah, I see. You think she's doing it or has Astaroth put this in place?"

"Astaroth, I think. I don't imagine her method would look like this. She'd want it to be strong so it would probably resemble something that demonstrates that, rather than a mist."

I exhale loudly, not needing to worry about disturbing Rory in her sleep, blocked to us as she is.

"Yeah, Emelia said she pictures a wall. Something solid. And big. Well, home, I guess."

I pass through the mirror into the office and smile weakly at Lee.

"No joy, huh?"

"Nope," I say. "I dunno what we can do."

"Team meeting?" she suggests, sympathy in her voice.

"Definitely. You call everyone here and I'll get Eremiel. It's cold outside today though, let's stay in here."

"Okay, boss lady. I noticed the leaves changing on my way here. Guess autumn came fast. I know you love the changes, but I wish summer could stay."

I laugh as she walks through to her desk, hearing her begin to chatter to Xan before the beeping tells me she's started the coffee. I sit at the round table and close my eyes, Mathim quietly taking the seat opposite as I send my thoughts to Eremiel. The cool breeze of him arriving even before I look around makes me shiver.

"Xan will be here any minute, he was already on his way when I rang," Lee calls.

"Okay, honey, we'll wait for both of you."

My phone rings and I reach across to the desk to pick it up.

"Hello, Jax speaking," I say.

"Hi, Jax," replies Joanna. "I just thought I'd call to see how things are going."

"Not too well, actually, Mrs C." A thought occurs to me and I narrow my eyes at Mathim as I consider it. "You're not free this afternoon, are you? We're at a bit of a standstill. A fresh mind might see something we're missing."

"Of course. How does two o'clock sound?"

"Perfect. Thank you, Joanna. I really appreciate it."

"Don't be silly, it's no trouble at all," she chides gently. "And, Jax? Cheer up, we'll figure it out."

"Okay, we'll see you this afternoon," I say with a smile in my voice.

"Alright, dear. See you then."

I put the phone back in its place and look at Lee as she comes in with coffee.

"Mrs C's this afternoon. Two?" I ask unnecessarily.

"Ooh, yay!" she answers happily, making Mathim grin.

I hear the door at the front of the house open and wait for Xan to join us before I start.

"Meeting with the surveyor," he explains as he sits next to me. "Sorry I missed everything."

"Hey, no problem at all. How's it all going?" I ask. It's been too easy to forget all he has going on at home as well as all of this.

"Ugh, don't. There's massive structural damage everywhere. They're not sure it's worth the money to salvage it, if it is even salvageable. That's a conversation I'm not looking forward to having with my parents later," he says wearily.

"How are they doing? Are they still at the hotel?"

"No, I sent them to stay with my aunt and uncle in France. There's no reason they need to be around to deal with all of this. I'm just letting them know what I know as I find out. I think maybe my mum is enjoying the time there though. They've spoken about moving there before. Wouldn't surprise me if this is the thing that pushes them to it."

"Damn, Xan, I'm sorry."

"I'm okay, Jax, really. Now, why all the glum faces? What's happening?" he asks, refocusing my thoughts.

I fill him in on Rory and Jay, and the block put in place by Astaroth.

"Hmm, he's been busy," he says.

"Yeah, right? So, suggestions anyone?" I look around the table, expecting them all to start talking at once, but am greeted by silence. "Or not?"

"You can't remove the block, I take it?" asks Xan.

"I cannot," confirms Mathim.

"And even if we could, I don't think she'd listen. Jay is the key, right now. He's the big brother she doesn't have," I add.

"Yeah, but we have the real big brother," says Lee. "I know you're not gonna like this idea, Jax, but hear me out. I don't like it either."

"Go on," I prompt.

"If there's no way you can win her over, then you might just have to leave her. They need her for something, so they're not gonna hurt her. Not like he did you. Then, when we figure out where and when that ritual you saw is taking place, we turn up with Gabriel. At the very least, it levels the sides." Lee's words speed up at the end as if to try and stave off any argument from me.

I rub my temples with my fingers as I try to think of any alternative, but to no avail.

"Yeah, you're right," I concede. "There's no other way I can think of. As much as I hate it, that's exactly what we're gonna have to do. Unless anyone else has any ideas?"

I look around at them but see no lightbulb moments occurring with any of them.

"Unless Joanna comes up with something this afternoon, I think it is the only thing we can do," says Mathim, turning to Eremiel for his opinion.

"We must hope that having two of Lucifer's children is enough to stop him. If you manage that, then Aurora may be able to be swayed after things have played out," he agrees. "I know how much this goes against everything you would wish, Jax. I am sorry, but I see no other way."

"Thank you, Eremiel. But in this case, I'm with you. There's just no other option."

I stand and walk to the patio doors, looking out at the rain as it falls in the garden.

"Hey," says Xan, coming to join me and putting an arm around my shoulders, "I know we'll get her in the end. Don't worry."

I rest my head on his shoulder and sigh.

"I hope so, Xan. She's too innocent to last long once Lucifer has what he wants from her."

"Which is why we're gonna stop him before it even gets that far," he states, leaving no room for argument.

"How are you always so sure we'll win this?" I ask. "Every time we talk about it, it's like there's not even a possibility we'll lose."

He puts his hands on my shoulders and turns me to face him.

"We're team Jax, doofus. Unbeatable," he says, pulling me into a hug and resting his head gently on top of mine. "How do you not know that?"

I chuckle and hug him back, wondering for the millionth time how I'd ever cope without my friends.

***

"Oh, that poor child," says Joanna. "But, yes, I agree. There doesn't seem to be anything you can do for now. Perhaps if you had her brother, Gabriel, did you say his name was? But even then, she may not be able to see him. Just because she is a child of Lucifer doesn't mean she will have the sight."

I sit back in my chair, shocked. How did I not think of that?

"Here we all are wishing Gabriel was here already and never even considered she might not be able to see him. I guess with Xan coming back with that gift, I just assumed that the kids would have it too," I reply.

"What about Em? She has all kinds of weird stuff going on," asks Lee.

"I don't think it's ever come up for her. Not yet anyway," replies Xan.

"How much longer do we give Gabriel before we worry about him?" I interrupt, my mind going in a different direction, and I look to Mrs C for an answer.

"Everyone is different, Jax. It takes a lot of energy for spirit to make contact, as you know. He not only has to do that, he has to find his way to you first. Some spirits communicate easily, others have more difficulty. Especially at first. He may have to wait for a while before making contact once he has found you," she explains. "I don't have all the answers, Jax. I'm sorry."

"Any help is definitely appreciated," I reply, smiling at her over my coffee cup.

"Help? Help," she repeats thoughtfully, staring into the distance.

"You got an idea?" I ask hopefully.

"Maybe," she says. "Let me think for a minute."

We sit quietly, waiting for her to start speaking, but the silence is broken by Lee's phone.

"Oops, sorry," she giggles, "I'll take this outside."

"Okay, chick," I agree.

"I think I have it," says Joanna, after a few more quiet moments. "Is Lizzie around, Jax?"

"Umm, let me try. Lizzie?"

"Hi, Jax," she answers in my mind.

"Hey, sweetie. We might need to ask you something, but I need Joanna to tell me what it is first. Gimme a minute?"

"Okay," she answers, humming quietly while she waits.

"Yeah, she's here," I say.

"She might be able to help draw him to you," suggests Mrs C.

"She said it was her job when we were in the Realms, didn't she?" asks Xan. "Ambriel told her?"

"Yeah, she did. Hold on." I switch conversations and start again. "Lizzie, when we were in the other place, you said that the lady angel asked you to help Gabriel to find us. Is he near yet?"

"Not yet. He's on his way though. Want me to go check?"

Her readiness to travel who-knows-where scares me and once again I mentally chastise Eremiel for bringing her so close to all of this.

"Sure, sweetie. Be careful, okay?" I warn.

"I will, Jax, don't worry. I'm too little for anyone to see anyway."

My mind feels suddenly empty and I know she's gone to do what we ask. I realise everyone is waiting for me to tell them what she said and speak quickly.

"Sorry, she's gone to see if she can find him. She said he's on his way. I have no idea how any of this works. She didn't seem worried though."

"Well, the sooner the better so we can start figuring some of this stuff out," says Xan. "We have way too many unanswered questions at the minute."

"Don't we always?" I laugh.

"Well, yeah, that's true," he agrees with a grin. "I guess life would be boring if we knew everything all the time."

"Now, Xan, while we wait, what about you? I was really sorry to hear about your home. What will you do?" asks Joanna.

"I spoke to my parents again just before we set off to come here," he begins, and I turn to him, having not heard of this until now. "I think they've pretty much decided to move to France near my aunt," he says.

"What about you? And the house?" My questions sound as surprised as I am. I never thought they'd actually leave their home permanently.

"Well, the house is up to me. I can fix it, if that's even possible, with the insurance money. They've agreed with the fire people that it was accidental. A gas leak, they said, from a faulty appliance in the kitchen. They haven't figured out which one yet though. Anyway, like I said, I can maybe fix it, or I can sell the place and buy somewhere else. For now, I'm happy enough at Jax's. I'll sort it all out later."

"I don't know how you're managing to cope with all of that, as well as this stuff," I say.

"Cos I'm awesome," he replies simply, making us all laugh.

"Jax," Lizzie says, silencing me as I listen.

"Yes, honey, I'm here."

"He's stuck."

"What? What do you mean stuck?" I ask, trying to keep the panic from my voice and accidentally speaking out loud, making everyone look at me at once.

"I dunno. I looked for him, but I couldn't find him, so I asked the lady angel and she said he can't get through. That he can't find his way. We need to help him, Jax. Me, you and Xander," she explains.

"How?"

"I have to be the light and you have to help me guide him, I think," she replies. "But we need to make it as easy as we can for him. And she said that I have to save my energy up a bit first so I can shine really bright."

I grimace at the idea of this little angel doing something that requires so much energy that she needs to rest first but bite my tongue.

"What's wrong?" asks Lee, as she comes back in and takes her seat, and I hold up a hand to ask her to wait.

"Okay, Lizzie. How long do you need?"

"Tomorrow? We need to do this quick," she says. "The lady angel is making Gabriel rest too."

"Okay, sweetheart. Go, rest, and I'll come get you tomorrow. Sleep well, Lizzie."

"Thank you, Jax, I will. But it's not really sleeping, you know."

I chuckle at her answer.

"Well, in that case, rest well, angel."

"You too."

She leaves again, and I bring my attention back to everyone around the table.

"He's stuck between Realms. Lizzie is gonna help bring him through but they both need to build some energy before we try, so we're gonna get him tomorrow night," I explain. "I hate how much they're involving her in this. She's just a child."

"In this, they might be right though, Jax. Child spirits shine the brightest," says Mrs C, making my eyes snap to hers. "Did I say something wrong?"

"No, you just used the same words she did. 'Shine' was what she said too. She also said we have to try and make his crossing as easy as we can. What can we do?"

"You're welcome to use the house, if you'd like. It might make things a little easier, as the veil seems to be thinner there. I think that's why it's so active," she offers.

"Wait, what did you say, Joanna?" Mathim interrupts.

"The house?" she asks puzzled.

"No, the veil."

"It seems to be thinner there. You know there are places where the barrier between here and the afterlife is weaker, surely," she says.

"I do. Times too," he agrees, looking at me.

"Mathim, I love you dearly and I know we're close, but my link with you hasn't evolved to mind-reading yet. What are you thinking?" I say with a grin. "Please make my day and tell me you have something."

"The thinning of the veil. It's a kind of transition period during which the barrier weakens, just like Joanna said. The most noticeable time being Samhain." His eyes watch mine for the realisation dawning but when I take longer than he wants, he carries on. "Halloween?"

"I know what Samhain is, doofus," I chuckle. "I just don't know what you're talking about."

"Your description of the images you saw? The darkness turning to light and back again. Samhain has been represented as such in many depictions."

"Holy crap," exclaims Lee. "Halloween? That's next weekend."

I take a huge breath as I realise just how close to the end of all this we really are and huff it back out when I think of everything we still have to achieve.

"We need Em," I say hurriedly.

"These devil kids are really talented, aren't they?" replies Lee. "Psychic isn't the word for it. That was Em on the phone. She's boarding the plane as we speak, she'll be here this evening."

"Awesome," I say, relieved.

"Better than awesome. She'll be here to help with Gabriel and that

way we'll know if she can see him. Another question answered."
Xan leans forward to cover my hand with his. "See, Jax? One step at a time makes nothing impossible."

"Amen to that," agrees Joanna. "Now, who wants another coffee?"

25

A Homecoming

"Welcome home, Rory," Jay says as he pushes open the door to his apartment.

She looks around, eyes shining with excitement.

"Thank you, Jay," she answers.

"For what?" he asks, his eyes flitting to the mirror through which he knows I will be watching.

"For everything. For letting me come here, for picking me up from the airport, for just being here for me. I don't think I would have coped without your support. No," she corrects herself, "I know I wouldn't."

"You've got more support than you know," he says, half under his breath and I know he means for her to hear it.

"What?" she questions. "What do you mean?"

"Umm, nothing." He pauses and looks at her for a minute. *"Look, let's get you unpacked and settled in. We can get to all that when you've slept. You've got to be tired after your flight. And you need to be prepared and fully awake when I tell you everything, if you're gonna believe me."*

He manages to look worried at her reaction and she crosses quickly to reassure him.

"Jay, look at me. I will always believe you. Look at what you've done for me. This time last week I had nothing. I felt so alone all the time. Now, I have a brother who's saved me from everything I was going through. You rescued me, Jay. How could I doubt you?"

He surprises me by pulling her into a hug, but when he looks over her head and into the mirror, grimacing, I realise the show of affection was only to mask his feelings, written as they are on his face.

"Just remember that when I tell you later, okay?" he asks quietly.

"I will, Jay, I promise. We can talk about it now, if you like?" she offers, pulling back to look up at him.

"No, Rory. You need sleep. Are you sure you had enough to eat though? Drive through burgers are not my idea of a decent meal."

She giggles and nods.

"It was perfect. I've been needing cheeseburgers forever!"

"Okay, well let's get you settled," he concedes, leading her down the hall. "This is your room. Do whatever you want to it to make it yours."

She steps inside and lets out a little squeal, and I see Jay tense at the sound.

"It's perfect. Thank you, Jay," she says, stifling a yawn.

"See?" he replies, pointing a finger. "Tired. Sleep."

She finally agrees and he pulls the door closed as she crosses to the bed, climbing into it fully dressed as exhaustion hits her, allowing Jay to return to the living room alone.

"Ugh, how long do I have to listen to this?" he grumbles quietly.

"I do not know, Jay. The time of the ritual has not been revealed to me yet," I reply. "Until then, she must feel safe and secure with you. I do not think she would cope with meeting your Father just yet, do you?"

"No," he laughs. "Definitely not. I'm not sure she'll ever be up to that. I'm not even sure she'll deal with the idea of being the daughter of Lucifer."

His words spark an idea, loaded with truth as they are. This girl may not be able to cope with that thought, and then what use would she be? How are we to keep her calm enough to accept her parentage?

"What's wrong, Astaroth?" he asks, seeing my expression.

"I do not know if presenting her to your Father is a good idea at all, Jay. You are home for the rest of the night?"

"I am, I'll be here if you need me," he confirms.

"Very well, I will return shortly."

The mirror clouds and clears to the normal reflection, and I pace as I think. How can we have Aurora join our side, to make her decision in *our favour, without her having to meet my Master? Knowing that the answer is beyond my understanding, I do the only thing I can.*

"Sire?" I say as I cross back to the glass.

"Yes, Astaroth?" he replies quickly.

"My Lord, I need to know how best to continue from here. I am at a crossroads and am unsure which path would be the wisest."

"Tell me," he says. "We will work it out together."

"Master, you have seen the girl, you have witnessed her character for yourself. I do not think she would cope with knowledge of her Father. Is it written that she must know everything before she makes her decision?"

"Hmm, I do not know. Hold for a moment." He raises a hand, and I see the script of the prophecy burn itself into the glass. "It says only that the children must choose a side. I think that if you were to persuade her to join you and Jay, that would suffice. Yes, I'm sure of it. When Jay agreed, I felt a bond form with him, although at the time, I did not realise the cause of the feeling. If, when you get her to say the words of allegiance to you, I feel the same, then we will

know you have succeeded. If not, then we will know that she needs to pledge it to me. Does that seem like a fitting solution?" he asks.

"Yes, Sire, I think it does. And now I know how to move forward, I will not take up any more of your time. The girl sleeps, but when she wakes, she is expecting Jay to tell her all. It will not be long until we know."

"Good. I will await your news then."

He fades from view, and I take the opportunity of silence to work out how best to instruct his son on the direction in which his next conversation should go. I muse on this for a while, only moments seeming to have passed before I am disturbed from my thoughts.

"Astaroth," says Jay's voice, making me lift the block on the glass, "she is waking up."

"Tell her of me, Jay. But not of your Father unless she explicitly asks. I will join you when she is ready."

"Okay, Astaroth. Here goes."

He turns his head to the hallway, pasting a smile on his face as he *does.*

"Sleep well?" he asks. "I thought you'd be out cold for longer than that."

"I've always been a light sleeper. Too used to being woken up at home, I suppose," she says with a shrug.

"Coffee?"

"Please. I have a feeling I'm gonna need it. You said you have things to tell me that I won't believe. Better be wide awake for a conversation like that."

He does not take the bait, rising from his seat instead to make her drink. He waits patiently while she sips at it, curling her feet up under herself in the large chair that somehow makes her look even smaller.

"Okay, big brother," she says, the strength in her voice surprising me, and I suspect Jay too. "I'm ready."

"What do you know already?" he asks. "What has Astaroth told you?"

I raise my eyebrows in surprise at his allowing her to lead the conversation but have no choice than to see where it goes.

"He said I was destined for greatness and that Jax and Mathim would try and stop me. I laughed at the idea cos I just couldn't believe it, but then I found the person whose name he gave me not only existed, but also managed to find me. So, I guess there's gotta be some truth to it all, somehow." *She pauses and takes a breath.* "See, the thing is Jay, when he says I'm destined for greatness, I scoff. But, as you're my brother, I think we share this 'destiny', and I'd easily believe it of you."

"Thanks, sis," *he jokes.*

"I mean it. I can see you'd be doing great things in the future. I can't imagine what they'd be, but I know you could do anything. Me? I'm not so sure." *Her eyes drop to the floor, showing the version of Aurora that I first met, but then lift to his defiantly.* "No. That's the old me talking. The one who had nothing and no one. Tell me, Jay. Tell me what I can do."

"I'll do better than that," *he says with a wicked grin.* "Come on, let's go outside and I'll show you."

"Wow, Jay, and you can teach me how to do all of that? It's like magic!" she exclaims as they come back through the door. I did not follow them, trusting to Jay to demonstrate his gifts.

"I can't, but Astaroth can. When you're ready to meet him, that is. If you're to stay with me and learn all this stuff, he'll have to be here," he replies.

"What's he like?" she asks curiously.

"He's okay, Rory, honestly he is. I know all of this must seem scary, but Astaroth really helped me. He showed me what I'm truly capable of, and he'll do the same for you."

"Do you need to call him to see when he can come?" she asks, pulling a laugh from Jay.

"Rory, you're gonna have to get used to the idea that you're important to us all. It's not a matter of when he can fit you into his busy schedule. You're his priority. And mine. We want you to be as happy and strong as you can be. We have important stuff to do for our family, and if you're gonna be part of that, then we need you *ready as soon as possible. Just gimme the word whenever you decide," he says, his calm tone reassuring her as he speaks.*

"Jay, can I ask you something?" she almost whispers.

"Anything," he replies.

"My mom was crazy. She used to drink a lot and would say some really weird things, especially when she thought I was sleeping. She'd come into my room and stand over my bed, looking down at me and crying." She pauses to get control of herself and he reaches for her hand. Smiling gratefully, she takes a breath and continues. "This is gonna sound insane."

"Go on," he encourages. "I just showed you I can make fire with my mind, how much crazier can it be than that?"

"Was my mom right?" she asks, lifting her eyes to his. "Am I the Devil's daughter?"

26

A Surprising Move

The sound of a car on the gravel driveway has Lee leaping from her chair to run to the front door, opening it wide, and bouncing on the spot when she sees that it's Xan with Emelia beside him.

"They're here, Jax," she yells without turning around, so not realising I'm already walking towards her.

"Right here, chick," I say, "and now I'm deaf."

"Oops, sorry," she giggles. "I can't believe we're gonna have everyone here at once. For more than a few hours, I mean."

"Me either," I agree. "It'll be good for her to be with us for a while."

"It'll be good for everyone," she corrects.

"Yeah, for everyone."

Emelia walks towards us with a tired smile, hugging us in turn before coming inside.

305

"Oh, wait, my bags," she says.

"Nope, you go, I'll help Xan," Lee offers, running to the car before anyone can argue.

"Come on, sweetie, you look exhausted." I link my arm with hers and lead her into the main office, pointing to the sofa as I start making coffee. "Sit. Your flight was on time then?"

"Yeah. How come Lee's here so late? I thought she'd have finished hours ago."

"Umm, have you met Lee? You think she was gonna go home on time today? She demanded to stay until you got here. Marcus will be picking her up soon though," I reply. "Mathim has offered to take the sofa, so you have the guest room, by the way. It has a bathroom of its own, so whenever you're ready to sleep, just go ahead and make yourself at home."

"I don't wanna put anyone out," she complains. "Will he be okay?"

"He'll be fine. He's sharing the delights of that room with Xan. He told you about the house?" I ask.

"He did. Astaroth, by any chance? Xan said he thought it might have been but that you didn't think so. Was that true? Seems like a bit of a coincidence, if you ask me," she says.

"You know, it did to me too. I just didn't know. But now I see how much work he's put into getting Rory on side, I don't think he'd have had the time anyway."

"Yeah, I suppose. So, tell me about her while I can still keep my eyes open."

I fill her in on all that's happened, pausing in places as the others join us, one by one. By the time I'm done, we're all together and the sound of a cheerful voice tells me that Marcus has arrived too. Making sure everyone has a drink, Lee perches on the arm of the chair and looks around, smiling.

"What?" I ask.

"Just being here with all my favourite people. What could be better? Apart from the circumstances, obviously."

"Yeah, I know what you mean, kid," agrees Xan. "But back to business. So, tomorrow night we have the farm. Emelia is very excited at the idea of her first ever ghost hunt."

"Beyond excited," she says around a yawn.

"Emelia, you really need to sleep, honey. It's gonna be a long night tomorrow night. We're all used to it, but you're not. Tomorrow, just sleep as much as you can. We'll wake you up in time for everything. We might need your help to bring Gabriel through."

"Yeah, okay. I guess I'll head to bed then," she agrees.

"I'll show you where you're at, then we'll head home and let the rest of you get settled for the night too," says Lee, standing up and leading the way.

I hear her chatter as she goes and I look at Xan.

"Think she's happy?"

"Lee?" replies Marcus. "You guys are family to her. To both of us. She's glad to have everyone here."

"You're family to us too," I say. "Now gimme a hug before you leave."

He grins and obliges, Lee following suit when she comes back in the room, before they say their goodbyes. Hearing the door close behind them, I start to move from my place in the corner, but a flashing in the mirror in my office catches my eye.

"Mathim," I say, gesturing towards it.

He strides past me and up to the glass, frowning at the clock as he goes.

"Mathim?" I hear Scirlin's voice and tense. It's late for him to be trying to reach us, and I hope nothing's wrong as I join them.

"Here, Scirlin. What's wrong?"

"I don't have much time. I've been trying to get a moment to talk to you all day, I know the lateness of the hour there."

"It is fine. What do you need?" he asks.

"Nothing. I wanted to let you know something I overheard today that's all. Some demons that had been working on Earth returned home earlier. As they crossed, they were complaining about having to do Astaroth's work as well as their own. I couldn't question them without raising suspicion, but I heard them talk of a fire and a distraction. I'm guessing that he was, in part, responsible for what happened to Xander's home. I thought he should know," Scirlin says.

"Yeah, I had my suspicions, Scirlin, but thank you for confirming them."

Scirlin nods at Xan before turning back to Mathim.

"So, how goes it all?" he asks, and I realise how long it's been since we updated him.

Before Mathim can begin to tell him, I interrupt.

"I'm gonna go to bed, Mathim. I'll see you in the morning. Goodnight, guys."

"Goodnight, Jax," they answer, and I pull the door closed behind me as Xan and I leave them to it.

"You okay, Xan?" I ask.

"Yeah, Jax, I'm fine. I think I knew all along," he sighs. "Look, go and get some rest. We have a busy night, like you said. I'll be okay, I promise. I'm tired too."

"Okay, sweetie. Goodnight."

With a heavy heart, I climb under the sheets, hating that all of this has cost so many people I care about so dear. And try as I might, I can't help but wonder what else it might cost us all before the end.

***

"Holy crap! You mean it?" Lee's excited squeal is the first thing I hear as I make my way from my room to the office.

With a frown, I realise that her voice came from the opposite direction to where I'm heading and turn around to walk back towards the living room rather than the office.

"Mean what?" I ask as I enter.

"You might wanna sit for this," Xan says, waiting until I do before he starts.

"Okay, I'm ready. Why does Lee sound so excited when that sounds like bad news?"

"It's not bad news. Well, maybe it is," she chatters, handing me my cup.

"I'll do it, Lee," interrupts Xan. "It's early and she hasn't had coffee so it needs to be as simple as possible."

"True," I agree. "Go on."

"Well, last night after you went to bed, Mathim and I were talking. We began to wonder just how safe it was for everyone to be here. The fire at my house is a little too close for comfort. I know that if Astaroth could reach us here, he probably would have, so the angels' protection must be working. But I'm not a hundred percent happy that all our eggs are in this little basket, so to speak." He pauses to see how I'm taking this so far.

"Yeah, I can see where you're going with this. Where are you wanting to move us to?" I ask, blowing my coffee to cool it a little. I get the feeling I'm going to need the caffeine to hit quickly.

"Rose Hill Farm," he says, almost choking me on my next sip.

"What? We can't all just rock up to Joanna's with our bags packed," I exclaim.

"No, not Joanna's farm. The old farm. Hear me out," he says, seeing the look on my face. "I spoke to her this morning. The building is actually sound, she told us that the first time we visited, remember? There's nothing wrong with it essentially, not even any holes in the roof or broken windows or anything. They built the new one cos of the weird things happening and as an investment."

"Yeah, I remember that," I concede.

"So, all it needs is heating up. The power is even still on. Lee and I can go on a shopping spree today for everything we need until this is over. Mrs C says she's more than happy with the idea, as long as she gets to feed us."

I shake my head in wonder at the generosity of the woman, but frown at the thought that strikes me.

"What about her family? We're gonna be in the way."

"No. They're always working, they keep late hours at the minute, she says. It's actually very doable, Jax. Won't be as comfortable as here, but until this is finished, it's gotta be safer if Astaroth doesn't know where we are. Eremiel can do the protection thing, there's that huge mirror in the front room for Mathim to use to talk to whoever he needs to, and Em can block herself and even Gabriel, when he comes through. It'll make things easier for him too, if we stay there." His excitement is easy to see as he explains all of this as fast but as clearly as he can. "Come on, Jax, camping out at your favourite place? You've gotta be tempted."

I chuckle at his boyish expression, trying to persuade me. But for the life of me, I can't think of a single reason to say no.

"I can rerecord the answerphone message to tell anyone who wants us, to call your mobiles," chimes in Lee. "And it's not as if we'll be working now 'til it's all done."

"The new house has Wi-Fi," Xan adds. "We can catch up on work when we're there. Joanna already said that when I spoke to her."

I see them both staring at me, waiting for my decision, and decide to put them both out of their misery sooner rather than later.

"Okay, let's do it," I say, my last words drowned out by Lee's excited squeals and the laughter of Mathim and Xan at her impromptu happy dance. "I take it you'll be joining us?"

"Hell, yeah. No way I'd miss it. Marcus can survive without me for a few nights, I'm sure," she replies.

"He's welcome to join us after work, if he wants. He's seen what we do. And he's part of the family," Xan tells her. "He won't want to let you out of his sight anywhere near this, if he can help it, Lee. Especially after the last time."

I shudder when I recall those images. Lee and Xan's lifeless bodies being lifted out of the wreck. Marcus and I keeping our vigils at their bedsides.

"Xan's right," I say. "He's been through all of this with us. He's definitely part of the team."

Xan's eyes meet mine and he smiles, probably able to guess where my thoughts went.

"Alright then, that's settled. So, kid, you ready to go shopping?"

"Always ready," she says, jumping from her chair. "Any requests, Jax?"

"Nope, whatever you think we need. Oh, but we really need to remember to take Carlos. No coffee, no deal."

"Jeez, talk about stating the obvious," Lee groans rolling her eyes. "He was the first thing on my list."

"You gonna be able to get all this done in time, Xan? What can we do? Emelia, Mathim and I make three pairs of hands just sitting around all day otherwise."

"Pack whatever you need and take it up to the farm?" he suggests. "Office stuff included. The bedrooms are in good enough shape to sleep in, so pick a room to work from and to store the gear in. We can work everything else around it. It'll be cold in there though, until we get the heaters up and running. Other than that, just get rid of the dust sheets and stuff, I suppose. There's still some old furniture around. We'll make do with that for now."

"Okay, Xan. I dunno how you expect to fit everything in your car though," I laugh.

"I don't," he says. "What's the use of money if you can't use it to get what you need one way or the other? If I can't bribe them into delivery today, we'll hire a van."

I laugh as they leave, looking at Mathim in delayed shock.

"Why do I feel like I just got hit by a steam train?" I chuckle.

"I think we should name it the Lee effect," he answers with a grin. "Doubly effective when combined with Xander. They plotted together for it to go just as it did, so you wouldn't have time to argue."

My jaw drops when I realise how well I was just played, but I'm soon recovered, hearing Mathim's laughter and joining in with my own.

"What's funny?" asks Emelia, as she walks sleepily to the sofa and sits next to him.

"I just got railroaded very successfully by Lee and Xan," I groan.

"Ooh, how?" she asks, eyeing my cup a little jealously. "Where's the java? I can't sleep any more, I swear."

"I'll get it, Jax. You tell Em the news."

I hand him my cup for a refill with what I hope is a winning smile, before turning back to Emelia.

"It's probably a good thing you're up and around, chick. We're about to have a very busy day."

***

"Okay, guys, last trip," I call. "Clothes and personal items. And I suggest a shower and food for everyone back home before we lock up and move here for the night."

"Yes, boss lady. Marcus is gonna meet us back there, so there'll be another car to fill with stuff if we need it."

"Awesome. Xan, are you taking the van back tonight?" I ask.

"Yeah, I'm gonna go do that now and pick up my car. I'll meet you there," he answers, coming into the hallway from the dining room, his arms full of crumpled sheets.

"Here," says Lee, taking them from him, "Mrs C says she'll wash these and store them so they're out of the way."

"I think we're just about done here."

I look around at the now much brighter house. Lee's idea to wash the windows seemed a little silly at first, as we're only here temporarily, but now seeing the light stream into the building, I have to admit I was wrong.

"I think you're right, Xan. If we close all the doors, the rooms will warm up while we're gone."

"Yeah, good plan. Em, are you still upstairs?" he calls.

"Yeah, I'll be down in a minute," she yells back. "You want these doors closing to keep the heat in?"

"Yes, please," he replies, turning to me with a grin. "See? Told you. Devil's kid. Psychic."

I shake my head at him, laughing, and realise just how good I feel. This place really does have an effect on us. Footsteps bouncing down the stairs draw my attention to a smiling Emelia as she comes to join us.

"Okay, I'm ready," she says as she reaches the bottom. "This old place rocks. I love it."

"We all do," I reply. "Come on, let's go and get the last run done so we can relax for a while before we start."

I'm about to climb into Vinni, when Joanna comes out of her house, waving to get our attention.

"Don't you even think about eating back at home," she warns. "You're all eating here tonight. No arguments."

"Really, Joanna, you don't have to feed us tonight," I start to argue but quickly change my mind when I see the look she gives me.

"Nonsense. I want to. What do you all like?"

"I have a better idea," says Xan. "A compromise. Mrs C, how about you cook whatever you like from tomorrow and tonight we order Chinese food, but all eat together here. My treat to say thank you. Not that one meal is anywhere near enough to do that."

"That would be lovely, dear," she agrees, surprising me.

"It's a deal. We'll make this last run and then we'll be back, and I'll order it all then. We won't be long."

We all set off down the driveway, a little convoy of our own, and as I look in my rear-view mirror and see the old farmhouse getting smaller, I smile to know I'm coming back in no time at all.

27

Introductions

I watch as Jay's eyes widen in surprise and see him look quickly to the mirror.

"I think Astaroth can probably answer that better than I can. Do you want me to call him?" he asks.

She gulps and takes a deep breath before answering.

"Yeah," she says, "I'm ready."

Although I could step through immediately, I wait for Jay to speak before I make the connection properly.

"Astaroth, are you there?"

I smile when I realise he does not wish to give away my having overheard their conversation and I congratulate him silently on it.

"I am, Jay. Does Aurora wish to meet me properly? I would not want her to be made uncomfortable by my presence."

"It's fine, Astaroth," she answers herself. "I'm ready."

She watches curiously as I appear in the room, standing to greet me when I get near.

"Nice to meet you, Astaroth," she says politely.

"And you, Aurora. You must have questions. Please, sit."

I pull up a chair to face her and force myself to smile kindly.

"I do. Is my father the Devil?"

I feign surprise at her words, keeping up Jay's pretence, and sit back as though shock has made me pause before answering.

"I do not know quite how to answer," I begin.

"Just tell me the truth, please."

"Very well. Then yes, you are the daughter of Lucifer. That is why you and Jay are destined for great things. You are capable of far more than you have ever dreamed, child."

My words have no effect on her at all. She merely nods and looks ready to ask something else, and so I await her reply.

"And in doing these 'great things', do I get to stay with Jay?" she asks.

"You do."

"And what about Jax and Mathim. What do they have to do with all of this?"

"Ah, now that is a very different thing," I say. "Jax is the Chosen One, the one human who is allowed to approach you. I myself could not talk to you like this until you requested it. Indeed, I did not know if you merely asking me to talk to you would be enough, but happily it was. She wishes to talk you into siding with the angels. They would stop the work of your Father if they can. They need you to be able to do this."

She chews on her bottom lip as she hears and considers my words, looking thoughtfully at Jay when I am done.

"And how do I get them to leave me alone? Will they just give up now?"

"Perhaps. I blocked their approach through your dreams when first we met. I do not think they can break through that. I can teach you to put your own barriers in place though, until you make your final decision. You have until next week to do that. Your birthday, in fact. I will be honest, Aurora. If you choose to stay with us, with Jay, you may have to do things you are not comfortable with. Humanity is about to face great changes. As part of the cause of those changes, you will work closely with your Father and may see things you do not think you can cope with."

I take the risk with saying this only to save time later. She is not as weak as she originally appeared, and I would rather begin to prepare her now for the road which lies before her.

"But I will be with Jay?" she repeats.

"You will be with Jay," I confirm. "And eventually with your Father."

"Then I don't need time, Astaroth. What do I need to say?"

"There are no special words, Aurora. Just tell me what you wish."

"Okay, Astaroth, I take the side of my Father. I will do whatever it takes to help him achieve his goals. I am with you." Her words ring

with clarity and strength, only to end with a gasp as the mirror begins to flash, catching her attention.

"It appears your Father wishes to be introduced. Are you ready for this, child, or shall I ask that you be excused until you are more prepared?" I ask, genuinely unsure of how she will answer.

"No, I'm tired of running away from everything. I want to meet him," she says, her eyes moving past me to Jay, wanting his approval.

"Good choice, Rory," he says, infusing his words with pride and getting a smile from her when she hears it. "Come here, we should be together when you meet him."

She crosses to his side without a second's hesitation and I arc my arm over the glass, bringing my Master into view.

"Well met, Aurora. I have seen much change in you this last week. Are you ready to learn all that Astaroth and your brother can teach you?" he asks.

"I am, Father," she replies. "I am ready to do whatever you need me to."

Her voice trembles a little, but I do not blame her for this. She has made such progress of late that I would be surprised if she was not a little nervous.

"Very good, child. I think it is time you all came home. There are things we still need to discover and to learn. Aurora's training can be done here," he ends, looking at me.

"Yes, Sire," I reply. "When would you have us return?"

"Whenever you are ready. Call to Scirlin for the doorway," he says.

"Of course, Sire."

As much as I'd like to stay on Earth, I know that my time with Bathin approaches and so am not too disappointed to be called back to Hell.

He disappears from the glass and I turn to face his children.

"How long do you need?" I ask.

"I'm ready now," says Jay, unsurprisingly.

"Me too," agrees Aurora a second later.

"Very well," I say. "There is no time like the present. Scirlin, when you are ready."

The mirror blurs and then refocuses on the Transportation Room when the connection is complete. I step through, barely acknowledging Scirlin as I pass him, and I turn to watch as Aurora and Jay follow, hand in hand.

***

"I have to admit, Aurora, you had me a little worried for a while," says Lucifer with a smile. "I thought perhaps the world had beaten you."

"No, Father," she answers timidly. "It almost did. But then Astaroth and Jay came into my life. And now you."

She looks up at him almost bashfully and he descends the stairs to stand in front of her.

"You will be part of the new order of things, child. You both will. Emelia too, if I have my way."

I look to him a little too sharply, my quick movement not going unnoticed.

"While you were busy with Aurora, I thought it wise to test the strength of the blocks she has put in place. She is annoyingly good at creating them it seems. No matter though. You can take over trying to get past them now, Astaroth, if you wish. I know you have a score to settle there. Meanwhile, as you wait for her to sleep, I have another task for you. Aurora needs training, as did Jay. You can do that here as well as anywhere else."

"Yes, Sire. And thank you. I would be glad to be able to bring Emelia to you, at last. Aurora's training is to be the same as Jay's?" I ask, hoping she will pick it up just as quickly as he did.

"Yes, the same will suffice. Unless you uncover anything else worth working on," he says. "Also, we have still to discover where and how the ritual is to take place. The details are still shrouded from us. I will let you know when I find out more."

Hearing the unspoken dismissal in his voice, I shepherd his children out of the Throne Room and lead them down the passageway towards an empty training room, before changing my mind and bringing them to a halt.

"Are you hungry? Perhaps food and something to drink first, before we start."

I change direction, taking them into the Great Hall. All eyes turn to us as we enter, and silence descends upon all demons inside.

"Umm, Astaroth?" murmurs Aurora. "Are we meant to be in here?"

Her words make me laugh aloud, startling her a little and I am quick to explain, I would not wish to lose the small amount of trust she is building in me.

"Aurora, you are the daughter of Lucifer," I explain, trying to sound kind and caring. "This whole Realm is your home. There is nowhere here that you are not 'meant' to be."

She relaxes and smiles widely.

"Good, cos I'm kinda hungry," she replies.

"Me too," seconds Jay. "Come on, let's eat so we can get started on your training."

I sit and listen to them talk as they satisfy their appetites, joining in *the conversation when questioned or required. I still see the rest of the demons staring, trying not to be noticed as they talk closely in hushed voices, but I pay them no mind. Curiosity or jealousy, whichever fuels their interest is of no importance to me. I have far more important things to concern myself with. This training for one, and ensuring it works quickly. I would not waste a moment that could be better spent on stealing Emelia back from under the nose of Jax. And Bathin.*

28

The Rescue

"You got all that, Emelia?" I ask, happy when she nods quickly in answer. "Good, cos it can be a lot to take in."

"No, I'm good," she replies. "You kept it simple enough for me to pick it up. All this stuff looks way more complicated than it actually is."

She gestures to the gadgets laid out on the dining room table. Lee's excited voice approaches from the hallway, as I agree with her.

"Yeah, it really does. When we first had it delivered, we were all a little nervous about using it."

"Are you still gonna use it all though, Jax?" asks Lee as she joins us. "It's not like you need the Ovilus or the spirit box to talk to them any more, is it?"

"Well, no, it isn't, but I wanna give Gabriel every chance. Something might be easier for him to use than the rest, you never know. At least if we have everything running, it'll give him a fair shot."

"Yeah, good point. Oh, speaking of which, I put the EMP pumps in a few rooms. Did you want them anywhere in particular? I have some out already and others are charging so we can swap them over and it'll load the place with constant energy to help him."

I look at her in surprise and then shake my head.

"No, wherever you have them will be good, honey. Thank you. I dunno why I'm surprised when you do stuff like this, but you never fail to impress me, Lee. I hadn't thought of doing that," I say, grinning at her. "I think you can cross the 'in training' part out on your ghost hunter top."

She chuckles as she reaches past me for a voice recorder.

"These run for hours, right?" she asks.

"Yeah, they do. Why?"

"Cos we could be using them now. You never know what we'll catch while we're setting up. And I see you frowning at me, Jax," she laughs, "I don't mean to review later. I know this is a totally on-the-spot thing tonight. I just mean if we think we hear something then we can check on here."

"Damn, Lee, you're on fire tonight, kid. Definitely. Can you make sure everyone has one and that they're running? I think we're almost ready to start soon anyway."

She takes the box, hands one to each of us, and hurries away calling for Xan and Mathim as she opens the door to the hall.

"Wow, she's really good," says Emelia admiringly.

"Yeah, she is. She hasn't been doing this side of it long, but she's a real natural. Plus, she loves it, which is always a bonus."

"Hell, yes, I love it. My job rocks! And I can still hear you, by the way," Lee says, pushing the door open. "I'm only out here. I really am lucky to work doing this though. I have the best job in the world. Apart from the demons, obviously. They suck."

I look over her head, seeing Mathim staring at her, and have to force myself not to laugh.

"Umm, Lee—" Emelia starts to warn her.

"What?" she interrupts. "They do. They're always trying to hurt people or end the world or something."

She sees us both looking past her rather than at her and turns around to see what we're looking at, giggling when she sees the demon behind her.

"You were saying?" he asks, somehow managing to sound serious.

"Not you, obviously. You're not one of them. I mean, real demons. Well, you're a demon, but you're not like a real demon-y demon. You know?" She ends her hurried explanation with a dazzling smile and his mask slips as he bursts into laughter.

"Oh, little one, you make my heart lighter every day," he says, ruffling her hair.

"Yeah, she's good at that," I agree. "Okay, chick, we just about ready?"

"We are. Go, smoke, charge up or whatever. It's still dry outside if you wanna get that hoodoo working. I'll just check on Xan, and I'll be there." She ushers us towards the door before turning around and running up the stairs.

Walking to the lawn, I slip off my shoes and settle for standing barefoot on the grass. I feel pretty charged up already and wonder if it has anything to do with Emelia being here.

"Are you all prepared?" asks Joanna, coming up the path.

"I think so," I reply. "We're as ready as we'll ever be."

I bend my head to shelter from the breeze as I light my cigarette, blowing the smoke away from her as she gets closer.

"You know those things are bad for you?" she asks with a grin.

"Yeah, I know. Maybe I'll quit once this is all over. I mean, if we beat Lucifer, then nicotine cravings are nothing, right?"

"Right," she laughs. "I won't offer to be part of your night, Jax, but if you need me, just send Lee."

"Thank you, Joanna," I say simply. I know she doesn't want to join us, so I appreciate her words.

"Have you spoken to Lizzie?" she asks.

"No, not yet. That's the first thing I'm gonna do when we start. I'm just giving her all the time I can before I call to her. I still say she's too young for all of this." My lips purse in displeasure but I shrug my shoulders and force myself to relax.

"She will be fine, Jax. She's stronger than you think, I'm sure. They wouldn't include her if she wasn't."

Her reassurance makes me feel a little better and I bend to put out my cigarette, smiling at her when I straighten up.

"Well, no time like the present, I guess," I say. "I'll send for you if we need you, I promise."

She pats my hand and goes back to her house, leaving Emelia and I to walk back inside.

"Ready?" she asks.

"Always ready," I answer.

***

"Lizzie? Lizzie, are you here, sweetheart?" I ask aloud, holding out the spirit box as it clatters its way quickly through the radio frequencies.

"I'm here, Jax," she says in my head. "What's that? It's noisy."

I muffle the speaker against my leg as I answer her, still speaking so the others can at least have half of the conversation.

"It's a machine that will let everyone hear you, honey. Is it too loud?"

"Just turn it off, Jax," says Lee. "Whatever makes it easiest for Lizzie."

I nod and switch off the little box, handing it to her and watching as she puts it on the table behind her.

"That's better," Lizzie says, "I can hear you properly now. I've rested all day, have you? It was really boring though."

"I've rested enough, angel. Do you know where Gabriel is?" I ask.

"No. The lady angel does though, she's gonna show me. But I need to hold onto you, she says. And Xander. How do we do that? Oh, and I have to make myself shine really bright. You have to help with that too. And the lady with the red hair."

"Emelia?" I say. "Hmm, okay. Can you talk to her?"

Emelia looks at me, eyes widening at the mention of her name, and waits for me to tell her what's going on.

"I dunno, Jax. Want me to try?"

I don't know what to do for the best. I don't want Lizzie using energy unnecessarily, but if she says she needs Em, then I can't stop her from working to create a link.

"Jax, what's wrong?" Mathim asks, seeing the frown on my face as I try to work out what to do for the best.

"Gimme a minute, Lizzie, okay?"

"Okay, Jax," she says, humming quietly to herself while she waits and making me smile.

"Right, guys, I dunno what to do. Lizzie needs me and Xan to hold a link with her while she goes to find Gabriel. She also needs to make herself 'shine bright' and needs Emelia and I to help with that. She says she can try to make a link with you, Emelia, but I don't want her burning herself out, she's already doing too much as it is." I rub my forehead, feeling tension building.

"I can create the link," Em says simply. "I did it with Sal and Malaphar. That way Lizzie doesn't have to. I can send her my energy through it to help her 'shine', as you put it. Does that work?"

I blink in surprise at her easy solution and huff a laugh.

"Umm, yeah, that works. Now, Xan, we need to hold a connection with her, I guess to keep her anchored here."

"Yeah, Jax," Lizzie interrupts. "Like a boat."

"Yes, sweetie," I answer. "Just like a boat."

Xan grins at my two-way conversation before he answers.

"So, how do we do that? I'm still new to all this, remember?" he asks.

"Like you did with me, Jax," says Mathim. "The strand between us. Do the same."

"Oh, of course," I breathe, relieved. "Right, Lizzie, we've got it figured out. But it'll be easier if Xan can see you while he visualises it. Can you come through properly for a while?"

"Yup," she replies, popping the 'p' sound, and appearing in front of me.

"Hi, Lizzie," says Xan, but it's the echo of his words a fraction later from Emelia that grabs my attention.

"You can see her?" I ask.

"I can. And she's a very beautiful little girl," she replies, smiling at Lizzie.

"Thank you, Emelia," Lizzie says. "You're pretty too, I like your hair."

"Okay, let's get this done," I say, gently bring everyone back on task. "Xan, I need you to picture a strand or a cord linking you and Lizzie. When you have it, then build it up into something stronger. It needs to be something you can see easily, I can't give you exact instructions. It's gotta work for you, so it needs to be personal. Do you know what I mean?"

"I think so," he says. "Let me try."

"Whenever you're ready. Lizzie, when you see it or feel it, I need you to make it really special, okay?"

"Yes, Jax," she says.

"I've got it, changing it now," Xan mutters, going quiet again for a minute before opening his eyes and grinning at me. "Done."

"Me too, Jax. It's shiny now. Your turn."

I follow Lizzie's prompt, seeing the golden strand turn to thick metal chain before glowing brightly and turning pink.

"Yeah, that works," I sigh in relief. "Lizzie, you made them extra strong, so they'll keep you with us no matter where you go."

"I know," she agrees. "Emelia, I'm ready."

She turns to Em, who breathes deeply and focuses on the little girl in front of her. When I hear Lizzie giggle, I glance back to Em, who nods.

"All done," she confirms. "When you're ready to shine really bright, Lizzie, just let me know and I'll send you lots of light. Jax too."

"Yup, we both will. Okay, angel, time to work your magic."

My stomach lurches at the thought of sending her who-knows-where, but I know there's nothing else I can do.

"I'll be back soon, Jax," she says. "Don't worry."

And before I can answer her, she fades from view, leaving us all in silence with nothing to do but wait.

"Now what?" asks Lee, seeing me slump and realising she's gone.

"Just listen and watch for anything showing any sign of activity. Xan, Em, you guys hear or feel anything, shout up."

As the time passes, I begin to pace the floor, my concern rising with each minute that goes by.

"I've found him," Lizzie says, after what seems like forever.

The three of us connected to her stiffen at the same time, and I see Lee nudge Mathim and gesture towards us.

"Good job, sweetie. Can he reach you?" I ask.

"No, he's got to find me on his own. I need him to be able to see me so I can lead him here. But it's dark. I'm ready for you to help me now," she replies.

"This is it, Em. Now."

I envision a huge ball of the brightest light growing inside me, filling me from my head to my toes. I allow it to connect with the chain I forged before Lizzie left, and send it travelling down the links, making the whole thing glow so bright I can hardly look at it. But even as it goes, I replace it with more, a never-ending stream of light going from me to Lizzie.

"Wow, Jax, that's bright," she says, and I grin in response. "Ooh, Emelia, yours is pink."

Em shrugs at me quickly.

"I thought she'd like it," she offers, before closing her eyes again to focus.

"He's seen me!" Lizzie squeals. "He's coming."

"Lizzie, that's awesome!" praises Xan. "Can he reach you now?"

"Yeah, he's almost here. Got him." But after these words she goes silent.

"Lizzie?" I ask, repeating it more sharply when she doesn't reply.

"He's heavy, Jax," she grunts. "He's heavy cos he's stuck."

I look to Xan in panic, not knowing what to do.

"Stay calm," Emelia says, and I feel a strange tranquillity wash over me. When I hear Lizzie sigh, I know she feels it too. "This must be why she needed to be anchored. You need to pull her back. Both of you."

"Okay, we can do that," replies Xan. "Lizzie, get ready, sweetie."

"Ready, Xan. I'm holding him really tight." Her little voice so infused with bravery brings tears to my eyes, and they escape over my cheeks as I shut out the world around me to concentrate.

"Pull, Xan." I focus on the glowing chain, pulling it back to me arm over arm, all the while still sending light through it in the hopes it'll keep her strong.

I hear his breathing quicken with the mental exertion and realise mine has done the same. I force myself to relax, reeling them in like fish on a hook.

"Stop," says Lizzie. "The lady angel said he has to do this bit on his own. We're nearly back."

I do as she asks and stop pulling, but I keep the chain in place just in case.

"What do you need, Lizzie?" asks Emelia.

"Nothing. It's up to him. You can open your eyes now."

I do as she says, and the air rushes out of my lungs in relief when I see her standing in front of me.

"Am I glad to see you," I breathe.

Her tiny face screws up in concentration and I see her begin to glow. A small ball of light in the middle of her body at first, it spreads and grows until it radiates from her and I'm silenced by the beauty of it.

"Holy shit!" exclaims Lee. "I can see her!"

But as soon as she's spoken the words, noise erupts from behind her. Alarms from the emf meters spiking fight with the spirit box and Ovilus for our attention, sending Lee running to the table to check them.

I …. Am …. Here

"Okay, Gabriel, we've got you," I shout over the noise. "Just follow Lizzie's light. Eremiel said this wouldn't be easy. Picture your sister. Think of how much you want to be able to help her. Imagine a link between us, any kind of link and pour all that into making it a strong one. And when you've done that, then pull as hard as you can."

I feel a strange buzz starting around my wrist and look down in confusion.

"Jax, it's you," Lizzie says excitedly. "Help him."

I zone out, away from the noise, focusing only on the feeling in my arm and soon see a rope appearing, tied around my hand. I change it to the chain that worked so well with Lizzie and grip it mentally with both hands.

"I've got you, Gabriel. Now, pull."

I feel the air shift somehow around me and open my eyes quickly. There standing beside Lizzie is the smiling but exhausted-looking figure of Gabriel. My knees buckle under me and I stagger briefly before Mathim catches me and helps me to the chair.

"You good?" I ask Gabriel.

"I'm good," he replies. "Now, how do we get my sister?"

29

Getting Ready

"Good, Aurora. Again."

I watch as she parries another attack from Jay, using her height, or lack of it, to her advantage and throwing him off-balance.

"We do not expect you to fight. We only wish for you to keep yourself from harm, should the situation call for it," I explain. "We need you safe."

"Yeah, okay," she chirps, her breathing at a normal rate. She has the same natural abilities as her brother, but even quicker in her movements than he is.

I watch them face up to each other over and over and see her progression with every move. But when Jay's mask begins to slip as he becomes increasingly frustrated, I know I must end the practice.

"Enough. You have mastered those skills very easily, Aurora. I am impressed. But now let us see how you fare with some more difficult."

"Nice work, Rory," Jay praises after I give him a hard stare. "Don't worry about the next part, I'm sure you'll pick it all up just as fast."

I give him a quick nod and turn to the girl.

"Are you ready?" I ask. "This will take more than speed."

"What?" she replies in answer to the calculating look she sees on my face.

"I am trying to decide how best to teach you."

"Just tell me what you need me to do, and how to do it. I'll work it out from there," she says.

"It is not as simple as that, child. But as you wish. To use the gifts that we suspect you have, you must channel your rage, your grief, even. Any emotions to give power to your intentions. Let us begin with an attack," I instruct. "The forms you see around the room are used to train newly created demons. I want you to imagine a ball of energy in your hands, focus on one of them, and unleash your bolt at them."

She watches me carefully as I explain it, and then nods and turns to the dummy on her left. She closes her eyes and takes a deep breath, holding it for a moment before exhaling it slowly. Bringing her hands together, she opens her eyes and pushes her arms out before her. The human shape explodes into pieces, catching me off-guard as the fragments fly across the room.

"Well, shit," exclaims Jay, recovering enough to add, "nice job, sis."

I look at her in astonishment, before signalling for her to do it again. The wide grin that appeared at her success vanishes immediately as she focuses on her next target. One by one, she destroys them until I call an end to the task, knowing she has mastered it.

"Well done, Aurora. I am impressed. Now, let us see what other hidden depths you have."

As the time passes, I instruct her in the use of fire, wind, glamour and control, commandeering a few demons passing by the room for the last. When she makes them do all manner of harmless actions, I know this skill too has been honed to perfection in no time at all.

I see Jay watching her, an almost petulant expression on his face, and I know it is borne of jealousy at the ease with which she has picked up the instruction. I raise an eyebrow at him when he glances *at me, seeing his eyes drop from mine in shame.*

"Wow, I thought all this would be way harder to figure out. It really was as easy as you said, Jay. You told me Astaroth would teach me."

Her happiness lights her face as she waits for his approval once more.

"Yeah, you're a real natural, kid," he agrees, managing to make the sentiment look and sound genuine enough to amplify her smile.

"Yes, well done, Aurora," booms my Master's voice from the mirror overshadowing the room. "I have watched your progress."

"Th-thank you, Father," she stammers. "I didn't know you'd see."

"I did not want to distract you or put unnecessary pressure on you. I do not think I needed to worry," he replies. "Astaroth, are you satisfied enough with her progress to leave them to train alone for a while? There are things I would discuss with you."

"Of course, Sire. I will come to the Throne Room at once." I turn to his children. "Keep going. Either practice your powers on the targets or defence against each other."

Jay sees the stern look I give him and nods in agreement.

"Yes, Astaroth."

"I will return as soon as your Father has told me all he wishes."

I walk to the door, pausing briefly when Aurora calls after me.

"Bye, Astaroth. Thank you for teaching me."

"You are most welcome, child."

I open the door and make my way to Lucifer, wondering what it is I am to be told. When I reach the Throne Room, I see the door already open, Lucifer awaiting my presence still in front of the glass he has just spoken through.

"My Lord," I greet, as I approach him.

"Astaroth, the mists have cleared further. It would seem that, as we have two of my three children onside, we hold the advantage in more than numbers. It is down to me to choose where the ritual is to take place. I thought it wise to confer with you regarding this, as you have spent so much time in the human realm. Do you have any

suggestions?"

The question, so unexpected, leaves my mind blank of any immediate answer.

"I am unsure, Sire. I had not considered this." I set my mind working quickly, scrolling mentally through images of all of the places I have seen of late, and one stands out from all of the others. "Although, perhaps, I do have a suggestion. The place in which I created the gateway through which I brought Jacqueline. Broken Scar, it is called. The barrier between realms will still be weaker there."

I watch his face for his reaction, seeing a knowing smile appear there as he turns to look at me.

"I know that you do not expect me to think this a choice made solely for that reason, Duke. It is another hit to the Chosen One. It is, after all, her 'special' place, is it not? Her place of solitude and tranquillity?" He chuckles and brings it into view before us. "Yes, I agree, Astaroth. Not only would the veil be thinner there, another slight to Jacqueline would be something I would encourage. Very well, Broken Scar it is."

"Yes, Sire," I agree, somehow keeping the malicious smirk from *showing. "Will the angels know?"*

"I assume so. Just as we are given sight of what is to come, I would think that they will too. I am not ashamed to admit that I do not understand how all of this works, I only know that whatever is prophesised will come to pass somehow. Speaking of which, it would seem that my children are to receive instruction of the ritual itself. Much as Jacqueline received images of them when she crossed over into our realm."

"Do we know how soon?" I ask.

"That is why I have brought you here, Astaroth, and left them alone. The time of our success grows near, I expect the visions are imminent as we approach the day of my ascension."

He clears the green vista from the mirror, replacing it with the sight of Aurora and Jay, still battling. As Aurora ducks and runs under the arm Jay swings at her, Lucifer laughs beside me.

"Who would have thought that the downtrodden mouse of a girl could have that much potential? My son must be very disappointed," he muses.

"He is, yet he manages to hide it," I reply. "He will do whatever is necessary to maintain your favour, Sire."

"Yes, I see that. He is very keen to continue to make a good impression upon me. That will be more than useful in the coming days. I need him to return home soon though. My word needs to be spread. Your plan to make Aurora's disappearance known is still the way you would move forward, I take it?"

"It is, my Lord. By making the world care about her more, we guarantee that she has their attention upon her return. She is gifted in what she does there, I will just make that more so. And her words and music will spread your message as you require. People will start to pay attention without even realising, while your son informs them of the decline of their world, following any moves Agares or anyone else makes in your name."

He nods thoughtfully and smiles.

"Very good, Astaroth. And once all of this is completed and I have my victory, you will be rewarded for all your work. I could not imagine anyone else having this much success had I charged them with the task. It will not be forgotten."

"As you wish, Master," I answer, not allowing my voice to betray my thoughts at his words. The seat at the right hand of my Father is surely guaranteed.

A sudden movement catches my eye and brings my attention to the glass. Both Jay and Aurora have collapsed to their knees.

"The vision?" I ask.

"It must be," he says. "The time really does grow near."

I watch them closely and see no movement from either of them for a few moments. It is almost as though time has stopped, as still as they are in the room. Only when I see them both heave a huge breath simultaneously do I realise it is over. They both turn to mirror at the same time, and I hear Lucifer's low chuckle as he sees when I do that their eyes are flecked with red.

"My children are definitely coming into their own. Go to them, Astaroth. Find out what they know."

30

A Time to Rest

"It's not as simple as that, Gabriel," I say, holding up my hands to stave off the argument I know is coming. "You'll be no good to her if she can't see you or if you're burned out from the journey you just made. You can see that, right?"

His determined glare softens as my words sink in and he sighs and nods.

"Yeah, I guess so. How long do we have for me to recover? And how do I stay with you guys more easily? It's kinda taking a lot for me to keep myself here."

I look to Em, hoping she has an idea, and relief washes over me when she smiles at him.

"You used a helluva lotta juice crossing over, Gabriel. I think we need to recharge your batteries." She pauses while she looks at me, still sitting on the chair and attempting to catch my breath.

"Actually," she continues, "on second thoughts, I think I can do this solo. Jax, you need to go outside. You look terrible."

"Wow, thanks," I laugh. "I seem to be hearing that a lot lately. Are you sure you can do this alone?"

"Yeah, it's just the same as we did for Lizzie. You already used more of your juju than I did when you pulled him through. Go, I got this," she says, and knowing she's right, I cross the room a little unsteadily, heading for the door.

"Woah, there, boss lady. Let me come with you. Em's right, you don't look good."

"I'm fine, Lee, honestly. Or I will be," I reassure her. Seeing she's unconvinced, I compromise. "Tell you what, you make me coffee and meet me outside?"

"Yeah, okay, that's a better idea," she agrees. "Just be careful, okay?"

"I will."

I take my time, reaching the grass with huge relief as I sink down gently onto the chair. Kicking off my shoes, I wince briefly at the cold wetness of the lawn before the tingling warmth I've come to depend on takes its place.

"Is that gonna be enough?" Lee asks as she approaches carrying two cups, passing me one when she sits next to me. Rummaging in her jacket pocket she produces chocolate and I take it gratefully.

"It will be, honey. I'm really fine, it just took a lot to bring Gabriel through, especially after feeding Lizzie all the energy she needed first."

I sit back in my seat, stretching my legs out properly, munching quickly and feeling better almost immediately. When I've eaten, I reach for the cigarettes Lee brought out and light one, blowing the smoke high above us so it doesn't get her, and sipping my coffee as it cools.

"Well, you're starting to look better, I guess. A little," Lee concedes. "So, now I don't apparently need to worry about you passing out or anything, what's the plan?"

"It looks as though we're gonna have to teach Gabriel to form attachments to all of us like Lizzie did. We need him to be able to come through easily when we need him. I don't know if he'll be able to stay with us all the time. I don't think his spirit is strong enough for that. Not yet, at least. I wonder if Lizzie can help us to teach him. I mean, she figured it out easily enough, I think."

"She's already started," Lee laughs. "Even while Emelia was sending him the good stuff."

"Cool, I'll go help in a minute."

"And after that?" Lee asks. "It's two days to Halloween, or whatever that word was that Mathim used for it."

"Samhain," I offer.

"Yeah, that. And we don't know what's gonna happen or where or anything. Do you think you'll get to find out or are we meant to figure it out on our own? Cos, Jax, you know I'll hunt anything down for you, but I kinda need to know what I'm looking for."

Her worried expression makes me frown, but I can't comfort her.

"I dunno what to tell you, chick. I hope we'll find out, either through visions or something, or that Eremiel will turn up with the info we need. This whole thing has been geared towards some kind of final showdown, or at least the chance to stop Lucifer and Astaroth doing what they plan to. Surely, we must be given a chance to stop it, or what's the point in all this?"

"Hmm, yeah that seems sensible. If any of this can be sensible, I mean. Oh well, I guess we'll have to wait and hope for the best."

"It's all we can do. Tell you what, if we haven't heard or seen anything by the morning, I'll call to Eremiel and we'll all figure it out together from there. We have everyone with us, one of us might have a brainwave," I say, hoping to lift her mood.

"If anyone can, we can, right?" she replies a little more cheerily, making me grin at her.

"Exactly, honey. Now, how about we head back inside and turn Gabriel into a super-spirit?"

Giggling, she stands up, watching me closely as I do the same and nodding when she sees I am actually okay.

We walk back into the house in much better shape than we came out of it, our smiles and chatter pulling the attention of everyone to us when we enter the room.

"Oops, sorry, did we interrupt?" asks Lee.

"Nope," says Emelia. "We're taking a quick break while Lizzie and I figure out how best to teach Gabriel all he needs to learn. Lizzie, how did you do it? How did you teach Jax to keep you close? And how did you learn it?"

Lizzie's voice sounds in my head and I look around to see where she is.

"I'm resting, Jax. Em told me to. She said I might need to save myself for teaching Gabe tomorrow."

"That's a really good idea, Lizzie. Why don't you do that, and I'll fill Emelia in on everything we did. When you feel strong again tomorrow, you can come back properly and help us show him how to do it," I suggest gently.

"Okay," she agrees, sounding happy enough about it. "I'll go and stay with my mum tonight, she always makes me feel good."

"That sounds like a very good plan, sweetie. You go rest, and we'll see you tomorrow."

I feel the link break and turn back to Emelia.

"Gabriel?" I ask.

"He's tied himself to me, like he did to you. He's resting now. We'll start all this in the morning. I can't believe how long this took today. And how much it took out of us all. Poor Xan's exhausted too. He went to make calls about his house when I said I was okay to be left here. Mathim had an eye on us anyway," she adds, giving him a grin.

"Oh, okay. So, it's still early, I guess. Food then chill for the night, ready for another busy day?"

"I promised I'd go tell Mrs C when we were done. I'll check on Xan too while I'm gone," says Lee, jumping to her feet again and jogging out the door.

"You know, it's a real shame she doesn't have the gift," muses Emelia. "She's got enough energy for all of us."

"Now that is very true," says Mathim. "She never stops. I admit sometimes she makes my head spin."

"She does everyone's," I chuckle. "It's one of the many reasons we love her."

"So, while it's just the three of us, I need to talk to you both," says Emelia.

"Sure, what's up? Everything okay?" I ask, settling back on the sofa as she sits in the chair opposite.

"Yeah. Well, at least, I think so. My dreams are getting really weird lately, and I thought I should mention it."

I look at Mathim and see my concern at her words mirrored in his face.

"Weird, how?"

"I dunno. It's almost as though there's some kind of pressure building while I sleep. Like something is pushing somewhere. I can't explain it. I still build my wall and put up the bubbles every night like Sal showed me, but lately something is different. Is it Astaroth again?" She turns to Mathim as she asks, knowing he'll know better than anyone.

"It could be, Emelia. We should have seen this coming. With him having secured Aurora, it gives him a few days to try and convert you over to them," he says.

"Two days and it's done though. I can keep him out for a few more nights. I just wanted to let you know."

"There is, of course, a more worrying possibility," says Eremiel from the doorway, startling us all.

"Yeah, there would be," I grumble. "What are you thinking, Eremiel?"

"When Lucifer created all of his demons, he created a link that cannot be undone. It is possible that such a link exists between him and his children. It may not have been Astaroth who was attempting the contact."

A heavy silence drops over us as we take in what he's suggesting.

"Can I keep him out too?" Emelia asks, a slight tremor in her voice.

"It sounds to me as though you have been doing a good job of that up to now," he replies, smiling at her. "Try not to worry. It is as you say, two days until all of this is over."

"Hmm, okay," she agrees, uncertainty in her voice. "I'll just put up two walls instead of one."

"As many as you need to feel safe." Mathim's tone is kind and seems to put her at her ease and again, I thank my angels for sending him to us.

"Thanks, Mathim," she says, but then frowns at him. "How aren't you linked to him any more?"

"I disavowed my name. The one he gave me upon my creation. Bathin," he explains, as I realise that Emelia hasn't heard this part of Mathim's story.

"Yeah, but how?" she asks.

"It was only words but witnessed by another demon. Sallas, to be precise. I drew on the powers within me to abandon the name and all ties belonging to it. I swore to take on new life and new spirit by renaming myself. And so, I am Mathim."

She looks as though she wants to question him further but stops herself and closes her mouth. Instead, she sits back and crosses her ankles in front of her, her gaze becoming unfocused as she lets her mind mull all of this over.

Giving her time to work through her thoughts, I turn to Eremiel.

"What happens next?" I ask, voicing Lee's question from earlier. "Do we get to find out where and when the ritual will take place?"

"I would assume so, yes. You have been given all pertinent information up to this point, one way or another. I would guess that this will be no exception. Lucifer has his three chances to succeed, but the Chosen Ones have their three to stop him. It would be logical to assume that the final day would be shown to you somehow."

His words don't exactly infuse me with confidence, given the "somehow", "guess" and "assume" within them, but I nod anyway.

"Mathim?" Sal's voice echoes through the mirror over the fireplace, and I grin when he appears looking as cheerful as always.

"Sallas, how goes it?" asks Mathim, standing to face his friend.

"I will take my leave for now. I will return as the time approaches," Eremiel states. "Oh, time. You asked when? I agree with Mathim. Samhain was definitely shown in your last vision. And as that is the day chosen, then there can only be one time. Here on Earth, some call it the 'witching hour', in truth it is the time when the veil is the thinnest. Combining this with the thinning on Samhain, and you have the best possible opportunity to break through."

"The witching hour. That's two am. On Halloween night. Yup, that's definitely spooky enough to seem appropriate. Are you certain?" I ask.

"As I can be," he says simply.

"Thank you, Eremiel. You haven't been wrong so far. I'd still prefer to see it somehow too though. For confirmation. No offence."

He chuckles and shrugs his shoulders.

"None taken. I would prefer you had it confirmed. Now, if you need me just call to me."

"I will," I reply to the empty space he's just vanished from. Shaking my head in amusement, I turn to the mirror. "Hey, Sal."

"Hey, Jax, how are you? I am glad you got Gabriel back safely." He looks over my shoulder, seeing Emelia rise from her seat. "Hi, Em."

"Hi, Sal. You good?" she replies distractedly.

"I am well, thank you."

"I'm glad to hear it. Guys, I'm gonna go sleep for a while. Can you call me when we're leaving to eat?" she asks.

"Of course, Em. You okay, sweetie?"

She doesn't seem herself at all, but I can't blame her.

"I'm fine. I'm just tired. I'll catch up with you next time, Sal," she says, giving him a half-smile before she leaves.

"What's wrong with her?" he asks when she's gone. "That's not the Em I know."

"She's been having dreams. We think Lucifer was trying to turn her. I was hoping they would just leave her alone once she made her decision," Mathim replies. "She will work through it, I am sure."

"Definitely," Sal states firmly. "She will figure it all out. She just needs time. I have never seen anyone with a stronger intuition than she has. When I was teaching her how to harness any powers she had, I was surprised at how quickly she picked up the knowledge. But when she figured others out on her own, I was astounded. She just needs to do the same now. Follow her gut instinct."

"Yeah, you're right, Sal. Maybe a sleep will do her good. Okay, I'm gonna leave you guys to it, and go see Joanna. Just call if you need me," I say.

Hearing Mathim agree, I make my way outside, breathing in the cool evening air and crossing the driveway to the newer house. Joanna sees me through the kitchen window and beckons me inside, a wide smile on her face and I push open the door, looking forward to coffee and a chat before I have to face the chaos I know is coming.

***

"Hey, Mathim. Hey, Xan," I greet as I come into the room, smiling to see them sitting and talking like old friends.

"Hey, Jax. Mrs C fix you? You looked grumpy when you left," Xan asks.

"Yeah, she did. She always does. Lee's still over there, putting the world to rights. They're set for the night, it seems. Oh, and she says dinner is in ten minutes. Joanna, obviously, not Lee," I say with a chuckle.

"Thank God for that," quips Xan. "Lee is awesome, but I'd much rather Mrs C did the cooking out of the two."

Mathim laughs and sits forward, looking ready to join in the easy conversation but is cut off by the door slamming open and a breathless Emelia running into the room.

"Em, what's wr—" Xan begins but she cuts him off before he can finish.

"I know how to do it!" she exclaims. "I know how to break the bond."

31

Details

"Two days from now, by the way time passes on Earth, Sire. Both Jay and Aurora described depictions of the thinning of the veil at Samhain. They described the summoning ritual down to the smallest detail. They have all of the knowledge they need. I set them to practising the words they need. I assumed you would wish to go over the details of the night," I say, waiting for him to reply as he takes in what I have just told him.

"It is as I thought, the knowledge became clear to them as the time approaches. I wonder though, that it was left so late, so close to the event, as it were."

I jump on the chance to bring up the subject I wished to discuss without raising any suspicion.

"I have thought of this too, my Lord. As time passes more quickly here, would it be better to take your children to Earth to prepare? They will have more time there to be ready for their efforts to be successful."

He looks at me carefully, and for a moment I think he has seen through my ploy.

"Excellent, Astaroth, I had not thought of this. Yes, you will take them back as soon as we are done. The more time they have to prepare, the better."

"As you wish, Master," I reply, keeping my face blank.

"Now, as for the final confrontation. I know that you always prefer to work alone, but you realise that on this occasion I must insist on sending others to help you. I cannot think that there will be no involvement from the angels. Bathin, too."

I grit my teeth at the thought of other demons alongside me on this, but I know he is right.

"I do, Sire. Your children, however, saw only a few accompanying Jax. Perhaps that must be obeyed too?"

"How many? And who?" he asks quickly.

"Jacqueline and Emelia, obviously, Xander, Bathin and one they did not know. I assume that to be the angel that works so closely with

*them. They also saw two figures in shadow. For our part, they saw
the three of us accompanied by three others."*

*"Hmm, yes, I think that too must be obeyed, as you say. Very well,
three demons will accompany you. Who would you have?" he asks,
surprising me. "You would wish to choose your own, would you
not?"*

*"Indeed, Sire, thank you. I would prefer having those I trust at my
back. May I suggest Loray, Valefar, and Forali? They have served me
well for so long, I would have no problem in trusting to their
defence."*

*I offer the names of three soldiers from my own legions, knowing
their loyalty and obedience is mine to command in any way I see fit.
Indeed, it was those I employed to take Lilim when the time came. I
watch Lucifer's face as he considers them, inwardly breathing a sigh
of relief when he agrees.*

*"Very well, I will have them briefed and sent to you when it is time. I
would not have them get in the way of my children's final
preparations. Is there anything else?"*

"I do not think so, my Lord," I reply. "I think all that can be planned

for, has been.

"Very well then, Astaroth. I will send you on your way. I do not need to reiterate the importance of success, I know you will not fail me."

I bow to him and leave the room, walking through the passageways to reach Jay and Aurora, my entrance making them pause mid-sentence.

"Ready for home?"

***

"What do we do while we wait?" asks Jay, once we had made the crossing into his home.

"You will go and spread the word of Aurora's disappearance some more. While you are doing that, she can continue to practice. When you return there are things that I would discuss with you."

I look pointedly at him and then glance to his sister, seeing the realisation hit him that I have things I would share with him alone.

"No problem, Astaroth. I'll go and plant the seed. My editor thinks

I'm off chasing down stories anyway, I can just call into the office and raise it to him as something to keep an eye on."

"Good. You do that. I will wait here. Aurora, you may begin whenever you are ready."

"I have a question," she says.

"Go on," I prompt. "Ask what you will."

"The ritual. Do we need to draw the symbol?"

I turn to face Jay, who shrugs, then back to Aurora who nervously continues.

"Cos if we do, I can do it. I know what it looks like and I used to be good at drawing stuff. Here, I'll show you." She looks around and takes paper from the machine in the corner of the room. The pencil flies across the page, not stopping until the second before she turns the sheet around and holds it up to Jay. "That's right, isn't it?"

"Yeah, it is," he says, sounding genuinely impressed.

"It is settled then. Aurora, you will create the symbol when we get there. Does that fit with the vision you both had?"

Seeing them both nod, I mentally cross another thing off my list of things to check.

"Okay, I won't be long," says Jay, and picks up his coat before leaving us.

I watch as Aurora duplicates the image over and over, all the time repeating the words of the summoning in an almost melodic way. A thought occurs to me upon hearing and seeing her efforts. If the symbol required someone with at least some artistic talent, and the summoning easier for someone with a musical ear, then is it merely coincidence that my Master's two daughters fit that criteria so well? And if not coincidence, then what is Jay's purpose during it all? I cannot place his talents, and so cast the thought aside, sitting back and taking rest while I can until Jay returns.

Before too long, I hear the door open and close, and stand to head him off before he comes in.

"Carry on, Aurora. I have things to discuss with your brother and would not wish to disturb you."

"Okay," she replies happily, not pausing in her movements at all.

I signal to Jay to turn around, and lead him back outside, leaning on a low wall opposite him.

"What is it, Astaroth?" he asks.

"I would discuss our plan, before the time arrives when we must act not talk. We know now that Aurora will be busy with the symbol before you begin the summoning. Normally, I would lead you in this, but I am beginning to think that I should leave that to you. Aurora looks up to you and will do as you ask without question. I know that I do not need to give you instruction as to what to do. You are quite capable, I think."

"Yes, I am. Thank you for trusting me with this."

His choice of words gives me the opportunity I have been waiting for.

"And what of you, Jay? How much can I trust you?" I ask.

"What do you mean? You know you have my loyalty, I have sworn it from almost the first time I met you," he replies.

"Ah yes, loyalty to your Father. I know that is unwavering," I agree.

"And to you too, Astaroth. I would not be here now doing all we're about to, if not for you," he adds. "You know that, right? That my loyalty is not only to him?"

"I do. I was just making sure, Jay. Very well, let us return to your sister. You also need to repeat the summoning to ensure it is in your mind clearly," I say pushing myself away from the wall and walking towards the door.

"Wait," he says, making me turn around to look at him. "Aurora draws the image, I wait 'til it's complete and I lead the ritual? That's it?" he asks.

"That's it," I repeat. "I will keep anyone who tries to stop you at bay. With the help from my soldiers. Complete your task, Jay, that is all we ask of you."

"I can do that," he says confidently. "Then what happens?"

"Then," I answer, "then your Father rises from Hell, he comes to Earth and humanity will not know what has hit it. Such sights they will all see, such horrors they will be forced to witness, and through *it all, you will be the one to spread his word. I hope you are ready,*

Jay. You are about to be very busy indeed."

32

Last Steps

"What?" I exclaim. "How?"

She looks a lot more focused than earlier, her eyes still lit by her discovery as she crosses the room towards us, looking briefly at the chair but dismissing the idea.

"It's like this," she begins, pacing the floor as she explains. "I was thinking about the link between me and Lucifer, actually, stressing might be a better way to describe it. Anyway, it struck me that there might be a way to break it like Mathim did. A human disavowal, if you like. That's why I went weird and disappeared upstairs. I needed time to work it out. Sorry."

"It's fine, honey, but carry on with what you were saying."

"Yeah, you're kinda turning into Lee here," Xan laughs. "I can always follow your conversations normally."

She grins at him and takes a breath before continuing.

"Right, focus. I think as the link between him and the demons is different to the one he has with us but works the same way then the same thing Mathim used would work with just a small change. Our link is through blood, so I imagined the same kinda words but with a symbolic spilling of the thing that binds us. Ugh, I'm not making sense. Hold on, I'll rephrase it."

"No, I think I got it. You disavow all connections with him but instead of disowning the name, which is what ties him to the demons, you shed the blood you share?" I ask.

"Yes!" she almost shouts in relief. "Thank God for that. I couldn't get the words right."

"Can you do it now?" I ask.

"I don't wanna risk it. I know that Lucifer obviously felt nothing when Mathim broke from him, but this is a blood link. He might feel it. You have to trust me, Jax, I know it'll work."

Her eyes bore into me as she says this, and I quickly recall Sal's words about the strength of her intuition.

"Okay," I agree.

"Just like that?" she asks surprised. "Wow, I thought I'd have to convince you for a while. But in that case, we need to figure out how to best use it. In fact, the whole thing needs planning. We can't go into this completely blind."

"I know, I spoke to Er—"

I stagger forward, bending and bracing my hands on my knees as my mind is assaulted by a series of images so fast, I can barely keep up. Jay and Rory around the strange symbol on the ground, chanting like before, but this time I see where they are.

"Jax?" I hear Xan call worriedly and manage to lift up a hand to hold him off.

The scene seems to rewind and instead I see a standoff between us all. Emelia and Gabriel flank me, Mathim, Xan and Eremiel behind us. I stare down Astaroth as he smirks at me, gesturing to Jay and Aurora standing at either side of him, three others I've never seen before behind them. He snaps his fingers and trees burst into flames around us lighting up the scene just as the vision ends.

"Broken Scar," I gasp.

Emelia falls to her knees, panting for breath.

"Well, that sucked," she manages to say. "And where?"

"Astaroth had to have chosen it. It's the place I go to ground myself, it's really special to me," I reply, hating that he'd try to mar it again.

"So, he made a mistake then, didn't he? You being there, surrounded by nature? That's only ever gonna be an advantage to us, Jax," reminds Xan.

"Xander is right," says Mathim. "Astaroth clearly either does not know or he severely underestimates the power it gives you. This is a good thing."

"Yeah, I guess you're right," I concede. "I still hate it though."

"Hey, guys," calls Lee from the front door. "Mrs C sent me to get you. Dinner's ready."

"Coming, Lee," I call back. "Okay, as you were saying before all that happened, Emelia, we do need to figure out the plan. And now we know a little more than we did. So, let's go eat, and we can work everything else out when we get back."

"I have a better idea, I think," suggests Mathim. "Perhaps dinner and then sleep. We have yet to see how effective Gabriel will be. Until we know that, we can make no plans."

"Hmm, good point. Okay, food, sleep, and everything else in the morning. Sounds like we're gonna need an early night," agrees Xan.

"With all the food Joanna's prepared, trust me, you're gonna be in a food coma for at least ten hours," I laugh, linking my arm through his and walking to join an increasingly impatient Lee.

***

"Try again, Gabriel. Just picture the rope you tied around my wrist when you came through and try to replicate it for Xan," I say calmly.

It feels like we've been doing this for hours, without much success. The link he made with Emelia isn't very strong and he's finding it impossible to create with Xan at all.

"I can't do it, Jax," he replies, panic edging into his voice. "How can I help Aura if I'm not there and can't get to her?"

"Stay calm, sweetie. We'll figure it out. It's what we do. Let's try something else for a while. Test the link with me first though."

I barely finish my sentence before the pull on my wrist makes me grin, feeling the strength of our connection hasn't faded at least.

"Yeah, that one's fine," he says, sounding a little happier.

"Okay, Lizzie, are you here?" I ask.

"Yeah, Jax," her little voice answers.

"Okay, angel. Can you take Gabriel to hide with you and show him how to send pictures like you do? To all three of us?"

"Come on, Gabriel, this is a fun game," she says with a giggle.

My mind feels emptier immediately and when I know they've gone I turn quickly to the others.

"What do we do now?" I ask. "He can't do it and he doesn't have time to learn or build the strength."

I look at them all, seeing only blank expressions, and my heart sinks. We need him to get Rory, there's no other way.

"Wait, can I ask a question?" asks Lee. "It might sound stupid though."

"Just ask, honey. Nothing is stupid," encourages Xan.

"Well, do we really need him to link with Em and Xan? Why isn't the bond with Jax enough?"

"Because we need for him to be able to be there with us at Broken Scar," I reply, missing her point completely, I realise when she sighs and shakes her head.

"No, Jax, listen. When Astaroth had you, Lizzie came through to you, right? There was only you, there always was until Xan died and Emelia got here. Maybe the problem isn't that he can't link to them, maybe it's just that he's not meant to. Like it's diluting his energy by trying to spread it out between you all." She glances around self-consciously. "Yeah, stupid idea, isn't it?"

"Actually, little one, I think you have it exactly right," Mathim interjects, making her smile. "Lizzie has been around for a lot longer than Gabriel, and so is more practised and has built more reserves of strength over time. But even she only bonded with Jax at first. And as long as he has a strong connection with one of you, then it doesn't really matter which of you it is. His bond with his sister will do the rest when we reunite them, I would imagine."

"Oh wait, something else," adds Lee. "You said Broken Scar? That puts you both at a huge advantage. Even before the nature thing came along, I always saw what that place did for you. But now, with the whole Jax hoodoo thing you have going on, it's gonna be so much bigger. It's awesome it's you he's bound to, you can help him build his energy while you're there."

I hold up a hand to stop everyone talking, rubbing my temples as I process everything they're saying. I can see that one strong link is better than three weak ones, but to concentrate on feeding him the energy through me while we're facing Astaroth? It'd take me out of the game completely.

"How am I meant to defeat Astaroth if I have to focus on Gabriel?" I ask.

"You're not," says Emelia simply. "We are. You're not doing this alone, remember. Yeah, you're the Chosen One and all that, but we're a team. You saw the vision, we were all there. Divide and conquer, Jax. It's the only way we win."

An image of Rory appears in my mind, but a younger version of her, sitting in an old rocking chair and strumming on a beaten-up guitar.

"Nice job, Gabriel," I send. "Just focus on me. Let's build the link we have."

"Em is right, Jax. We need a plan that involves us all," agrees Xan.

"I know, guys. Really, I do. I have two conversations going on again," I reply with a laugh. "I didn't mean that I was meant to do it on my own. I'm not stupid or arrogant enough to think that. I just mean that if I'm focused on Jay, I dunno how much help I'll be to any of it."

"You'll be doing the most important thing," says Lee. "You'll be helping Gabriel get Rory on side and out of harm's way. But once you have her, what then?"

I huff out a breath, trying to sort my thoughts out and get them into a logical order. Only when I think I have it do I open my mouth to speak.

"Right, let's work through this. I have Gabriel and we get Rory. Once we have her, how do we get Jay? Do we need him? Cos there's no way we can get him to disavow himself."

And as we go through every part of the plan, weighing up our options, I begin to feel hopeful again. Seeing all my friends around me, hearing them talk everything out and offering ideas and suggestions, I realise Xan was right. One step at a time and nothing is impossible.

***

Despite the cool temperatures and the dampness of the ground, I pace the lawn barefoot, my shoes in one hand and my cigarette in the other. Now that we have as much planned as we can, I needed some quiet time. Normally, these are the days I'd go to Broken Scar, but I'll be going there soon enough anyway. For now, the garden at the front of the big old house I love so much will do me just fine.

"Penny for them," says Joanna quietly as she approaches.

"Hi, Joanna," I greet with a smile.

"You look full of thoughts, girl. Do you need to talk?" she asks gently.

"No, not really. I'm actually trying not to think too much. Now that we're here, at the end of it all, some of those thoughts are kinda scary." I take a shaky breath and try to push them away yet again.

"You've heard the phrase 'energy follows intent', yes?" Seeing me shake my head, she carries on. "It's used in healing mostly, but often when talking about affirmations and the like. In its essential meaning, it is true. You know yourself, how valuable an asset energy is. Don't waste it by giving it to negative thoughts. It only empowers them. Focus on the positives. How good life will be again when all of this is over. The ways you'll all move forward from here when you win. Focus on the things that deserve your energy and it'll bring them into being."

"Does it work?" I ask. "I mean, can it really be that simple?"

"Really, Jax, you're going to ask that? You of all people. The most determined, positive girl I've ever known. Of course it works. You live your life by it, even if you don't realise. You just need to apply it to this. You're 'always ready', I hear. This is no exception. You're ready for this too. I'd trust no one with the world more than you, sweetheart. All of you." She smiles reassuringly and I'm overwhelmed by her words.

"Thank you, Joanna. For everything. For all your support, your help and advice, and for letting us stay here too. Somehow I feel that being here is helping."

I see a twinkle appear in her eye, and a mischievous smile that she doesn't quite hide quickly enough, and I frown at her.

"What?" she asks innocently.

"I saw that look. What's going on?"

"Hi, Xan," she says, looking past me and sounding a little relieved at the interruption.

"Hi, Mrs C. Hey, Jax. What's that look for?"

"Hmm, Joanna's keeping secrets. I don't know what I said but it definitely triggered a suspicious reaction," I tease.

"Ooh, I like secrets," he replies, joining in.

"No secrets," she says. "I don't know what you mean. I came over to have a sensible conversation."

I close the gap between us and wrap her up in a hug.

"Thank you, Joanna. I mean it. We all love you dearly."

"I love you all too, flower. And I'll be here when you get back."

She steps back to lock her eyes with mine, not dropping her gaze until I nod in agreement.

"We'll see you then," I promise.

She turns away, her hand wiping quickly at her face as she walks back to the new house and I have to swallow the lump that's made its way into my throat.

"I love this place," says Xan randomly, changing the subject and lightening the mood.

"I do too. We all do," I agree.

"I know," he says, leaning towards me conspiratorially. "That's why I bought it."

"You what?" I ask, not believing what I'm hearing.

"Ssh! It's a secret. Don't tell Lee until this is all done. It hasn't gone through yet, we've only just agreed the sale. But given the state of my house, I think this is a better option. I don't need somewhere that big anyway. My parents have found a place in France. So, Jax, am I okay to move us all here? Work, you, Mathim, everything?"

I squeal and wrap my arms around his neck, hugging him tight while I bounce around on the spot.

"Yes! Definitely yes!"

He grins and hugs me back.

"You're all my family, Jax. I wouldn't wanna be anywhere without you."

"Love you, Xan," I say easily.

"Love you too, Jax. Now come on, we have a world to save. But you have to help me redecorate after, okay?"

I look at him for a minute before bursting into laughter and agreeing.

"Not a problem. Fate of the world as we know it, then interior design. I promise."

Grinning at each other as we walk, I push open the door and go to the living room to join everyone, smiling wider when I see them all in good spirits.

"Perfect timing," says Mathim. "The reinforcements are on their way."

"Huh?" I reply but go no further when I see Sal and Malaphar stepping through the glass.

"As if we'd miss out on this!" scoffs Sal.

"But how?" I ask. "Lucifer will be watching and Astaroth will see you."

"That's easy," says Malaphar. "Watch."

And before my eyes they both begin to change, turning into totally different people.

"Just when I thought things couldn't get any worse," Sal complains, jokingly. "I have to impersonate an angel."

"I have the doorway prepared, whenever you are all ready," says Scirlin from the glass. "I will not be of much help beyond this point. My attention will be required here."

"Understandable, friend. Thank you again, Scirlin. We are almost at the end," replies Mathim.

"We are," agrees Tez, appearing at the other side of the mirror. "Good luck to you all. I wish I could be there with you."

"For our girls," says Sal, and we all take a moment to echo the sentiment.

"Jax, are you ready to call to Gabriel?" Mathim asks, breaking the silence.

"There's no need," Gabriel says in my head. "I'm here and I'm ready."

"He's here," I inform everyone else. "I'm not even gonna let him try to link with anyone else."

"Good. Well then, are we ready?" Mathim asks.

"Always ready," I answer firmly, stepping through into the cool air of my most sacred place and breathing deeply.

"I'm glad we're here early," Xan says, stepping through behind me. "I know you were worried about the trees burning in your vision."

"I know it seems silly considering everything else we have going on, but I can't help it," I reply.

"Nope, I get it. But given the fact we probably have an hour or so to prepare, let's take away the need for him to burn anything by creating a few fires of our own. Sensibly. Emelia," he calls, "a little help with your superpowers please?"

She grins and jogs over to us, nodding when Xan explains what he wants. I watch them as they busy themselves, as much about keeping their minds occupied while we wait as about providing light and warmth. In no time at all, piles of broken branches sit dotted about the hard earth, made safe by impromptu stone circle pits made by Xan. I watch intrigued as one by one, they spark into flame and grow in brightness, accompanied by an orange glow in Emelia's eyes.

"Nice job, guys. Thank you," I say.

"Jax," says Mathim, from a short distance away where he stands with Sallas and Malaphar. "We must prepare. The time approaches."

With a nod of my head to him, I turn to the others.

"Looks like it's almost showtime."

Determination takes over both their expressions and they take up the positions we discussed previously. I take a deep breath and attempt to steel myself for whatever is coming.

"Gabriel, you with me?" I ask.

"I am," he says, tightening the invisible band I can feel on my wrist. "Just tell me when it's time and I'll be there."

"Good. Ready, everyone?"

I look around at these people I'd trust with my life and see them all nod, eyes still focused on the horizon ahead. I stretch my gaze, eyes straining to see any movement whatsoever, but I need not have tried so hard. There in front of me, as described by Scirlin, rises the doorway within the river. And as I watch, the tall frame of Astaroth steps through, followed by Jay and Rory, and then three others I don't know. His eyes meet mine, before flicking to Mathim, then back again as he walks towards us, bringing his group to a halt when they reach the riverbank. His lips curl into a smirk and my skin crawls at the sight of it.

He takes a step forward from his companions, looks along the line of us and focuses on me once again.

"Well met, Jacqueline."

33

The Ritual

I see her face twist in distaste at my greeting and chuckle to myself. I will take so much pleasure in destroying her when my Master's work is done.

"And you, Bathin. I see you are in the company of the vermin. Very fitting for you, I must say."

"The only vermin I see is the one standing and talking to me," he replies through gritted teeth.

"I will not waste the precious time we have exchanging bitter words. I have a task to complete. Aurora, you may begin."

When she hears the words, she steps back behind us, dropping to her knees and beginning to drag her hand through the loose earth, outlining the design that comes so easily to her. I turn my attention back to Bathin and see them beginning to approach. I raise my arm in the air, placing a barrier around her and nod to Jay who drops back to guard her. My three captains come forward to join me and I grin at my opponents.

"And so, it begins."

My words are greeted by movement within their ranks, Bathin and the angels stepping between Jax and Emelia to take their places in front of them. I roll my shoulders, readying myself for the moment I have awaited for so long. Finally, I can take down the traitor.

"Now, Jax," orders Bathin, but before I can see to what his instructions refer, the scene erupts into chaos.

The two angels flanking him charge towards us, a third appearing to join the melee at the last minute. Trusting in my captains to deal with them, my eyes lock with Bathin's and I shake my head at the arrogance as he takes his time in approaching me. I mirror his steps, the bloodlust beginning to sound my quickening pulse in my head, as I take a final deep breath before launching myself at him.

Pent-up rage that has built over the months since his betrayal combine with the hatred I have always had for him, creating a blur of the rest of the world as I focus solely on him. He leaps forward suddenly, but I expected it, and I duck to avoid the blow, unleashing one of my own that connects with his jaw. A sudden rush of pure joy travels through me as I hear him grunt in surprise.

"Your time here has weakened you, Bathin," I taunt. "This may be disappointing."

He swings a fist at my head, and I begin to move to parry this blow too, realising too late that it was feigned, the air being pushed out of my lungs when I feel a rib crack under pressure from his intended strike. Shoving him backwards to catch my breath, I summon power between my hands, allowing it to explode from them and sending it towards him. He slips to his left, sensing its path and escaping the hit.

"Really, Astaroth? You have never been able to best me, what makes you think you can do so now?"

His arrogance pulls a growl from my throat, the need to spill his blood growing with every breath. I look behind him quickly, a tree bursting into flame at my will, creating the distraction I require for the briefest second. He turns his head slightly, and I make my move. Running towards him and dropping my shoulder, I charge into him, my momentum pushing him onto the ground, and I drop to kneel across his chest. Blow after blow I send crashing into his face, feeling flesh and bone give way to the assault.

And in the midst of the thrill of causing him pain, my mind vaguely wonders at such a weak defence. Surely he cannot have taken such a demise by being here.

He pushes me off-balance and attempts to reverse our positions, but I counter quickly as I'm moved off him, jumping to my feet to prepare for his next move. But when his eyes flick past my shoulder, I realise what my mind was trying to grasp. He is not so weakened, he is keeping me busy.

I spin on my heel, turning to see Jax and Xan approach the barrier protecting Aurora, but before I can react, I am shoved onto my knees by a boot in my back. I move to regain my stance, but not fast enough. And in that instant, Bathin allows his true skill to come out. Pinning me as I did him, he rains down strike after strike to my head and torso, each blow more painful than the last. I taste my own blood as my lip is split open, another trickle running into my eye from some other wound he has created, and I know I must get out from this dangerous disadvantage. Summoning all the power I can, I focus it as a burning ball of flame inside me, creating a blast wave when I allow it to be released.

He grunts in pained shock as he is lifted into the air and thrown back from me, and I stand to face him once more.

"Astaroth!" I hear the concern in Jay's voice and call to reassure him.

"I am fine, Jay. Concentrate on what you are doing," I command.

"No. I mean, the barrier!"

I turn quickly and see the focus I used to escape Bathin has pulled away power from Aurora's protection, Jax and Xander running to her side. Jay starts towards them and I begin to move towards them but see him stop suddenly.

"I can't get through," he says, panicked. "Something is stopping me."

"That would be me," Bathin drawls. "With a little extra help from the angels. Would you like to try and do something about that, Astaroth?"

I snarl at his tone and face him once more, seeing red flash in his eyes at my approach.

"Your arrogance astounds me, Bathin. You truly believe that you can win this?"

"Keep going, Rory," I hear Jay shout. "It's working."

I manoeuvre around Bathin so that I can see what is happening without turning my back on him.

"That is the difference between us, Astaroth," says the traitor. "You need to make sure they do as you say, you do not trust to their ability to complete your tasks. I have no such worries. I know that even without my help, Jax and the others will succeed. That is why you will not win. Distraction is such a dangerous thing."

I check on Aurora's progress as he speaks his words, seeing her chanting continues even as Jax nears her, but just before I answer him, I notice a faint red glow begin to emanate and build from the lines of the symbols so carefully drawn in the earth.

"Let us test your theory, shall we? Let us see just how well they manage without you."

I end my sentence with a sudden step towards him, not wanting him to see Aurora's progress, but his words strike a chord. I must trust to the training that Lucifer's children have received in order to focus on my target.

I lean back sharply to avoid the fist he aims at my temple, sweeping his legs from under him and hearing the air rush out of him as he lands hard on the ground once more. Too quickly, he pounces back onto his feet, dropping his head and running at me and I find myself once more at his mercy. Grabbing a rock within my reach, I slam it into the side of his head, feeling him lurch to the side once it makes its impact, and I work my way out from under his weight as he shakes his head, trying to clear it.

And although I should end him, I cannot resist checking briefly on Aurora, seeing her ignoring the pleading from Jax kneeling beside her, and her lips still moving in the repeated words. And, I notice with a grin, Jay's inability to join her for now does not seem to be holding back her progress. The glow from the seal has brightened even further and I think I can see a crack forming in the centre of it.

Jax looks hopelessly at Xander, but then her eyes meet mine as she scours the scene for her angel comrades.

"You will not win her, Jax," I scoff. "I offer everything she needs."

An unseen attack from Bathin takes me off my feet once more, and as I fall to the ground, I notice something else beyond the barrier. A shimmering form begins to appear behind it, just behind Aurora, and Jax begins to smile.

34

Blood is Thicker

"Rory, please, you have to listen to me," I plead. "Astaroth isn't what you think he is. Neither is Jay."

Despite my words, her monotonous words continue on their loop. I look to Xan who shrugs in response, shaking his head. Knowing he's as lost for answers as I am, I lift my eyes to the chaos past the invisible wall Mathim has put up. I sweep the scene for him, but my eyes lock with those of Astaroth and I see a smirk appear on his face.

"You will not win her, Jax," he says. "I offer everything she needs."

And for a minute, I believe him.

"Hi, Jax," Lizzie chirps in my head. "I did as you said, I stayed hidden until I could hide here with you."

A peace washes over me and I watch Astaroth's confusion as I begin to smile.

"Hi, Lizzie. Yes, you did just as I asked, thank you. Are you ready to bring Gabriel?" I think back.

"Yeah, gimme a minute."

The link drops for a few minutes and when it returns, it isn't Lizzie I hear.

"Okay, Jax, I'm ready."

With Gabriel's words comes the tingling band on my wrist and I slide my other hand into the long grass I'm kneeling beside.

"Now, Gabriel, as soon as you can manage it."

"I can feel the energy you're sending. I'm almost there," he replies, and before any more than a minute passes, I see him begin to take form behind his sister. "Aura?"

She stops her chanting and glares at me, before resuming her chorus once more.

"Aura?" Gabriel repeats. "This isn't a trick. Turn around and look at me. Please."

She turns to look behind her to where she hears the voice coming from, a sneer on her face, expecting to see nothing. But when her eyes come to rest on the full form of her twin, they fill with tears as she blinks in disbelief.

"Gabe?" she breathes, astounded.

"Yes, Aura, it's me. Now, listen. Astaroth lied to you. He used Jay to get you to his side. You need to change allegiances. Jax and Mathim are the ones you need to be with."

I see the battle playing out on her face as she glances between the spirit of her twin and the very real figure of Jay as he paces outside of the barrier.

"Gabe, but Jay. He took care of me. He rescued me from Ted. You don't know."

"I know enough, Aura. Look at Jay now. Does he look as though he's concerned about you?"

I glance up as she does, and wince at the mask of hatred on his face while he watches her.

"Aura, please. We've lost so much time already. If you do this, it's all gonna end. Aura, look at me."

She turns back to him and he kneels to face her.

"You thought you'd never see me again, Aura. Jax did this. She brought me back. We need to help her."

And as she reaches out a hand to his, I know we have her.

"Okay, Gabriel," I interrupt, "we're almost out of time. Get ready, you know what you have to do. Rory, just listen to what he tells you. We need to stop them." I watch until she nods in agreement and turn to Emelia. "You ready?"

"Umm, Jax, we have a problem." Xan's voice interrupts my focus

I open my eyes to assess the scene, and puzzle at what I see. All the demons have stopped fighting, each taking a step back. I see my confusion echoed on the faces of my friends, but when they all charge at once, I realise Astaroth's intention.

"The barrier," I warn, and as the words leave my lips, I see Jay stalk towards us.

"Mine," Xan says, leaving no room for argument as he walks to meet him head on.

I see Jay smirk as he covers the ground between them, an evil glint in his eye.

"No," breathes Emelia, running past me as I see what she noticed just before I did; the red glints in Jay's eyes betraying his powers. She lifts her hands in front of her, pushing them forward as hard as she can, and I see the demons battling Sal and Malaphar lifted off their feet and slammed into the trees ahead. Eremiel runs to them and I'm blinded by the blue flash I remember him using at the castle to destroy Abbatu's helpers. "Sal, I need you."

Xan catches Jay with a fist to the jaw but he's hit right back and staggers off-balance even as Emelia runs towards them. He regains his feet and gets ready to attack again, and I groan at not being able to help him. Tied as I am to Gabriel, helping him stay with Rory, I can't so anything but watch as they trade blows.

"Go, Jax," Gabriel says, and I feel the band around my wrist fade and disappear.

"I've got him," reassures Rory, with a shy smile. "I promise I'm not letting him go."

I don't need to be told twice, leaping to my feet and running towards my friends.

"Jax, look," Lizzie cries. "He's gonna do it again."

I see the moonlight reflect off the blade even as Jay slides it from his sleeve into his hand.

"Xan! Knife!"

This time my warning doesn't come too late and Xan raises his arm in time, knocking it from Jay's hand and I breathe a quick sigh of relief when I see it fall harmlessly to the ground.

"Now, Sal," says Emelia, making Jay turn quickly to see who is approaching but still too late to avoid them.

I watch as he's wrestled to the ground by Sallas and Malaphar, held in place for a moment before they drag him over to the seal, still glowing red under the night sky.

I turn back to check on Mathim, seeing him still in battle with

Astaroth, Eremiel starting to run to help him but stopping when Mathim raises a hand. And although I would prefer he had the help, I understand why he would want the fight to remain between the two of them. What he did needs repaying. Knowing that Eremiel has his back, I return my attention to the matter at hand.

"Okay, Em, when you're ready."

She picks up the knife as she walks back to join her siblings, kneeling next to Rory. Drawing the blade across her palm, she hands it to her and gives her a short nod. Gabriel reaches out and laces his fingers with those of his twin, speaking calmly as he does.

"Go on, Aura," he encourages. "More than the others, we share the same blood. I've got you."

She slices the pale skin of her hand, wincing a little as she does and then looks questioningly at Jay.

"No way," he spits.

"No problem," growls Xan, taking the knife and cutting the hand Sal forces out towards him, pulling it over the seal when he sees the blood begin to drip.

Emelia and Rory do the same, Gabriel following his sister's movements and the marking on the ground flares brighter.

"I am Emelia. I draw on any power bestowed upon me and of those around me. I renounce the blood I was given by my Father. I disavow any connection with it and caused by it. By spilling the blood, I reject any ties it created. I am reborn afresh and untainted."

The night somehow goes eerily quiet for a moment before the noise of the wind and of Mathim battling in the background crashes back down around us and my eyes flash to Emelia's.

"Your turn," she says quickly to Rory and Gabriel.

"I am Rory. I draw on any power…"

Echoed and prompted when needed by her brother, she repeats Emelia's words as I cast a wary eye all around us, only the repeated silence bringing me back to the group around the seal as they finish together.

All eyes turn to Jay, sarcastic laughter issuing from him when he realises we need him to complete the task.

"You really think I'd do that? I am loyal to my Father. You've just done exactly what I wanted you to do all along. He'll know I'm the only one he needs."

I turn to Mal, giving him a quick nod and seeing him move to the other side of Jay in response. Jay begins to struggle more in Sal's grasp as Mal leans close to him, whispering in his ear.

"I am Jay," he says, and I can see the struggle on his face as he fights against the words coming out of his mouth. "I draw on any power bestowed upon me and of those around me. I renounce the blood I was given by my Father. I disavow any connection with it and caused by it. By spilling the blood, I reject any ties it created. I am reborn afresh and untainted."

His words are halting, his sentences jarred, yet as he finishes, the air grows heavy and the sudden silence is deafening. And then, out of nowhere, the sky lights with a huge flash and a thunderclap sounds, the force of it shaking the ground I'm kneeling on. And when it ends, the howls of Jay take its place. I look quickly to the seal and see the cracks beginning to narrow.

"Mathim," I cry over the noise, "we did it!"

Knowing our work is done, he squares his shoulders and I gasp as he lets the bloodlust he's been reining in overtake him, his eyes turning red as he succumbs to it. And as much as I want to see him destroy the demon who has single-handedly destroyed the innocent life I once knew, I can't bear to see my friend become the violent demon he was. I know I need to be there for him though, to share his final success and to witness his revenge for those he loved and lost at the hands of his enemy, so I stand up to run towards them. Sal does the same and I'm glad he's here to see his friends avenged.

The sudden noise of a scuffle breaking out behind me makes me halt my step and spin on my heel to see what's going on.

"Shit!" exclaims Malaphar, his attention having slipped for a second, allowing Jay to jump to his feet and gain some distance from him.

"No!" yells Em, seeing Jay raise his hands towards me.

And somehow the world seems to go into slow motion. I see a flash of red in Jay's eyes, I see Emelia raise her own hands and aim them at her brother, and out of the corner of my eye I see a bright golden light from where Mathim fights with Astaroth. Almost like the effect is sucked out of the air, everything speeds up again and I know I'm about to die, closing my eyes and preparing for the pain as best I can.

But it doesn't hit. I open them again, failing to focus on the blur that somehow appears in front of me. It's lit up impossibly bright as Jay's energy bolt hits it, Emelia's making contact with him a second later and throwing him backwards, crashing him into the boulder I usually use to sit on. Mal is on him instantly, speaking quickly and rendering him somehow immobile on the ground. But Sal is staring at the shape on the ground at my feet. I look down and see the form of a still body, looking around to take count of everyone, trying to figure out who just saved me. I see Rory and Gabriel together on the floor next to the seal, Emelia standing to my right, breathing heavily, and Mathim and Eremiel holding a bloody and beaten Astaroth.

But when Mathim's eyes follow the gaze of everyone else, he drops the hold he has on his enemy and runs towards me, dropping to his knees.

"No," he whispers. "It can't be."

I hear Eremiel approaching too, still dragging Astaroth with him as he nears, but Mathim holds my attention.

"I don't understand," I say, confused.

"Not again," he groans, and the realisation hits me before he even speaks her name. "Sabnak."

Tears spring to my eyes as I drop to the ground beside him, watching as he turns her lifeless body over and brushes back the hair from her face.

"H-how?" I ask Eremiel.

He opens his mouth to speak just as I see Astaroth straighten up and shove the angel into me, running towards the seal.

"Return, Astaroth," booms a commanding voice from the almost gone cracks in the image.

"Astaroth," cries Jay, his body still pinned against the rock. "Take me with you."

"Leave him," orders Lucifer's disembodied voice. "I have no tie and no use for him now."

Before anyone can react, Astaroth races to the river, diving through the watery doorway that must have been created as we were all distracted, disappearing from view and leaving Jay sobbing in his wake.

I look from Mathim to the still body of Sabnak and then accusingly at Eremiel.

"This has got to be your doing. Fix it now."

"For once, Jax, I will not argue with you," he replies quietly.

Kneeling beside her, he gently pushes a resisting Mathim back, looking to me for help as he does.

"Mathim, honey, we need to give him room," I say gently. "Come on, big guy, move back."

The use of Lee's name for him seems to filter through somehow and he sits back heavily, his elbows on his knees and his head in his hands as he watches.

Eremiel works silently, his hands over Sabnak's brow and chest. He lets his head fall back, his eyes lighting the brightest blue I've ever seen, and the air seems to charge with power. Emelia looks at me briefly before joining him at the other side of her and mirroring his movements. Her eyes glow white as her hair blows wildly and I hold my breath and pray.

Mathim's head snaps up the same moment I hear it. A deep rasping breath, then another. I can't stop the tears from falling over my cheeks as I see her eyes flutter open, widening in disbelief when she sees Mathim.

"Mathim," she croaks. "I am here."

35

The Return

I see the lightning and hear the thunderclap and I know something has gone drastically wrong. The angel and the traitor have me held, and for now, I allow it. I must gauge the situation before making any move. I manage to lift my head to see what has happened and look over to where Jay sits, slumped against the rock. He struggles against an invisible hold and I realise that one of the angels has him pinned in place. I see Emelia with the others all looking down at a half-hidden figure at Jax's feet, only Aurora left alone by the seal. Except she is not quite alone. Beside her on the ground is a young man with blonde hair, his features although masculine, similar to her own. The brother.

How did they get him? He was dead. I look again at his face and realise just how similar he is to her. Her twin. I clench my jaw in anger. How did we miss that?

The seal on the ground flickers, despite its narrowing and I know it is time I made my move. Mathim gasps beside me and drops the hold he has on me, abandoning it to run towards Jax, and giving me my opportunity. When the angel pulls me forward, I put up a show of a fight against his movements but allow it anyway.

"I don't understand," I hear Jax say.

"Not again," Mathim groans, and the temptation to see what his painful tone is being caused by almost gets the better of me. I do not have to do that though, his next word answering that question, but creating so many more. "Sabnak."

The body on the ground is Sabnak? But I watched as she was ruined, destroyed and eventually killed by my Father.

"H-how?" asks Jax, voicing the first of my astounded questions.

Knowing that this is the best chance I have, I push the angel vermin off me, sending him barrelling into Jax and run towards the glowing image so lovingly created by Aurora before things went so wrong.

"Return, Astaroth," commands Lucifer from the cracks.

"Astaroth," says Jay, pleading from his place on the floor. "Take me with you."

"Leave him," orders my Master. "I have no tie and no use for him

now."

I see the watery doorway glimmering unnoticed in the moonlight and run towards the stream, expecting an attack with every step. I leap through, landing in front of Lucifer, and drop immediately to one knee.

I do not cower and plead in front of him. I stand to face him and await his reaction.

I am Astaroth, Grand Duke of Hell, I doubt he will cast me aside so easily.

36

Long Road Back

"Sabnak?" breathes Mathim.

"Yes, love," she replies, sitting up as he moves towards her, disbelief slowing his movement.

"But how? I saw him kill you."

"Eremiel. He gave me a chance to come back to you," she begins to explain, but the uncertainty of our situation makes me look around worriedly.

"Umm, guys, I'm really, really sorry to interrupt, but is there any way we can do this back at home?" I ask.

Mathim's eyes lift to mine, as though only just realising we're all here, and he nods numbly.

"Of course," Eremiel responds. "Sauriel, can you walk?"

I frown at the strange name, but see Sab open her mouth to

answer.

"You disavowed your name too?"

"I did not have to. My demon name died when I did. My new name was given to me on my rebirth. I will explain it all, I promise." Her last words are addressed to Mathim as she starts to get up from the ground.

"Wait," he answers. Giving her a look that not even I would argue with, he scoops her up and carries her towards the doorway Scirlin created for us earlier. "Jax, would you lead? I am not up to the questioning from Lee should she greet us first."

I nod with a knowing grin and walk through into the living room of my beloved Rose Hill Farm and it hits me that it's about to become my new home.

"Jax!" squeals Lee, running towards me and wrapping me in a tight hug. "Is that it? Is it really over?"

Her questions are soon forgotten though when she sees Mathim and Sabnak come through behind me.

"Coffee. And chairs. Here, big guy, you two take the sofa. I'll move everything else around it. And get you a blanket."

"And so, the fussing begins," jokes Xan, having just made it through in time to hear Lee. "I hope you're up to it."

Sal and Malaphar follow his steps, Emelia in between them, and Gabriel and Rory are close behind. No sooner have we all made it home than the mirror flashes and returns to its normal reflective state.

"Thank you, Scirlin," mutters Sal. "Jay is not one I would wish to have know where we have come."

"Amen to that," I respond.

"Come on guys, sit," bosses Lee. "But don't start with anything good 'til I'm back with coffee."

***

"Hi, Jax," says Lizzie, appearing in the corner of the room.

"Lizzie!" I exclaim. "You were awesome, angel. Thank you for your help. Through all of this, I mean. We couldn't have done it without you, sweetie."

"You're welcome, Jax," she replies with a shy smile.

"Wait 'til Ambriel hears how awesome you were," Xan adds. "She's gonna be so proud of you, sweetheart."

"Who?" she asks, screwing her little face up into a frown.

"Ambriel. The lady angel?" I say, confused. "Oh, wait, maybe you know her as Jayne."

"Nope," she says, popping the "p" and giggling. "Do you have more than one name? That's weird."

I struggle to make sense of the question before I realise she's looking past me.

"You? You were the lady angel?"

"I am," replies Sabnak. "And I am very proud of you indeed, Lizzie."

"Wait," says Lee, rubbing her brow. "I am so freaking confused right now. Please explain before my head explodes."

"Very well. Eremiel, would you like to tell it, or should I?" she asks the angel beside me.

"It is your story, Sauriel, not mine," he answers.

"Upon my death, I was gone. In blackness. In the void. Eremiel offered a chance at redemption. For Mathim's sake, as he was sacrificing everything to help them. He said if I proved worthy and strong enough, then I could return. I will not go into all of the details, but suffice it to say, I worked as hard as I could and did all that I had to in order to get back. Lizzie was the only link and only help I had. With her, and because of her, I was successful. And now I am here." She reaches for Mathim's hand. "Once I had the chance, there was nothing that could stop me getting back to you."

"The glow," I almost whisper. "That makes sense now."

"Huh?" Lee says.

"Nothing, honey, it's not important."

"Sauriel's sacrifice to protect you, Jax, was the final proof I needed that she was indeed redeemed. She threw away all she had worked towards to save you, as far as she knew," interjects Eremiel. "And now she has a place in Heaven. As do you, if you want it, Mathim."

Mathim looks at him in shock and then to Sabnak, who shrugs with a smile. He looks around the room and finally back to the angel.

"I am grateful and honoured by your offer, Eremiel. Thank you. But I think I would rather we stayed here. Together." That last word is said so forcefully that I know it will not be argued with.

"Very well, Mathim, you have more than earned the right to decide. Sauriel, I take it this is your decision too?" he asks and seeing her nod, he goes on. "I will leave you to your home. Gabriel, you too have a place with us. But I realise you have lost time to catch up on with your sister and so I will return for you when you are ready."

"Can't he do what I do?" asks Lizzie. "Live in Heaven but play here?"

"He can, child. Speaking of which, I think it is time you returned to your mother, little one. You can come and see Jax tomorrow."

"Okay," she agrees happily, skipping across the room and taking his hand. "Bye, Jax. Bye, everyone."

They fade from sight leaving us all smiling after her, before Lee's curiosity gets the better of her again.

"So, what now? Sallas and Malaphar? Emelia? And what about Rory?"

"Woah, slow down chica. One at a time. They're all welcome to stay if they want to. But let's not demand answers right away," says Xan.

"I can answer now for us," replies Sal. "We must return. But we will stay in touch as we have. I wish to tell Tezrian the good news, if Scirlin hasn't seen it for himself and told her already. Sab, I am so pleased you made it back. I will never let you out of our lives again."

She stands and hugs him, holding him tight as she blinks away tears.

"And I will never leave any of you again," she states. "Please, give our love to them both."

She pulls him tight again, not letting go until he chuckles.

"I'll tell them as soon as I can move."

She steps back and sits down with Mathim, settling against him as he lifts an arm to put around her shoulders.

"My friends, thank you will never be enough," he says solemnly.

"It was truly our pleasure," replies Malaphar. "Now, we should return before we are missed. I would not be here if Lucifer decides to check on us."

Knowing he speaks the truth, we say our goodbyes and watch them leave.

"Me too," says Emelia. "Not now, obviously, but I have a life and work in New York. I'll visit loads though."

"You're welcome here as long as you want to stay and whenever you want to come," offers Xan.

"Thank you," she answers, an easy smile on her face and I realise how much better everyone is beginning to look already.

"Rory, that goes for you too," he continues. "You don't need to go back to your old life if you don't want to."

I watch as her jaw drops in surprise before she manages to stop it.

"Really? You really mean it?" she asks.

"Of course I mean it. Plus, the veil is thinner here. Gabriel can cross more easily here than anywhere else."

I nudge Xan and nod towards Lee, who's looking at him in puzzlement.

"You mean when we come to see Mrs C? Ooh are we gonna start visiting her more often?" she asks excitedly.

"You could say that," he chuckles. "Welcome to your new workplace, kidda. And part-time home, I guess, given how often you stay with Jax."

She catapults herself out of her seat towards him and he barely has time to brace for the impact before she lands on his knee and almost suffocates him with a hug.

"Oh my God," she squeals, making me worry about poor Xan's hearing. "How did my awesome job just get even better? Wait 'til I tell Marcus!"

"Yeah, where is Marcus?" I ask.

"Working late again," she says. She looks around the room at all of us, her face changing as she becomes serious. "Is it really over?"

"It really is, chica," reassures Xan. "I'm sure Astaroth is safely chained up in Hell right now. Lucifer is stuck there forever, and I don't think he'll be thanking his Grand Duke for that."

She looks to Mathim for confirmation.

"I am certain that it is done. About Astaroth, however, I am not so confident. He has a way of coming out of such things unscathed."

"Yeah, I know he has in the past," I agree, "but how does he come back from this? Come on guys, he's done, it's over, and we have an awesome new life to start. Right?"

"Right," they respond in unison, and finally, after literally going to Hell and back, I can see a bright future for all of us.

Epilogue

"I did not see this coming, I should have known. We should have been told of this other. And now I am here. Trapped. Limited."

He paces the floor, spitting his words through gritted teeth, fury having turned his eyes crimson as he spins to face me. He raises a hand and I await the outcome, unflinching under his stare.

"It is yours, Astaroth," he says, gesturing to the throne beside his. "For although my time on Earth has been taken away from me, that does not mean my impact upon humanity must be lessened. I may not have any children to raise me, but I do have my true children."

I keep my face neutral as he laughs sardonically.

"I almost made the same mistake my father did, turning my back on those most worthy of my care and affection in favour of others. No. I am not him. Together we will make humanity suffer more than ever before. The centuries to come will be filled with nothing but horror and blood. Are you ready to take your rightful place, my Grand Duke?"

"Yes, my Lord. I am ready to serve in any way I can," I reply.

I arc my arm over the glass, bringing the human world into view once more as I climb the steps to take my seat. And as I do, I wonder if, now they have achieved their goals, the angels' protection over the Chosen One might dwindle.

For really, it would be a terrible thing if she were to once more become prey for the Devil.

THE END

Printed in Great Britain
by Amazon